GUILT BURNS HOLES

An absolutely gripping crime thriller full of twists

EMMY ELLIS

Detective Carol Wren Mysteries Book 3

JOFFE BOOKS

Revised edition 2023
Joffe Books, London
www.joffebooks.com

First published in Great Britain in 2022

This paperback edition was first published
in Great Britain in 2023

Cover art by Nebojša Zorić

ISBN: 978-1-80405-892-3

PROLOGUE

21 Larch Lane — Scudderton

The house had a scary feel to it now the shouting had stopped. Mam and Dad had been arguing, and Carol sat halfway up the stairs, watching through the balusters, the pair of them raging in the living room. Mam rarely shouted, but tonight, after he'd come in from out the front, she'd gone for him.

Carol wished she hadn't heard what he'd said to his friend. About the woman he was seeing, his "girlfriend". How could you have a girlfriend when you had a wife? It didn't make sense, and Carol had asked Mam.

"A girlfriend? What do you mean?" Mam had frowned then let out a silly laugh.

She thought it was a *joke*?

"That's what Dad's got, you and a girlfriend."

Mam had paled. "You go on up to your room and play for a bit. Tea won't be long."

Carol didn't do that, hence her sitting on the stairs, and when Dad had come back in saying he was off up the pub, Mam had stood there in the hallway, hands on hips, and called him out.

"What did you let Carol overhear?"

"Eh?"

"A *girlfriend*?"

He'd shoved her into the living room, where they'd rowed, lots of nasty words coming out: "If you weren't shit in the sack . . ." and "You're not much of a wife, so what do you expect?" and "Don't you dare tell me who I can fuck!"

Carol had grasped her knees, tears streaming, and listened to it all.

Now, she held her breath as Dad raised his fist and punched Mam in the face. She fell back onto the swirl-patterned carpet, hitting her head on the corner of the hearth, her cry of pain hurting Carol's heart.

Carol made a move to get up, to go and help, but Mam stared at her through the doorway.

"No," she said. "No."

"No what?" Dad shouted. "No fucking what, Eleanor?"

Mam struggled to her feet, her cheeks flushed. "Get out of my way. I'm leaving and taking Carol with me."

"Like fuck you are."

The living room door shut, and Mam screamed, but it didn't last long. Carol ran upstairs, knowing Mam was getting a smack like Carol did when she'd been naughty. She sat on the bed, listening, but it was quiet now.

Until the front door slammed.

"That's it, fuck off, run away!" Dad raged.

Carol lay on her side and shivered, a cold tear slipping along her nose. Where had Mam gone?

Footsteps thundered on the stairs. Oh God . . .

Her bedroom door flung open, and Dad glared at her. "Your mam's left us, gone, all because you're a little rat. *Don't* come downstairs. You get in bed and stay there. No tea for you."

He walked out, thumping downstairs, and Carol cried, missing Mam already.

She'd come back, wouldn't she?

Later, waking from a fitful sleep, Carol listened to a strange sound. *Shum, shum, shum.* She got up and knelt on her bed in front of the window and, seeing nothing, carefully opened the latch and pushed the window outwards.

She peered down.

Dad was out there in the dark, close to the house, digging a hole.

CHAPTER ONE

Truth-Hunt Cottage — Midnight

Grim Reaper loved his nickname. It gave the sledgehammer of a hint that he might well be the last person *they* saw. He'd been called it ever since he was a child, the little group he'd hung around with all choosing what they wanted to be known by when they got together. His name was even more fitting many years later when he'd set his mission in motion. Something to stimulate fear in the people he'd taken to his isolated cottage on the moors, their only outside companions two big trees so close together they appeared as one, branches and leaves intertwining. Rolling grass and moss stretched all around, his long driveway cutting a curving ribbon through it.

He kept his subjects in the former living room, the thirty-by-twenty space kitted out with three soundproofed boxes on the left-hand side, pretty ribbon bows on the front doors. He'd even pasted on facades with red-brick wallpaper and fashioned windows out of white tape for the frames, and instead of having glass, he'd painted replicas of what lay inside each box, minus the person, so they appeared just like real homes. He enjoyed rapping the brass cow-face knockers as though he visited the inhabitants, as though he was only there to have a chat and a cuppa, not to change their way of thinking and burn them with cigarettes until they screamed.

In the other half of the room, he'd put down fake grass, cutting it so each "house" had its own concrete garden path, and either side of them, potted plastic plants and flowers lined the walkways, pretty little soldiers that guarded his sinful guests. He'd given his subjects a nice place to live, and if they were grateful, if they answered him satisfactorily enough that he felt their incarceration had mended their ways, he'd set them free with threats to kill their families if they told anyone where they'd been.

Will you? Will you really?

So far, they'd all lived here for three years, give or take a month or two. Mind control was a long old road, one he'd prepared himself for from the start.

Steady wins the race

He called the room the Guilt-Ridden Estate, because that was his aim, to prove guilt, to inspire it, to get these people to understand you couldn't just gad about doing whatever you wanted. One of them had been rude and accused *Grim* of doing just that, but it only showed they didn't understand the work of a vigilante. They couldn't expand their minds enough to know he was doing it. They didn't *listen* to what he'd said.

In his eyes, the boxes held those who'd committed the cardinal sin. At the time of kidnapping, he hadn't *known* them as such but had heard many a brag in the Little Devil, the pub opposite the marina in Scudderton, somewhere he'd once frequented for an hour after work to gather gossip. Drink tended to loosen tongues, handing him his test subjects on a silver platter. If only they'd realised at the time that their tales would bring them here to Guilt-Ridden, their homes for the foreseeable.

Grim pushed his silver hostess trolley up the path of number one and parked it in front of the red door. He had a disguise on — he loved dressing up for each resident — but he'd hidden his face beneath a prosthetic over-the-head mask, adding a Dolly Parton wig to match the features. Grim *did* work nine-to-five, apart from the odd stint of overtime, but he wasn't jealous of the real Dolly's Jolene.

He raised the knocker, let it drop — *tap, tap, tap* — and ran his hands over the fake boobs beneath his red dress, pretending the inhabitant was coming to the door to let him in, just like she would have had he gone to her real house. She wouldn't know whether he was there or not, seeing as all sound from this room was dead inside hers, but the illusion kept him happy.

He stroked the ribbon of the bow then fished his keys out and pulled the door outwards, propping it open with the trolley. Naked, Karen sat on her narrow bed to the left and placed her closed book on the wooden nightstand. A Perspex screen with a locked transparent door in the middle separated him from her, a hatch beside it that flipped inwards and acted as a shelf. The screen didn't reach the ceiling or floor, so the air could circulate.

He'd installed extractor fans in the walls, same as the one in his bathroom, operated from the other side by a string pull with a tiny white cone on the end. The plastic facias had three slats and were flush to the wall. The staleness of their bodies and breath filtered through into his lounge, where he opened the windows when he was home so they could smell the freshness and regret not being allowed outside. A torment. Another reminder that they'd been imprisoned. Each fan had a small, soundproofed steel door in his lounge that he snapped shut and covered with pictures if he was due visitors — precluding any chance of his subjects being heard shouting out.

Mind you, he hadn't had a visitor in a while. His last girlfriend had called things off, upsetting him as much as his ex-wife, Emma, leaving him, ending things when they should have fought to keep the relationship alive, to have *cared* enough not to throw in the towel. Emma had ruined him years ago, filing for divorce and sending him into a world of uncertainty where he'd focused his energy on getting the cottage just right, everything tidy, spick and span, a way to bring order into the chaos. It had calmed him, kept him from abducting Emma and locking her up — that would have been a silly thing to do, considering their split had been acrimonious. He'd have been the first suspect on the list.

While the girlfriend had come to the cottage, she hadn't explored his home, which was a good thing, considering what the locked boxes in Guilt-Ridden contained. She'd been too intent on going straight upstairs, taking what she wanted from him in bed, then going back to her place afterwards — without him.

She looked nothing like Emma, and he'd tried to mould her into his perfect companion, but she had a will of her own and refused to be directed. It had hurt him more than he liked to admit, her sacking him off. He was obsessed with her still, needed her, but she wasn't interested. She was too . . . headstrong, too dedicated to her single life, wasn't the type who was willing to bend. So yes, he'd been cast aside again, left to wallow once more in anger, to force other unscrupulous people to mend their ways instead of snatching the girlfriend and putting *her* in Guilt-Ridden, something he'd contemplated a few times.

That wouldn't be wise, though.

A sharp pain poked at his chest, so he closed his mind off from his disastrous love life and concentrated on the now, the things he *could* do something about.

These box homes had portable caravan toilets — he must clean those out at some point — and a shower in the far right-hand corner, the water feeding directly into a grate beneath, which then dropped into large receptacles in the cellar. He wasn't a monster, he allowed them some dignity, and besides, he didn't like smelly people.

"I thought you'd like a snack." He used a key to unlock the hatch, pushed it down, and placed a clingfilmed sandwich and a Styrofoam cup of orange juice on it. "Take them before I change my mind."

He had chocolate on the trolley too, a Freddo, but she wouldn't get it unless she pleased him. Each woman had something they loved more than anything else, and he used it to manipulate them.

Karen stood on spindly legs. He was proud of her figure; he'd been the one to ensure she lost what he guessed was now around six stone. When he'd taken her, she'd been what he considered piggish, too many rolls of fat, too many chins, but the loss had resulted in loose skin that hung off her as if she'd melted.

He had plans for that.

She approached the hatch, her gaze pinned on him, and stretched out a bony hand, grasping the sandwich, then she raised her other arm and took the cup. Her batwings swayed. Her elongated tits had no substance, empty bags of skin bar a bit of weight at the bottoms, the nipples beige and puckered. He could give her a boob job, no problem, and a facelift, but he wasn't feeling that generous.

But he could change his mind. Maybe, if she did what he wanted, he'd send her back out into the world a new woman, all fixed up and ready to go with her husband, Craig, who'd been raging about her disappearance. The man had no clue Grim was on his side, that she'd been stolen because she'd cheated on Craig with his best friend. Grim was doing the fella a favour in reprogramming his wife, something no one had done for Grim — something he couldn't do for himself with Emma and the ex-girlfriend or he'd get caught.

As for Karen's two kids . . . A pair of rowdy teenage girls who wreaked havoc, doing whatever the hell they liked, the excuse being that their mother going missing had upset them, therefore everyone had to turn a blind eye.

Society was going soft.

Grim gestured for Karen to step back. She reversed to her bed and sat, taking a sip of orange, her blue eyes sunken, her cheekbones great big hills on a rocky face, all angled granite. He gave each resident a monthly haircut, and Karen sported an inch all over, neat and tidy compared to the unruly, long blonde curls of old, her shiny scalp showing through in patches where she'd suffered from alopecia since the week after he'd brought her here.

Stress did mad things to the mind and body. Grim should know.

I mean, look at me, what I'm doing

He reached in and closed the hatch, locked it and pocketed the key. He sat on a foldout wooden chair in the front-right corner to observe her. Her latest cigarette burns looked particularly sore. She stared out of the front door at the fake garden, her eyes as greedy as her stomach used to be, round and distended; they seemed to have popped out of the hollows. "On stalks," his mother would have said. She unwrapped the sandwich, the only food he'd brought her for twenty-four hours, and took a bite.

Karen grimaced. Salmon paste, something she detested. He'd made it for his amusement, chuckling as he'd spread it onto the bread.

"Have you thought about what I said on my last visit?" Grim asked.

She nodded. Swallowed. "I want to say I'm sorry, I know that's what you need, but I'm not."

He sighed. Here they were again, this silly dance she insisted on performing. She wasn't sorry because her husband was a bastard and she'd been looking for love and affection elsewhere. She wasn't sorry because she deserved happiness, and so did Craig's best friend — with her. What Grim had tried to drum into her, time and time again, was that women shouldn't call the shots, shouldn't ask for more than they'd been given. She'd married Craig, for better or worse, and that should have been her lot. Instead, she'd gone off and spread her legs for the one man Craig should have been able to trust.

Like my ex-fucking-wife did

It really was a bit of a mess.

"Then you can't go home yet," Grim said. "I've told you before, you're not allowed to leave until you're clean. What I don't understand is, why you insist on not being sorry when you've got two children out there, running riot, who are apparently desperate for you to go home. Don't you *care*?"

Karen snorted. She was what some would call common, a chav who'd been slung up on the shittiest estate in Scudderton, and her manners and behaviour spoke of ill breeding. A joke had gone around about *in*breeding in her family, but that was a subject for another day. He wasn't here to chastise her about being a product of a slovenly bitch and her first cousin, suspicion of incest alive in the gossips of the town.

That's probably why her daughters are so odd. A skewed bloodline

She shrugged. "They'll be okay without me. I don't even *want* to go home. If you let me out, I'd go somewhere else. Down south maybe. London. The girls are as mean as their father. I . . . I never did take to them."

Grim reared his head back in shock. She hadn't told him this before. It was another misdemeanour to add to the original one. A flighty woman having sex with someone other than her husband *and* disliking her kids?

She's a cow.

"This changes things," he said, his body slumping. Why wasn't this going right? Why was she making it so difficult? "I can't let you go now. If you haven't realised in three years, I'll not be wasting any more time on you."

She slumped too, lowering the sandwich to her lap. "I tried to love them, but they're . . . they were ugly little aliens as babies and grew up to be bitches. I didn't even *want* kids. Craig . . . he insisted, he threw my pills away, and then there was—"

She clamped her lips closed.

"Then there was what?" he asked.

"I don't want to talk about it."

And now I don't even want to listen.

Grim didn't buy what she'd said about the pills. Karen would have been well able to source another form of contraception at a family planning clinic, one her husband wouldn't know about. The implant, a coil. If she hadn't wanted to get pregnant, she could have prevented it. A deception, yes, but it was better than spawning badly behaved girls who'd recently taken to mugging old ladies, and who knew, without the kids distracting her, she might have appreciated Craig better.

Grim rubbed his chest. "I can't wrap my head around this. It's too much. My mother loved me. She stayed with my father no matter what. She did the *right* thing."

"What's right for one is wrong for another, and like you've said before, your mam was beaten, treated like shit the same as me, so no, in my opinion, she *didn't* do the right thing."

Karen lifted the sandwich and ate some more, her sights set on the fake garden again or maybe the mural he'd painted on the wall opposite to give the impression the subjects lived on an estate — houses, trees, a road, cars parked in two lines at the kerbs, puffy clouds in a blue sky, a little boy in the distance.

"I can't help the way I feel," she said. "Being here . . . I see everything clearly now. I should never have married or had the kids — should have gone straight down for abortions. I want to be like I am here, reading, being myself, not caring for brats or running around after that bastard, Craig."

"That is *not* what this is all about." Grim's hot breath hit the inside of the mask, and anger spiralled inside him. She was ruining it. Taking his plan in another direction. He thumped his thigh. "You're supposed to have mended yourself. God, you haven't even lied like her next door or pretended to be reborn for my benefit."

Karen laughed. "Why should I? You want me to say what you want to hear, but I can't. That book —" she waved her free hand at the nightstand — "has given me a new perspective. I shouldn't have to live a life I hate. I should be true to myself. I should be who I am, not what you and everyone else wants."

She'd missed the point. He'd given her that book to show her cheating was wrong. She hadn't got to the end yet, the bookmark poking out three-quarters in, so she hadn't seen the part about the couple getting back together and starting again, fixing their broken family.

Would it make a difference if she *did* read it?

I don't think so. She's selfish.

He hadn't wanted it to come to this, but Karen was a lost cause. He sighed. It looked like tonight he'd be performing surgery on her dead body.

Such a shame. He'd had high hopes.

It just went to show the best laid plans could go to utter shite.

* * *

In what was once the downstairs snug on the other side of the hallway, now his home surgery near the kitchen, Grim, his wig and mask off, stared at her body on his operating table. The cigarette burns were scars in places, fresh wounds in others, resembling large freckles all over her skin. *She* looked like an alien, never mind her daughters. His handiwork with a scalpel had been completed. He'd sliced off all the baggy skin and sewn her up using green thread — green for the envy she'd felt for others' lives, green for the grass she'd thought was more vibrant on the other side.

His skills in the operating room hadn't failed him, and apart from the gaudy cotton and him deliberately hacking at the skin to make it look like he didn't know what he was doing (he had to throw the police off), he was pleased with his efforts. Had she still been alive and dressed, she'd appear toned, lithe, someone who took care of herself, a gym-goer.

Grim eyed the skin and flesh in the nearby bucket. He'd leave it with her body when he dumped her. If she'd turned a new leaf, the skin would have represented the old Karen, the rancid parts of her cast away, leaving only the good behind. She'd be whole, *clean*, and ready to return to her marriage and be a dutiful wife.

Instead, she'd fucked up by speaking her truth, and while he appreciated her not being a liar, not trying to dupe him like the woman next door, he detested it all the same.

He hadn't bargained for his teachings to go wrong. He'd imagined her transforming, becoming someone other, a brand-new person. But she'd taught him a bitter lesson: no matter how hard he'd worked on her conversion therapy, it hadn't produced the desired results.

He'd failed.

Again.

Rage festered in his gut, and he raised the scalpel, fighting the urge to ruin all his hard work. Instead of ripping open the wounds he'd carefully sewn, he sliced off the bulbous ends of her breasts and threw them in the bucket, the *thwack* of flesh hitting flesh doing nothing to satisfy him. He slung the scalpel on the shelf beneath the operating table and snatched up his needle and thread. Grim sewed her tits up, green cotton again. To his mind, he'd taken away her nipples, her ability to feed children, to show the world she should never have been given the opportunity in the first place, one she hadn't appreciated.

It fuelled his anger. His mother hadn't been able to conceive after having Grim. She'd have been grateful to have two children, unlike Karen, who'd squandered the gift. What an absolutely horrible woman.

He tossed the needle and thread on the shelf beneath and walked to the head end, standing to one side to admire the strangulation marks on her neck below the hideous sewn line where he'd removed her saggy extra chins. He'd throttled her with thick gardening gloves on, the imprints of his thumbs and fingertips larger than they actually were, the bruises livid purple. Her face, stuck in the death pose, bore the red-spotted signs of asphyxiation around the eyes, the whites of which were stained with crimson veins. Her fists, clenched, would further alert the local pathologist as to what had happened, although Grim suspected Rib Shears — funny, another man with a nickname — would be flummoxed as to why surgery had been performed yet all the internal organs were intact.

A puzzle for Carol Wren to solve.

Most people in Scudderton knew her on sight, the copper and her partner, Dave, in the news for weeks on end regarding some pervert case a while back. Grim drank in the Lord in Mollengate and saw them both on the regular. Were they a couple now Dave's wife had kicked him out? The pair certainly seemed pally. Too close. Too familiar. They'd moved in together — wasn't that indication enough?

Grim threw those thoughts out of his mind and steeled himself for the disposal, something he hadn't had time to plan as Karen had put an unexpected spanner in the works with her confession. He cleaned her using washing-up liquid and a loofah, hosing the bubbles off, the water showering onto the section of grated floor around the trolley, pitter-pattering into yet another plastic receptacle in the cellar. He'd use his bilge pump later to chug all of the waste water away, the hose dangling down into the dried-out well in his back garden, a job he hadn't performed properly as of late. The amount in the receptacles was getting to unacceptable levels.

God, he had so much to do.

"You disappointed me, Karen," he whispered. He exchanged his gloves for a clean set then switched his all-in-one surgery suit for another, going from bare feet to hiking boots. "I really thought I could get you to see the error of your ways. But you had other ideas, and this is where we are, you dead, me about to take you back out into the world. Still, there's a bright side. You've got a nice figure now. That'll save Craig some money on the size of the coffin."

He laughed at his cruel, fattist joke.

Well, he had to get his happiness from somewhere, didn't he?

CHAPTER TWO

Truth-Hunt Cottage

Lesley Johnson rocked on her bed, listening to the whir of the fan in the wall high above it. The man who'd taken her so long ago moved around in the lounge, shouting about things never going right, *you motherfucking bitch*. Weak from hunger, she stood on the thin mattress and peered through the fan slats and the gaps between the slow-spinning blades, her breath stalling at the sight of him in a balaclava.

She hadn't seen his face since the night he'd abducted her. He always had a mask of some kind on — the one that looked like the Queen being particularly unsettling, seeing as he paired it with a curly grey wig, a royal-blue skirt suit, a white silk blouse, and pearls hanging around his neck. She'd once asked him why he dressed like women when he visited, and he'd told her his disguises represented important people in his life, people who'd left him. The Queen was his mother, Dolly Parton his ex-wife and the other face was his ex-girlfriend in the form of an actress called Nicola Walker.

He seemed to sense her watching and turned his head her way, his suit similar to the ones the police used, the forensic type. He stalked towards the fan, disappearing when he got close to the wall, then his head popped up where he must have stood on something in order to see through. His eyes in the balaclava holes chilled her — they weren't the same as usual, darker now, glinting with malice. A click, and the fan stopped whirring, the air immediately thickening. Her box home would be stifling soon, and he might not turn it on again, likely her punishment for spying.

"Your next-door neighbour is dead," he informed her, his voice flat, bland.

Lesley sucked in a sharp breath. Dead? That meant she hadn't done what he wanted. She'd failed to become whatever he expected of them all. He'd threatened death for so long that after all this time with no action, Lesley had stopped believing him.

"Why?" she whispered.

"She told a bit too much truth for my liking."

Lesley frowned. But wasn't that what he demanded, the truth? "I don't understand."

"You wouldn't. No one does. But let this be a lesson to you. She was here for years and tonight messed it all up. She told me what I didn't want to hear — and she *meant* it — and I had to get rid. She'd never have gone back to Craig like I wanted."

"What will happen to her . . . body?"

"The police can deal with her. The transformation didn't work, so *they* can pick up the pieces. I'll find someone else."

Lesley's stomach rolled over. She'd been "someone else" once, a woman walking home from the pub, his car coming by, him stopping on the quiet road to offer her a lift. She'd seen him in the Little Devil before, the plastic surgeon who raked in cash from people's insecurities, from their need to fix their supposed imperfections. Of course, she'd trusted him and got into the passenger side. He'd smiled, asked her where she lived, and set off on the road towards the big Tesco on the outskirts instead of heading through the Coldwater estate.

The locks had clunked down, and she'd known then that it wasn't the usual lift home, that something else was going on. Like it had before when that other man had . . .

She'd panicked but held it inside, turning to look at him. He'd stared straight ahead, his jaw clamped, thick fingers gripping the steering wheel.

"I don't live this way," she'd said.

"I know."

She didn't want to recall what happened next so concentrated on the slices of his wool-covered face showing through the fan. "Who will you take? Do you know who it'll be?"

"I always know who it'll be."

He'd told her as much during his "visits", the long list of people who'd broken his rules of life spewing out of his mouth. All of them had cheated, so he'd explained, something he couldn't abide. Lesley had queried why she'd been taken, because she hadn't cheated on anyone, but he'd insisted she had, he'd heard the gossip.

What he'd *actually* heard was a rumour based on misplaced identity — another woman had been having an affair, not her, but her captor wasn't having any of it.

"Are you going to be good and get down?" he asked her.

"Yes."

"Then I'll put the fan back on."

The twang of the fan cord being pulled sent the blades spinning. Cool air wafted onto her hot face, and she crouched so he couldn't see her. His muffled footsteps told her he was walking away, then the slam of the lounge door came, but she didn't stand straight, not yet. She'd lied to him in the past, said she'd sit, then when she'd heard the door shutting, she'd stood to find his Queen face still there.

She counted for five minutes, and the faint noise of the main front door closing and the even fainter one of a car engine starting had her unfolding herself to stare through the fan.

"Did you hear that?" she shouted, her voice chopped up, reminding her of how she'd spoken into a desk fan as a child, creating robot voices.

"Yes!" Teresa shouted back through her fan, the word coming out stuttered.

So it was Karen who'd died, then.

With nothing further coming from her companion to the right, Lesley closed her eyes. She'd be next if she didn't give him the answers he wanted, but how could she when she'd already maintained she hadn't cheated, that he'd got the wrong person?

She'd have to lie and admit to something she hadn't done. Maybe that would be her ticket out of here alive.

But I know who he is, so why would he risk releasing me? How can he trust me not to talk? Why should I believe he'll kill my mam and dad if I do?

But he'd killed Karen, so maybe she *should* believe him now.

It was a game, it had to be. He had no intention of setting anyone free.

CHAPTER THREE

The Alley beside Buns 'n' Bread

Carol and Dave stood side by side in the early hours of Monday morning, the sun poking her mighty orange head above the horizon into the clear blue above. Summer had come around again, Scudderton full of tourists, and at 5 a.m., there was enough light to see, but a tall halogen lamp had been set up just the same, giving the alley a bright wash of whiteness.

Everything appeared too stark, too *there*, right in Carol's face. The muggy air asked sweat to join the sombre party, her skin clammy beneath her clothes and the protective suit, her palms sticky from the gloves. Her breath inside the mask bounced back and coated her skin, and she craved a glass of water. All things the dead person couldn't feel or see, her life stripped away by what could only be described as a sadistic, twisted fucker.

As usual, Rib Shears, the pathologist, knelt on an evidence step beside the body of a woman who'd clearly been treated abysmally. Thin to the point of starvation. Her bones prominent, the skin tight over them. Carol couldn't decide what stood out the most, all the cigarette burns or the savage wounds where she'd been cut then sewn up. The pattern of thread reminded her of the Smith case, the rows of crosses on the doll-like corpses, bodies pointedly handled with disrespect.

As far as Carol could see, the deceased had been cut above the pubic area, and at the neck and breasts. A pile of skin had been placed beside her, raw pork rind in a supermarket fridge. An interesting aspect was how she'd been posed — on her back, her ankles held together with nylon rope, her hands placed over her private parts, one on top of the other. To preserve her dignity? That seemed highly unlikely, given the fact her breasts were on display. Did it mean something else, something only the killer understood?

Strangulation bruises marred the neck, and the throat bothered her — it was as though the top of her neck, in the crease, had been sliced *after* she'd been choked, and joining the skin together meant the purple blots created by thumbs had distorted. Lower down were more thumb marks, so the killer must have repositioned their hands. It was a small mercy if she'd been killed first and cut afterwards. The other way around didn't bear thinking about. The pain. The terror.

No tent had been erected, Todd Butcher's SOCO team yet to turn up bar the photographer. As all the pictures of the body had been taken prior to Carol and Dave's arrival, Rib bagged the deceased's hands and moved them onto plastic sheeting he'd laid either side of her, revealing the abdomen wound in all its glory, the jagged slice from hip to hip. Had internal parts been removed? Would there be a missing womb, further lending weight to Carol's initial thought about the hands hiding the private parts? Was this about reproduction? With the lower half of each breast cut off and the legs being closed . . . was the killer trying to tell them something?

Rib raised one of the arms. Oh, another wound. He cocked his head to inspect the sewn-up slice from elbow to beneath the armpit. "This . . . it's botched batwing surgery — not a straight line, more of a wobbly one, so someone not used to doing it. The excess skin over there—" he nodded to the pile — "points to severe weight loss, too fast, so the skin didn't have a chance to shrink slowly. I can already see from the discarded bits that there are faded stretch marks and the elasticity has gone. Did someone perform an operation that went wrong? Was she desperate to get rid of the saggy skin but didn't qualify for NHS surgery?"

"Why the strangulation marks, though?" Dave said. "They don't make sense if we go with your theory."

Rib placed the arm down and leaned over to check the other one. It was the same. "Maybe she had a fit during the op and the person acting as a surgeon panicked. A guess, nowt more."

"Nope, it doesn't work for me." Dave adjusted his mask. "The fag burns. How skinny she is. Food's been withheld."

"Or she withheld it from herself," Rib said. "And *she* could have administered the burns."

"Depends. Check her back." Carol knew about self-harm, but the amount of burns, new and old, were a bit much. Could this be a woman who'd been desperate to lose weight, had starved herself, hated the baggy skin so had burned her body to release her anger, then she'd enlisted the help of a dodgy plastic surgeon?

No, too ridiculous.

Rib gently gripped the arm farthest from him and pulled the body towards him so the victim rested on her side. "She's still pliable enough, so rigor hasn't fully set in yet. What's behind there?"

Carol bent to look. "Burns. Sewed skin beneath each bum cheek and down the thighs. She couldn't have burned herself, some places are too far to reach, so someone else did it."

Rib lowered the woman to her back then gestured to the head. "Alopecia. Stress-related hair loss or a condition she's always had?" He bent to study the scalp. "Her hair's been cut recently, and it would take a skilled stylist to get the length all the same with scissors, otherwise clippers were used. She's extremely thin, so if she was anorexic, the alopecia could have come from that."

Dave let out a breath. "Okay, I'd agree with the anorexia and self-harm theory were it not for the burns on her back and the surgery, although whoever did it had no clue what they were doing. A proper surgeon would have cut her more precisely and sewn her up with dissolving stitches, surely, not that green thread."

Carol's mind ticked over. "What if she was held somewhere? That ticks all the boxes. Lack of food, alopecia from stress, fag burns from torture, her captor having a go at doing surgery, then for whatever reason, she's killed. We'll need to check the missing person's database."

"Might be no need." Rib indicated farther up the alley to a yellow marker. "Her handbag is there; I haven't had a chance to check it yet."

He stood, ferreted in his medical bag and brought out what appeared to be a drumstick. They followed him to the bag, and he crouched, lifting it with the stick beneath the straps.

"I'd need to change my gloves to touch it, so can you have a look inside, Bird?" he asked Carol.

She took the brown leather bag and twisted the silver clasp. Inside, all manner of things: a Freddo, lipstick, blusher, compact mirror, tampons, keys and the best thing — a pink purse. "Dave, grab that, will you?"

He took the purse out and undid the popper for the side that held cards. "Lucky for us, a driving license." He removed it and held it towards Carol. "Karen Stokes, forty-two, lives at five Kipling Close, the Coldwater estate."

"The rough end," Carol said.

"Doesn't mean *she* was rough," Rib said.

"I know, it was just an observation, Mr Jump-on-my-case."

Rib laughed. "You're too easy to wind up."

She poked her tongue out, despite him not being able to see it behind her mask. "It might mean something, where she lived. There's more likely to be someone there who'd be prepared to do this hideous surgery on her."

"It's not the olden days, like those women with knitting needles who claimed they were abortionists." Rib shook his head.

"I realise that — oi, are you winding me up again?"

"Might be."

She chose not to fling something back at him, opting to be the bigger person, although she was dying to say something caustic to keep the banter going, something to lighten the oppressive air around here. She enjoyed being in his company these days, now she knew he wasn't being an arsehole to her, that his way of being friendly was to grind her gears. "We're all aware that strange people live in plain sight. Who knows how she got this way, but we'll bloody well find out."

"Do you want a rough estimate on when she died? I've already taken her temp."

"Please."

"Between midnight and three."

"Okay, thanks, that gives us something to go on when asking her next of kin where they were last night. First, I'll ring Michael and get him to find out who it is. She might not have a husband or partner."

She walked to a cardboard box containing evidence bags and placed the handbag inside one. She handed it to Rib for him to fill out the relevant information, then passed Dave a bag for the purse.

"Can you take pictures of those, Dave, so we can show the NOK? The face on the driver's license is so different from what she looks like now. For all we know, they might not be the same person, so getting confirmation on the handbag and the purse will help."

She went to the end of the alley, stopping by the inner cordon. She smiled at the log officer beside her. PC Mulholland had drawn the short straw there, but he didn't appear to mind doing the most boring job on the planet.

"You okay?" she asked him.

"Yeah. So-so."

The street was deserted apart from uniformed coppers in booties, checking the ground inside the outer cordon, searching while they waited for SOCO to take over — the quicker they could find something the better. Buns 'n' Bread might not be opening today, nor any of the other shops blocked off with police tape.

Sergeant Richard Prince caught her attention, beckoning her.

She pointed to her booties. "I'd need to change these, so you come here."

Richard strode over and remained on the path on the other side of the alley cordon. "I've got officers doing door-to-door enquiries around here and the streets behind; not a thing so far, though. As expected, everyone was asleep and heard nowt, and nobody was happy about being woken up early."

"I don't suppose they were." Carol could do with picking Richard's brains. He'd been a bobby around here for years and knew many of the locals. She privately thought of him as the Oracle. "She's called Karen Stokes. Heard of her?"

His eyebrows hiked up. "Bloody hell, she went missing about three years ago."

Carol's heart skipped a beat. "Missing?"

"Well, I say missing . . . She left the Devil after a night out and didn't make it home, but it isn't like it sounds."

"How come I never heard about this?"

"You were on another case. There'd been talk of her leaving her husband, Craig — lots of talk. As in, she'd planned when she was going to do it, which was around the time she disappeared. She told a friend she wasn't taking owt with her except for her handbag and the clothes she stood up in. Oh, and the money. She'd opened a separate bank account in her name only and had been depositing cash for about five years prior, small amounts so as not to arouse her husband's suspicions."

"What was Craig's take on it?"

"He wouldn't believe she'd left him. Said she wouldn't dare — take that as you will, but *my* view on it was he'd been abusive. He's . . . brusque, shall we say. Not your cup of tea at all."

"Shit. Just what I need." A confrontational man always got her hackles up, reminding her of her father. "She's got cigarette burns all over her, and someone's attempted surgery — looks like it was to remove excess skin. She's as skinny as a rake."

Richard frowned. "That's interesting. She'd have been classed as overweight when she left, which is daft in my opinion. She just looked comfy in her body to me."

"So why was the case closed? Assuming it was, that is."

"Because money was withdrawn from her bank account afterwards. Different ATMs throughout the area — Robin Hood's Bay, Whitby, Sandsend, Runswick Bay, Scarborough. We checked out the first few, you know, had a look at the CCTV to see who'd been withdrawing, and it was her. She kept doing it until all the money was gone."

"How long was that?"

"A couple of months. The missing person's team had seen proof of life, so what else could they think but that she'd kept her promise and left Craig? There's only so much we can do, isn't there? People *do* leave to start again, sending no word back to their families. It happens."

Carol nodded. "What we're trying to work out is whether she starved herself and possibly shacked up with someone who liked burning her, or she was abducted and imprisoned. I was leaning towards the latter, but now I don't know what to think."

"Either way, she's come to a bad end, which is what Craig was convinced was going to happen. He's maintained all this time that even though she'd said she was leaving, she wouldn't really have done it."

"Any kids?"

Mulholland coughed. "Those two teenage girls suspected of robbing the elderly."

Carol pulled a face. "*Those* little sods?"

"Yep. We've yet to catch them at it or find any fingerprints — the last victim said they had gloves on and snoods over their faces. We've nowt to pin on them, see, just a description that it's girls with ponytails, and I've talked to them umpteen times. They swear it isn't them, but the rumours flying around say different. It's only a matter of time before they're caught in the act."

"Why are they even doing it?" Carol asked.

"Gone off the rails, haven't they, since their mother left them." Mulholland shrugged. "Doesn't excuse it in my book."

Carol winced internally. *Her* mother had left too, and she understood the girls acting out because of it. Although Carol had wanted to, she hadn't dared. Her father, Harry, had kept her in line with his fists and his bullying, reminding Carol it was her fault his wife had upped sticks. Telling tales, he'd called it.

"They might get worse when we go and give them the bad news." Carol stripped her gloves off and dropped them in the designated bag behind the cordon. She took her phone out. "Which reminds me, I need to update Michael so he can get going on this. Katherine's still in bed — she's got the school run to sort out as the woman who usually helps her is ill. Thanks for letting me know the NOK's name, Rich. It saves Michael the job of tracking him down."

"No problem."

"I assume Craig still lives in Kipling Close."

"As far as I'm aware. I'll give you a bell if the uniforms come up with owt round here."

"Thanks."

Richard walked away to direct the newly arrived SOCO van on where to park, and Carol swiped her screen. The connection rang twice.

"Are you properly awake yet?" she asked.

Michael chuckled. "Wide as. Have you got owt?"

"The deceased is Karen Stokes." She went on to describe the injuries, the story about her walking out on Craig and what her daughters were getting up to.

"Sounds like she left home and met someone, and whoever it is has been abusing her," he said.

"That's what I'm thinking now, that she lived off the money she'd withdrawn, then got together with a new partner who subsidised her, which is why there's no record of earnings."

"Her not being listed as living anywhere is a concern, though."

"Not if you think about it this way: Craig might have been abusive according to Richard, so she wouldn't *want* to be found."

"Okay, I'll look into everything."

"If we're not back by nine, which I bloody well hope we are, get Katherine poking into social media when she comes in, and if you're bogged down, she can also do her thing reading Karen's misper file."

"Will do."

"Got owt on the mobile used to ring the police?" There was no dog-walker or jogger to speak to, someone who'd stumbled upon the body. News of the death had come via an anonymous phone call.

"It's a pay-as-you-go effort. I'm waiting for news on where it was purchased, but with no contract, we don't have a name, and seeing as it's so early in the morning . . ."

"Well, we're off to see the husband, so catch you later."

"Ta-ra."

She slid her phone away and turned to call out to Dave, who left Rib with the body and walked to her. Carol took off her protective clothing and bagged it, Dave doing the same, then she dipped under the cordon, signed out of the log and headed for her car beyond the outer street cordon. In the driver's seat, she stared through the windscreen and thought about what she'd seen. That poor woman. Who the hell had done that to her?

Dave got in the passenger side and consulted his notebook. "So, number five Kipling Close."

"Hmm. I'm not looking forward to it."

"Why?"

She told him what Richard and Mulholland had said. "We might be greeted by an angry bloke who decides to take things out on us. Shooting the messenger kind of thing."

Dave sniffed. "So long as he offers coffee, he can blame us all he likes. My throat's well dry."

"Yeah, we were up too early to grab a brew."

She smiled. They lived together now, a cottage in the village of Mollengate, one she'd purchased with money left to her by her father. Dave helped to pay the bills, and she had extra money coming in from a static caravan she'd purchased. It was booked out until October, and she paid the site manager to clean it between lettings and deal with the holidaymakers.

"We could have had one in a to-go cup," Dave grumbled, "but you insisted on getting down here straightaway. I didn't even have a chance to wipe the sleepy dust from my eyes."

"Karen deserves us going without so we can give her justice."

"I know, I'm only messing."

She smiled. "I agree, though, coffee does sound good. We just have to pray Craig isn't the stingy type, or maybe he'll be too upset."

Dave put his seat belt on. "You know me, if I get the chance, I'll go and make one anyroad, give him something to hold in case he thinks about getting fisty."

Carol started the engine and drove towards the Coldwater estate. "He'd better not. I'm in no mood for arsey men."

"Me neither."

"Good, then we're on the same page."

CHAPTER FOUR

Kipling Close

Knitty Nora opened the curtains and nosed out of her bedroom window. It was ten to six on yet another muggy morning, and she had to get to work by eight. She rode her moped every day to what she called her *appointments*, the job list sent through the night before by her boss at Constant Cleaning. Knitty liked her work, scrubbing other people's homes. It helped to keep her guilty mind busy, although one client didn't need her there at all. He was a surgeon who lived out in Truth-Hunt Cottage, a weird name to call a home if ever there was one, but who was she to judge? He cleaned well enough all by himself, so why he'd asked for a cleaner was beyond her. Once she got home, she picked up her knitting, hence her nickname, and created things for the neonatal unit at the hospital.

It was something she did to make good on what she'd done.

Two people got out of a car parked outside next door. It wouldn't surprise her if they were police, going by the way they carried themselves, all stiff-backed and full to the brim with importance. They had that air about them, didn't they, coppers? It was about time the Stokes girls were reprimanded for what they got up to. They'd yet to try to rob Knitty, and if they did, she'd soon give them a clip around the earhole, but they'd hassled one of Knitty's elderly friends last week and nicked her pension.

Terrible children, but with parents like they had, it was bound to happen.

The officers walked up the Stokeses' garden path and knocked on the door. The woman took something out of her inside suit jacket pocket and opened it up. Ah, they *were* the police, that was some kind of ID.

Knitty rushed downstairs to the living room, snatching a glass from the sideboard that she kept there for listening and carefully placed it on the wall, her ear to the chilly end. Weird goings-on happened next door, and she liked to keep abreast of it. Today's episode might make her late for work, but if she caught the coppers as they were leaving, she could tell the boss she'd had to give a statement or something.

Excited that her somewhat boring life was about to have an injection of drama, she closed her eyes to concentrate.

CHAPTER FIVE

Kipling Close

"Craig Stokes?" Carol held up her ID and assessed the bulldog of a man, hoping he wouldn't give them any shit. It was too early for that.

He didn't have the kind of body where he'd toned it at the gym, but he was a beefy fella, his neck the widest she'd ever seen. He appeared rumpled from sleep — they must have got him out of bed — his greying hair standing every which way, and his white vest and boxer shorts needing a wash. Stains on the vest spoke of dribbled ketchup.

Unless that's blood

"Yeah?" he groused, clearly annoyed at coming to the door at this time of the morning. He peered at her.

"DI Carol Wren and DS Dave Waite. Can we come in, please?"

As if sleep had so far clouded his mind and he'd just realised why they might be there, his eyes lit up. "Is it about Karen?"

Carol nodded. "It is."

"Have you found her?"

"Please, indoors would be best."

"Doesn't sound good."

He turned, and another kind of stain on the back of the boxers had Carol holding back a heave. She dreaded to think if he'd followed through and hadn't bothered to change them. If Karen *had* left him, was it any wonder if he presented himself like that? Or had he only become slovenly since she'd gone?

Carol glanced at Dave, and he mimed poking fingers down his throat. She pinched her lips together — she couldn't laugh or smile, not in this situation, but God, she wanted to. Maybe it was a case of nerves more than anything.

She followed Craig into a living room that matched the man — dishevelled, uncared for, stained and smelly. The front door clicked, then Dave came to stand beside her. He coughed into his fist and glanced around for somewhere to sit, but the chairs were full of discarded jumbles of clothing, schoolbags and shoes, and the sofa had a quilt and pillow on it, neither of them with covers. They were no longer white but a shade of filth, what seemed to be spilled coffee on the duvet.

I bloody hope it's coffee.

Craig bundled the bedding up and threw it into the corner beside the TV cabinet, on top of which sat a huge flat-screen. He plonked himself down and gestured to the chairs. "Just dump that shit off and give your legs a rest."

Carol moved a pair of black skinny jeans out of the way and perched on the edge, tops and bras and leggings behind her, thigh muscles straining from the uncomfortable position. Dave moved to close the door and remained standing in front of it.

"Have you had a sighting of her?" Craig laced his fingers over the reddish dribble on his vest. To hide it?

"Yes." Carol wasn't lying, but the actual sighting wouldn't be what he was expecting. "I'm sorry to have to inform you, but a body was discovered this morning, and based on the ID we found, we believe it to be your wife, Karen."

"You what?" Craig bounced forward, elbows on shiny bare knees amid the thick hairs on his legs. "She's dead, is that what you're saying?"

"She is."

"How? I mean, I thought she was living along the coast a bit, the withdrawals proved that."

"We don't know why she's back in Scudderton, nor where she lived after she left, it's something we're looking into to determine how this happened to her. When was the last time you saw her?"

"In person? The night she went up the Little Devil with her friend. After that, I saw her in the photos the missing person's team showed me, the ones where she was taking cash out. I had to confirm it was her."

People took news like this differently, but Craig didn't seem upset by the death, more confused. He scratched his head, frowning, then his bottom lip wobbled. Some kind of reaction was better than none. Maybe it was only just sinking in.

"What happened, did she have a heart attack or something?"

Carol took a deep breath. "She was murdered. Strangled."

"Eh? That doesn't make any sense! Why would she be strangled?"

"She'd been abused." Carol sensed he could take the truth but wanted to be sure. "Do you want to know the details?"

"Of course I bloody do, she's my *wife*."

"We have information regarding her appearance when you last saw her, and since then, she'd lost a lot of weight. She appears to be about a size six now, but the signs are that she didn't eat well, was perhaps denied food. Is this something you think she'd have done to herself?"

Craig laughed. "Karen's a burger and chips kind of gal, chicken nuggets, chocolate."

Carol thought of the Freddo. The information on the wrapper could be used to find out where she'd bought it and whether it was an old one she'd had in her bag the night she'd gone missing or if it was a newer purchase. "Excuse me for a moment." She took her phone out and messaged Michael to ask forensics to give him details on the wrapper once the evidence had been processed. She put her mobile away. "Sorry, you saying chocolate . . . She had a Freddo in her handbag. Is that something she'd have eaten?"

"Yeah, she loved chocolate, especially those. She'd never starve herself, so if a Freddo was all that was on offer, she'd have eaten it. She was okay with her size, and so was I, it meant no one else would want her. So no, she definitely wouldn't have gone hungry if she could help it." He shook his head. "Size six. That's way too small for her."

"Okay, thank you, that helps us a lot. Are you all right for me to continue?"

"Yeah." He flapped a hand. "Get on with it."

"There are old and new cigarette burns all over her body. Did she smoke?"

"Yeah, but she wouldn't have done *that* to herself. Low pain threshold. When she had the kids, you should have heard her screaming." He guffawed.

Inappropriate, but maybe this was his way of dealing with it.

"We know she didn't do it because they're also on her back and thighs where she wouldn't have been able to reach. What I'm about to tell you next is harrowing, so if you'd prefer me not to say . . ."

"Look, I want to know everything, no matter how bad, so stop stalling and spit it out. Christ."

Keep your hair on "Someone had performed an operation on her. This may seem like an odd question, but was anyone jealous of her having children?"

"How should I know, and what the fuck are you asking me that for?"

"There's a cut on her lower region, like for a caesarean, and the ends of her breasts were removed."

"What are you saying, she was preggers and some sick fucker cut the baby out?"

Carol's skin pebbled. She hadn't considered that as an option. "The post-mortem will determine if that happened. What I'm trying to find out is whether anyone held a grudge enough to do that to her."

"She pissed a lot of people off, but not to that degree. Bloody hell, even I wouldn't stoop that low."

"What do you mean by that?"

For the first time, he seemed chagrined. "I pushed her about a bit, you know? Gave her a slap and that. I shouldn't have, and I regret it now, regretted it the moment she fucked off if you must know, but she had a way about her . . . I couldn't help but lash out."

"No one deserves that, even if they *do* have a 'way'." *Like me punching you for what you just said, it isn't right.* "Do you feel she left you because of the abuse?"

"Abuse? Shit, that makes me sound like a monster. All I did was clock her one every now and then."

"It's abuse, whatever you did." She aimed to throw him off guard. "Where were you last night until this morning?"

He stood and glared down at her. "Sod pinning this on me, woman. I haven't seen hide nor hair of her, and you'll find nowt of me on her body, you'll see. As for where I was, I had to go and sort something out to do with my girls. They'd nicked a necklace from one of the shops, and I had to speak to the manager, get her to let them off with a ban. She said that was fine, they weren't to go in there no more. They've been nowt but a handful since Karen buggered off."

"We've heard about the muggings."

He sat, slumping back. Defeated? "Yeah, it's them all right, and I'm sick of it. The minute I find out for sure, I'll be marching them down the station. They need more than a caution, embarrassing little cows."

Carol wasn't sure what to make of his attitude, whether it was a father pushed to his limit or he just didn't like his offspring. "What's your relationship with your children like?"

Craig shrugged. "Hard to describe. I love them because they're mine, but I don't like them at the minute. Truth be told, they were fuckers before Karen went, always up to something, but they got worse after. I can't control them. The threat of a wallop does nowt."

"You said *threat.* So you hit your wife but not your daughters?"

"I'd never hurt those girls, what do you take me for?"

Carol failed to understand his reasoning. Karen had been someone's little girl, yet he'd felt it was okay to smack *her* around. "Back to what you were doing. What time did you go to the shop about the theft?"

"Straight from work, so about half five. The manager's a mate, she phoned me."

"Where do you work?"

"The biscuit factory. Senior line attendant."

"Where did you go after the shop?"

"I took them to June's Chippy for our tea, then we went to the fairground on the pier for a bit. I know, it sounds like I was rewarding their bad behaviour, but I just wanted to see them smile again instead of going about with those bloody scowls like they always do. We left around eight, came here, and I grounded them until next weekend. They went upstairs while I watched a bit of telly."

"What did you watch?"

"Netflix. A film about some bloke with bionic eyes. Fucking boring, so I fell asleep. I woke up about eleven, checked the girls were actually in, because they've got a tendency to sneak out. They were out for the count, so I came back down, grabbed the quilt and pillow, and nodded off again."

"Do you sleep down here, then?"

"Yeah, have done since . . . I don't like the bed without Karen."

What a contrary bloke. An abuser who seemed to love his wife in the only way he knew how, which was ropey at best, but he *did* have feelings.

"So, back to the night Karen went to the pub. I realise you've probably been through this umpteen times already, but we're new to her disappearance, starting from scratch, so bear with us."

"Fine. If it means you find whoever killed her, I'll answer owt you want. She went to the pub with Lindsey who lives at number twelve. They've been mates for years, had kids at the same time, went up the school together, you know the sort of thing. Anyroad, Lindsey drank too much and had to go home. Karen said she'd stay behind because there was another mam there, think her name was Julia. Lindsey got home about ten, and according to Reg, the landlord of the Devil, Karen walked out at ten past eleven. She was pissed as a fart, weaving, but happy."

"Do you know where Julia lives? Have you got her phone number?"

"Nah."

"Her surname?"

"Bolton."

"When was it Karen informed her friend she was going to leave you?"

"A couple of weeks before she left. Lindsey, she told. I don't believe it. Maybe I'm being naive, but what with me slapping the wife about, she seemed too scared to walk away. I *did* love her, you know."

Carol didn't have a suitable answer for that, her diplomacy on the subject non-existent, and if she blurted what she really felt, she might well be looking at a reprimand if Craig complained to the DCI. If he loved her, he wouldn't have struck her, it was as simple as that. "She didn't take a suitcase?"

"No, all her stuff is still here. You can look in the bedroom if you want, just do it quietly, because I don't want the girls to wake up yet. I need time to . . . Yeah, I need time."

Dave slipped gloves on. Carol got up and whispered for him to find out where Julia Bolton lived while he was upstairs. He left the room, closing the door behind him. Carol took her notebook out to write things down now her partner wasn't here.

"Do you recall how much money Karen managed to put into her own bank account?"

"That was a shock, her doing that. Your lot said it was about four grand, maybe five, can't remember exactly, but I never noticed it going missing. Karen did the shopping and paid all the bills, so she knew how much she could skim without it being obvious. That's enough for a deposit in a rented place, plus the rent itself and whatever else she'd need — food, clothes and the like. That's what I reckon she did with it."

"There's no record of her renting or buying anywhere, no record of her existing since her night at the Devil."

"She's not clever enough to have got a new identity. I said that at the time. She's a bit thick. Plus, her taking cash out along the coast, it didn't fit. She was always banging on about London, she'd have gone there. I told the missing person's woman Karen wouldn't hang about up here, and I said something would happen to her, because I don't believe she'd have left me when push came to shove."

"We haven't had a chance to review the file yet, so if you could help me out here . . . Was there any CCTV of her leaving the pub?"

"Was there fuck. You must know what it's like down the marina. There's sod all security, even in town. She walked out of the Devil and vanished."

It was so frustrating. Karen could have left him, yet she could also have been taken. What were the odds of that, though? How convenient was it for the abductor to have nabbed her when she was about to leave her husband? Had someone overheard her talking to Lindsey about it? "Do you know where that conversation took place, where Karen said she was leaving you?"

"In the pub."

"The Devil?"

"Yeah."

There was a lot to think about. Was it possible someone had snatched Karen *because* she was leaving, and her disappearance could be blamed on that? What had they done then, taken her up and down the coast to withdraw cash? *Really*? That sounded too fantastical, but stranger things had happened.

What if she was having an affair and went off with the bloke and he turned nasty years down the line?

She had to ask. "Was your wife seeing anyone else?"

"She'd have had a right old shiner from me if she was."

"So that's a no, then?"

"As far as I know, she wasn't playing away at the time she fucked off, but I did catch her out another time, years before that. We got through it."

"What do you mean by that?"

"Well, I dealt with it, didn't I? And she didn't mess me about again. Wouldn't dare."

"Dealt with it?"

"I shoved her."

Carol had a hard time keeping her temper in check. Craig spoke as if it was his right to bully his wife.

The door opened, defusing the bomb about to go off inside her, and Dave stepped in. He shook his head: *Nowt up there of concern.*

Carol wrote down the gist of what Craig had said. She looked up at him. "What's that on your top?"

Craig lifted it. "Barbeque sauce."

"So you won't mind us taking it to check that."

"Nope." He tugged it off and sat there with his belly hanging out.

Dave took an evidence bag from his pocket and popped the vest inside.

"Can you get someone to come and collect that?" she asked him. They had to visit Lindsey and wouldn't be able to take it in.

Dave left the room again.

Craig got up and tossed a few clothes around on the other chair. He found a black T-shirt and put it on, returning to his spot on the sofa. "She suffered?"

"I can't lie, suffocation isn't a pleasant way to go."

"If I get my hands on that bastard . . ."

"I'd advise you to keep that sort of thing to yourself."

Dave came back, nodded to Carol, then got on with labelling the evidence bag.

"I can't imagine her skinny," Craig mused. "I called her my chunky monkey."

"That's abuse as well, you know."

"What? You're having a laugh."

"It's bullying."

"The world's gone mad! Don't say this, don't say that."

Dave pulled his phone out. "Can I ask you to look at these pictures? They're not of Karen, it's two items. Do you recognise them?" He found the images and held the phone for Craig to see, then swiped to the next one.

"That's her handbag and purse." Craig sagged. "It's got to be her, hasn't it?"

Carol didn't need to answer that. "What was Karen's hair like?"

"Long. Curly. Blonde."

"Did she suffer from alopecia?"

"I've no clue what that is."

"Patches of hair loss."

"No."

"Had she always had long hair?"

"Yep, wouldn't cut it for no one."

"Okay, I think that's enough for now." Carol smiled at him. "You've had a shock, and we can come and chat to you again after we've looked at Karen's file if we have owt we need clarifying."

"What about Karen? Where is she?"

Carol wasn't about to give him the location. She imagined he'd storm down there and demand to see her. "She's in situ at present and will be for some time."

"In situ? What's that?"

"Where she was discovered. She'll be under a tent, and the pathologist and Scenes of Crime officers are in attendance. They won't move her until they're satisfied they have all the evidence they can gather. It could take hours."

"When can I see her?"

"After the post-mortem, although you might want to think about giving that a miss. The injury to her neck and the burns—"

"I need to see she's dead, that it's her."

"Bear in mind the weight loss. She won't look the same as you remember her. I'll ask the pathologist to give you a ring — it'll be classed as a formal identification. Do you think you'll benefit from a family liaison officer?"

"What, them nosy bastards who listen in?"

"It's not like that." *Although it kind of is* "Whitney can offer support and help you with the girls."

"When you put it like that, yeah, I could do with someone like her coming. She'll know how to deal with them when I tell them what's happened, won't she?"

Carol nodded. "You can wait for her to arrive if you like."

Craig grunted. "Yeah, that's best. What time should I expect her?"

CHAPTER SIX

Kipling Close

Knitty pulled the glass away from the wall. Well now, the things she'd heard! She had a thing or two she could tell the police herself, so she put her slippers on and went to the front door, opening it a tad to listen to them saying their goodbyes. They told Craig they'd send this Whitney woman round before half past eight then walked down the path to the pavement.

Knitty waited for the door to shut, then she opened hers wider. "*Psst*."

The woman turned and looked her way, opening her mouth to speak, but Knitty placed a finger to her lips and beckoned them over. She moved farther down the hallway so they'd know to come in and, when they approached the door, she flicked her hand for them to enter.

Both of them inside, the bloke closing the door, the lady held her ID up.

"DI Carol Wren and DS Dave Waite. Can we help you?"

"It's more about me helping you. Come on, I'll put the kettle on."

They grinned as though that was the best news they'd heard all week.

"Dave, can you let the officer know they've got to pick the bag up from here?" Carol said.

Knitty eyed it. One of those evidence ones she'd seen on the telly. It had white fabric inside. That had to be the top they'd got Craig to take off.

"What's your name?" Carol asked.

"Nora Patten, but everyone calls me Knitty."

Carol smiled.

Knitty went into the kitchen and filled the kettle, saying over her shoulder, "Park yourselves. He didn't offer you a brew, did he?"

"No, but I don't think he was in the right frame of mind to think about playing host," Carol said.

"He wouldn't anyroad, the mardy git. I was listening, you know, a glass against the wall. Been doing that for years. Carol — can I call you Carol?"

"Of course."

"Well, Carol, I've seen many a thing in my time, heard a few things, too." Knitty collected cups off the draining board and put teabags in them. "He's a rum one, that Craig. A bastard, to be exact. I don't blame Karen for copping off with his mate."

Dave whipped his notebook out.

"I assume you want tea, or is it coffee you're after?" Knitty held a teaspoon aloft.

"Coffee, please," Carol said. "*Copping off*??"

Knitty took the teabags out of two cups and spooned in some Nescafé. "She was having it away with that fella Geordie. He's from Newcastle. He's lived here since he was a kid but still has the accent. I saw him coming and going while Craig was at work, and like I said, I *heard* things. Didn't even need to use the glass!"

"What did you hear?" Carol asked.

"Them sex noises. Grunting and whatever, the squeaky bed. And laughter. Never heard Karen laugh so much as when Geordie was round. She sounded so happy compared to when he wasn't there."

"How long had that been going on?"

"Oh, ages. She'd been squirreling money away for years before she started seeing him. I took it that they'd planned to run away together. It didn't surprise me when she never came home, but it *did* surprise me that Geordie was still about. I could have sworn he'd have gone with her, but then when news came that she'd been taking all that cash out, I reckoned she'd moved up the coast and Geordie had stayed here so it didn't look obvious he'd been seeing her." She poured boiled water into the cups. "He's a friend of mine, but I didn't ask him about it because . . . well, some men don't like you in their business, do they? And they let you know about it an' all. He stopped coming round to see Craig about a year ago, and I suspected they'd had a falling-out."

She poured milk and stirred, then carried the drinks to the table. Back at the worktop, she picked up her sugar pot with the spoon sticking out of it and placed it so everyone could reach. She sat, excited about having someone to talk to. She hadn't met up with her group of friends for a while and sorely missed the company.

"Oh, let me just send my boss a message." Knitty pulled her phone out of her pocket.

"Where do you work?" the man asked. Dave, wasn't it?

"Constant Cleaning. I ride out on my moped to the outlying places no one else wants. Cottages nearer to Mollengate."

Knitty tapped in a message: *Police here. I'm giving a statement. Will be late.*

"That's a fair old trek on a moped," Dave said.

"I don't mind. Anyroad, help yourself to sugar, and I'll get back to my story. I've got to rewind a bit so you get the full picture. I've always lived here, it was my mam and dad's before me, so I've known that lot next door since the day they moved in. They only had the one kiddie at the time, but the other one followed a year later — and Karen wasn't happy about it."

"Did she tell you that, then?" Carol sipped her coffee.

"I happened to be hanging my washing out one morning when she was talking to her mother — she's dead now, by the way, the drunken sop, and there's a rumour she went with her cousin, Karen the product of it."

Dave wrote that down.

"Do you have their names?" Carol cradled her cup.

"What, the mother and the cousin? Margaret and Billy Baker. I think he's dead an' all, now I come to think of it."

"Thanks. So this conversation you heard . . ."

"Oh yes, Karen was talking to her mam, and she said she shouldn't have had children, they were a bind. Her exact words were: 'I fucking hate them and wish they were dead.'"

Carol's eyebrows shot up. "Oh dear."

"Hmm, it's no wonder they've turned out the way they have. It wasn't a shock when Karen went off like she did. Those kids were shouted at by her more often than not, called names, so she would have been pleased to be without them, I'd say." Knitty took a breath. "I heard you telling him she's dead."

"Unfortunately, yes."

"And the abuse." Knitty shuddered. "Cigarette burns!"

"Do you know of anyone who'd want to do that to her?" Dave held his pen over his notebook.

"Plenty." Knitty chuckled. "Karen was . . . unpleasant at times. Always gobbing off and sticking her oar in where it wasn't wanted. She caused untold trouble in the street, but I think it was because she didn't have any control when Craig was around so she exerted it on others. A lout, you might say. Maybe whoever killed her was someone from around here." She stared at the adjoining wall to make her point.

"Mr Stokes has an alibi."

"I know, and he's telling the truth about being home and watching the telly last night, same as he was when Karen went missing. But maybe he got someone else to track her down and kill her."

Carol drank. "So you think he's the type?"

"Yes. You should have seen him when Karen didn't come back. Steaming, he was, ranting and raving, how dare she leave me this, how dare she abandon us that. I was the only one bold enough to tell him it was his fault, she'd gone because he tanned her backside all the time, but he told me to mind my own business and piss off." She folded her arms. "Did I help?"

"Very much so." Carol drank some more coffee and got up to place the mug in the sink. "Sorry I didn't finish it all." She smiled and handed over her business card. "In case you remember something and need to get hold of me. So, Geordie. You say you're friends. Where does he live?"

"Ask Lindsey over the road." Knitty gave them a sly grin, like she knew his address but wanted to keep out of it. "Because she was having it away with Geordie's brother."

CHAPTER SEVEN

The New Me Clinic

Grim had started work early as his client needed to be home by teatime. He'd set up his clinic when working for the NHS had become untenable — that job had been one of the reasons Emma had cited as grounds for having an affair. Starting up on his own had been his way to show her, after she'd walked out, that he was willing to cut down his hours for her, to do whatever it took to reconcile. Besides, he'd thought the extra money he raked in would lure her back. Sadly, that hope had gone down the shitter. His sharp rise in earnings hadn't bothered her one bit, not when she'd had her precious boyfriend to play with.

In his office, he clamped his teeth together, listening to the sounds his staff created while getting the theatre ready. If he could work alone he would, but couldn't perform without the anaesthetist and the rest of the medical team.

Today's lady, a fifty-one-year-old fitness fanatic, wanted her face and neck wrinkles taken away. She'd look twenty years younger by the time he'd finished with her, and he'd be all the richer. She was the only client on his list today, so he could get home and go to sleep for the afternoon, plus do some housework. He'd been up late disposing of Karen's body, going down the alley from the back of the shops — no cameras in the street behind. The police would question residents there, and he'd risked his vehicle being spotted, but no one had been awake as far as he'd seen.

He leaned back in his desk chair. Lesley, his guest living in box number two at Guilt-Ridden, the middle one with the blue front door . . . would she talk to him properly now she'd found out Karen was dead? And what about Teresa in number three with the pink front door? Would she realise it was time to be truthful?

He was well aware the women spoke to one another via the fans, and Teresa might have heard him telling Lesley about Karen. Communication between them wasn't allowed, but they did it anyway, even when he burned them with cigarettes as a punishment. He supposed, despite them knowing he'd hurt them if they were caught, it was human nature to reach out and connect.

Lesley had maintained she'd never cheated — that story was getting old — and Teresa was a lot like Karen, unrepentant, although she'd lied and said she was apologetic, likely in the hope he'd set her free. The thing was, he didn't believe her. She'd sounded glad about her affair, wistful, as though the man was the love of her life.

He thought about the new woman who'd take Karen's place. Maybe *she'd* come up with the goods. Maybe *she'd* understand what he was trying to teach them.

He smiled, remembering he'd left a Freddo in Karen's handbag. She'd told him she loved them, and it was his last gift to her, something to show her dead self he'd been in control right until the end; he hadn't allowed her to have it until she couldn't eat it, denying her what she craved.

Karen had wanted control, she'd said as much in one of their chat sessions. She'd lacked it in her marriage until she'd taken the bold and silly step of having an affair. It had given her a sense of accomplishment to get one over on Craig, even though he apparently hadn't suspected what was going on — if he had, he'd have beaten her black and blue. She'd told him about "the worst time", and it must have been awful, but wasn't it better for all concerned that Craig had shoved her that day?

Grim understood control. Wasn't that what he was after, a way to wrest back what he'd lost after Emma had ruined his self-esteem? He'd been wronged, had been in Craig's shoes, and he needed to do this, to make the women see that leaving a man behind meant their mind might turn and they'd end up like . . .

Me.

* * *

"I'm leaving you."

They were the exact words his mother had said on her deathbed, cancer from smoking gripping her, and it chilled Grim's soul. How could Emma do this? The girl they'd nicknamed Nymph when they were nine? The girl who'd promised to love him forever, who'd now announced in their bedroom she'd been sleeping with Shark, another group member?

This couldn't be happening. How could Emma have betrayed him like this? How could Shark? They'd been friends for years, still meeting up at the pub opposite the park they used to play in, sharing their lives and having a good old knees-up. Not only had Emma said she was moving out of his life, but it meant Shark would leave, too — there was no way Grim could tolerate him now. It would create a divide in the group. The others wouldn't want meet up if there was tension.

"What?" he said. "What?"

"You heard. I don't love you anymore. Shark's been seeing me through it."

"He's been seeing to something, all right."

She narrowed her eyes. "What do you mean?"

"You! He's been seeing to you! How long has this been going on?"

Emma shrugged and threw a brush into her suitcase. "A few months."

Grim processed that. They'd had several meetups as a group during that time. Shark had behaved as usual, no sign that he'd been poking Grim's wife on the quiet. Emma hadn't changed either, no flirtatious comments or adoring looks. The pair of them had been acting, hiding what they were doing, how they felt for one another.

What would Knitty think about this? Did she know? She was close to Emma, but surely she wouldn't have kept this to herself. What about Blitz and Thunder? Those two blokes wouldn't have kept quiet, would they?

"Does everyone else know?" he asked, dreading what she'd say.

Emma zipped her case up. "We've all been out without you."

That stung. "That doesn't answer my question."

"It wasn't meant to. What they do or don't know is nowt to do with this."

"What?"

She rolled her eyes. "You're not deaf, Grim."

"When did you all meet up?"

"When you've been called into the hospital. Why should I stay home on my own all the time when we've got friends I can be with?"

"It doesn't sound like you've been on your own, anyroad. Did you bring him here? Did you let Shark shag you in our bed while I was at work?"

She smirked. "I washed the sheets after."

That smirk set his anger alight. "Is that all you can say? You washed the fucking sheets? Is that supposed to make me feel better?"

"I don't care how it makes you feel anymore. You're married to your patients, not me. You're obsessed with fixing people, yet you failed to fix the cracks in our marriage when they first appeared, when I first told you your job was coming between us."

"You hardly banged on about it. I thought it was just sniping, nowt serious."

"You know I'm not one for expressing myself too much. I did tell you, and you ignored me, kept taking extra shifts. I took it that you didn't care how I felt, only about yourself and what you wanted."

"So it was just a lack of good communication. We can talk about it now. I'll get put on a different schedule and refuse overtime now I know how much it's affected you."

"It's too late for all that. It's something you should have done a long time ago. I got bored of waiting for you to do the right thing. Shark can see where I'm coming from, so why can't you?"

She was talking as if none of this bothered her and that the mention of Shark stepping into his role wasn't a big deal, that talking about him wouldn't hurt Grim, wouldn't twist his stomach into knots. She'd kept her deepest feelings to herself all this time. Yes, she'd muttered about him never being at home, but she hadn't gone on about it that much, she hadn't sat him down for a proper chat and laid it all out: "If you don't spend more time with me, I'll find someone else." If she had, he'd have listened, something his mother had told him was important in a marriage. If Grim's dad had been better at listening, maybe his mam wouldn't have lived the life she had. Maybe she wouldn't have been walloped whenever she didn't do something right.

Christ, Grim had only spoken to Shark this morning about going to play tennis. The bloke had said they'd meet up at eight tomorrow night at the leisure centre. Had he known at that point Emma would be leaving? If so, why had he agreed to it? What, was that so he could get Grim on his own and explain why he'd been fucking around with his wife? Did he want to smooth the ruffled feathers with a "Come on, pal, we can still be friends, can't we?"

No, they couldn't.

"Please," Grim said, "let's talk about this. We can work it out. Go to marriage guidance."

"I don't need any guidance where this marriage is concerned. It's over, has been for a long time." She hefted her case off the bed and stood it on the floor.

"Is that all you're taking?"

She nodded. "I only need a few clothes. I'll start again."

"Where are you going to live? Not with Shark, surely."

"Why not?"

Exasperation filled him. "He lives in a caravan, for fuck's sake!"

"So? What's your point here, that someone who doesn't own bricks and mortar can't provide love?"

"No, it's just . . ." Love. Was she saying they were in love? It was worse than he'd thought. He gestured around the bedroom. "This cottage is your dream home. What do you want me to do, put it up for sale so you get half the money?"

"I don't want owt from you. Nowt at all. You put down the deposit, you pay the mortgage, you bought all the furniture. The only

thing I contributed to were the household bills, so none of it belongs to me. I'm not a complete bitch. I won't take what's not mine. I'll sort something out with my solicitor to that effect."

"So you've got one already? What are you saying, you're divorcing me?"

"Ah, you've finally caught up." She clapped. "Well done."

Mam had told Grim never to turn out like his father, but fucking hell, each crack of Emma's palms against each other shunted him towards doing just that, becoming the man who'd wreaked havoc in their lives. He clenched a fist, imagining hitting Emma's smug face with it, breaking her nose, blackening her eye. Strangling her.

No, stop it. Don't be him.

She gripped the case handle and walked out. He rushed after her, anger and frustration, the utter despair he felt, pushing him to smack the back of her head — hard. She dropped the case and spun round, slapping his face.

"Don't you ever *touch me again," she seethed, hatred and tears of pain in her eyes.*

"I'm sorry. I didn't mean it. I panicked and—"

"There's no excuse, you know that better than anyone. Who are you, your father?"

He winced. She'd said the one thing guaranteed to hurt him.

"Emma, I'm begging you . . ."

"No. Even if we could work it out, I wouldn't stay now. You hit me. Fuck off into the bedroom until I've gone."

"But what about our vows? For better or worse?"

"What about them? We've had the best, and you've just done the worst. I want nowt to do with you." She grabbed the case handle again and marched to the stairs, staring at him through the balustrades halfway down.

She looked like she was in prison, caged up, unable to get out. Should he do that? Lock her in the cellar, forcing her to talk? They could fix everything then. She'd see this was just a blip. They could go back to how they were at the start, desperate for one another, laughing, so happy.

His breathing grew laboured, his lungs fighting for air, his heart pleading for her love.

They stared at each other for what seemed an eternity, Grim wishing he could change her mind, Emma probably wishing he'd shrivel up and die. It'd make her life a damn sight easier if he did.

"Maybe you'll learn from this and treat the next woman in your life as well as you treat your patients."

She continued down the steps, her head disappearing, and he dashed to the top of the stairs, hate and hopelessness filling his mouth, tumbling out: "I won't make this easy for you, you fucking bitch. I'll stall for as long as I can in signing those papers. I'll tell my solicitor you were having an affair."

Her laugh, bitter and twisted, rose to wallop him in the face. "I've already told mine and stated Shark's the man I've been seeing, so whatever you hoped to gain from doing it yourself . . . no need to bother."

The front door opened, and she stepped out, slamming it behind her.

Desperate to keep his marriage intact, Grim sped downstairs and outside, waylaying Emma by her car. "Please, I'll do whatever you want."

"Get lost."

"Slag!" he shouted in her face. "Fucking whore bitch!"

She got in the car and drove away as if what he'd said didn't affect her. He imagined her driving to the clifftop and knocking on Shark's caravan door, laughing as she told him she was there to stay, that she'd left her sad sack of a husband.

Hollow inside, Grim went back in the cottage. It was untidy, always had been, what with his long hours and Emma being lazy after work. His mind dancing with images of her in bed with one of his best friends, Grim got on with cleaning the place, concentrating on decluttering, getting rid of everything to do with her, only keeping the bare minimum. Tomorrow, he'd throw everything he didn't need away, making the cottage just his, no trace of Emma to be seen.

Then in the evening, he'd turn up for the tennis match with Shark and see what he had to say for himself, the traitorous bastard.

* * *

Grim blinked aside the memories, chastising himself — he'd let his mind wander during an operation. The woman on the table had paid a lot of money, and if he messed up, he risked getting his license taken away if she reported him for a botched procedure.

What did the police think of his hatchet job on Karen? He'd have to check the local news once he'd completed his work and see if her death had been reported. He'd leave his staff to deal with the woman coming round from the anaesthetic then giving her aftercare until she could go home late afternoon. She'd be in capable hands.

After his nap, he'd clean out Karen's room, empty all three portable toilets, and use the bilge pump. Then tonight he'd go and collect the next resident of Guilt-Ridden. She was in the Devil most evenings but especially on a Monday.

Bingo night, her favourite thing.

His manipulation tool with regards to her, no chocolate needed.

If she was good, he'd let her play it in her new home.

CHAPTER EIGHT

Undisclosed Location

The photos on Bones's phone had been bothering him since he'd taken them — not only the photos but the guilt associated with them. He'd asked himself whether he should say something, show someone, but that would mean people would know he'd been out in the dark, watching, and he couldn't risk that. Creeping out of the house and bolting over the back fence wasn't a good look, was it?

It was against the rules.

When Karen had gone missing, he'd shit himself, thinking: *What if I'm on CCTV and the police see me on tape and ask questions?*

They hadn't, and he'd assumed there weren't any cameras near the woodland where he'd been hiding, smoking stolen cigarettes. She'd cut down the alley beside the Devil to go home. The car had come along opposite the turning for Fisherman's Rest, stopped, and she'd got inside, maybe because it had been raining and it'd saved her getting wetter than she'd already been. And why *would* there be cameras anyway? Most houses on that estate were made up of poor people like him, ones who couldn't afford surveillance, although the streets closer to the woodland might. The residents there were much better off financially.

Bones lived in the rough part, where everyone seemed to be on benefits, or if they had a job, it didn't pay much. Although, that was a lie. Karen's husband had a job, and they'd got by. They must have had more cash than Bones had thought because the police had mentioned her saving it for years without Craig knowing.

In the end, Bones had convinced himself he was in the clear and thought about deleting the images, especially the one of Karen getting into the car on the night she'd "disappeared". He should have told the police about that too, but again, he'd have been caught being outside when he shouldn't be. That was the thing with curfews, you were supposed to abide by them, not sneak out and spy on people.

The birds had woken him up this morning, the noisy fuckers, plus the sunlight creeping around his bedroom blind. From the sound of it, no one else was up, which was nice. He could have a shower without anyone banging on the bathroom door demanding he hurried up, then he could make breakfast and pray the smell of it didn't get them running downstairs to ruin his pocket of peace.

He rolled onto his side and took his phone from beneath his pillow. He shouldn't do that, keep it there, it was dangerous, could catch fire, but what if someone came in while he slept and nosed on his mobile? They'd see the images, the videos, and know what he'd been doing, that he'd lied, kept important things to himself, things that might bring all those women back.

He had a good shot of Karen, Lesley and Teresa getting into that same car on different occasions over a span of two months. He had the number plate. He had images of the driver, and he knew exactly who he was, that bloke who'd worked at the hospital but ran his own surgery now. Bones knew him because he'd had to see him once for plastic surgery when he'd had a chunk of flesh gouged out of his shin by the Bully. He'd had to lie and say he'd fallen, not that he'd been flung across the room. The surgeon had put a graft on it, and afterwards, he'd patted Bones on the head and given him his nickname on account of the bone being visible when he'd hurt it.

"You'll be in my gang, then," the man had said. "All my friends have nicknames."

"What are they?" Bones had asked.

"I'm Grim Reaper. There's Knitty, because she's always knitted, right from a little girl — the amount of ugly hats and scarves she used to give us you wouldn't believe. Then Nymph, she's my wife. There's Shark, because he has pointed teeth, and Blitz, who acts like a bomb going off when he's angry, and lastly, Thunder, because he's a storm, always moody."

Bones had laughed, chuffed with his new name. Shame he couldn't hang around with them all, they sounded fun.

He closed his mind off from that, from how *nice* Grim Reaper had been, only to show his true colours years later by giving the women a lift and not coming forward to tell the police.

But I'm just as bad as him. I haven't come forward either.

Maybe Grim Reaper wasn't involved like that. Maybe he'd just taken them home and hadn't thought anything of it afterwards. He was a busy man, fixing people up, and he might not have heard the news at the time that the women had gone missing after he'd dropped them off.

I'm kidding myself.

Bones accessed the photos and swiped through them. He'd gone to stand in the shadows for weeks after the three disappearances, hoping to catch Grim Reaper doing it again, but there'd been nothing. These days, he snuck out and prowled the estate, taking snaps of anything that took his fancy. No one paid him any mind. Why would they? He wasn't anyone to be bothered about.

He swiped the other way to the more recent images. The Stokes girls breaking into that house and coming out with a DAB radio and laughing. They had the bottom half of their faces covered, but he'd recognised their voices. Bones should tell the police about them too, but his fear of being outside when he shouldn't outweighed his conscience. Fear of the Bully kept him silent. He didn't fancy a bollocking, and he'd get one, no question.

No, best to keep it all to himself.

Best to make himself ill and introverted with nerves.

CHAPTER NINE

Kipling Close

Carol stopped at the kerb while Dave handed the soiled vest over to two officers who signed for it then drove away. Whitney Faulds pulled up from the other direction and, conscious they might have an eavesdropper in Knitty, when Whitney parked, Carol got into the passenger seat and Dave got in the back.

Carol explained everything she knew about Karen, then continued, "The next-door neighbour, the one nosing through her nets right now, seems to think Craig's capable of getting someone to kill his wife, but I'm not so sure. We've taken his vest off him — it looked like there was some kind of sauce on it, but best to be sure. When you go inside, keep an eye out for other signs of blood. Oh, and it's a mess, so maybe you can offer to tidy up while you're chatting, get the girls to help you. It might stop them from thinking too deeply about losing their mother. There are piles of clothes on the chairs — something might be stashed underneath them. Then again, if there was, he'll have hidden it by now since he knows you're on the way."

"Have the children been informed?" Whitney asked.

"He wanted to wait for you to get here. I'm glad you're early, because they sound a right handful and might have chosen to skip out for school before half eight. I don't think they listen to their father, so if he'd have told them to stay home, they'd have likely ignored him."

"Did you meet them?"

"No, they were still in bed."

"So I've got nowt to go on other than them being thieves?"

"That's about it. Oh, and according to the neighbour — that's Nora Patten, but if you speak to her, I'm sure she'll get you to call her Knitty — Karen shouted at the girls a lot. Said she wished she hadn't had them — not to the girls as far as I'm aware, just to her mother, who's now deceased."

"Sounds like the whole household is a volatile one."

"You've got your work cut out for you, I'll say that much."

"Where are you off to now, in case I need you?"

"We'll be over the road at number twelve. Woman called Lindsey, the friend I said about. After that, if she knows where this Geordie lives, we'll be going to see him."

"Okay. I'll let you know if owt odd crops up, but it might just be the usual where I offer support and whatnot."

"I hope so. Chin up. It might not be so bad."

* * *

Number twelve had a brown front door with mucky scuff marks where someone might have tried to kick it in. The living room curtains were open, and a snotty little lad pressed his mouth to the glass, his cheeks inflating and showing his milk teeth. He pulled back, leaving a circle of condensation and a revolting smear of what had once lived up his nose.

Carol shuddered. She'd never wanted children so could empathise with Karen. Like people said, they were nice enough at times, but she couldn't eat a whole one.

A knock at the door produced a teenage boy in school uniform, a slice of toast with jam in hand. He had spots for

England and long black hair, his striped tie askew. "Mam! Door!" He walked towards a kitchen at the end of the hallway. "Did you not pay Provident again?"

"What? He was here yesterday."

The woman who owned the voice appeared, a blue-and-white-chequered tea towel draped over her shoulder, blonde hair in a high curly ponytail and eyebrows that belonged on a creature from the Black Lagoon. What was it with women having beetles on their foreheads these days? Her make-up was the plastic-look variety, a strange shade of yellow, and winged eyeliner gave her a Cleopatra vibe. Slender and pretty in skinny jeans and a tight spaghetti-strap T-shirt, she came to the door and frowned.

"Can I help you?"

"Lindsey?" Carol held up her ID. "DI Carol Wren and DS Dave Waite. What's your surname, please?"

"Reynolds."

"Thanks. Have you got a moment to talk?"

"What's this about?" Lindsey folded her arms.

"Karen Stokes."

"Oh fuck, has she been found?"

Carol didn't want to discuss this on the doorstep. "It's better to chat in private."

"But I've got to take the littlun to school in five minutes."

"We might need you for longer than that, I'm afraid."

Lindsey turned to her son, who loitered in the kitchen doorway. "Can you take Sammy in for me?"

"Aww, Mam! He's a little shit," he mumbled. The way of teens.

"I know, but I've got to talk to the police. Please? I'll pay you a fiver."

The lad ducked his head, his hair obscuring his face. "All right, then. Sammy?" he shouted. "Get dressed!"

He wandered into what Carol assumed was the living room. The snotty kid must be Sammy.

"He needs a wash first," Lindsey called out. "Take him upstairs."

The boys went up there, and Lindsey sighed at their thundering footsteps.

"Bloody elephants. Come in. Excuse the mess, like. I normally tidy up once I've got back from the school run — Sundays are where I don't do owt much except cooking, so it's not to my usual standard at the minute. Pointless cleaning when you've got a hurricane running around. Sammy's . . . well, it's like my Tristan said, he's a little shit."

Carol and Dave entered, and the closer to the kitchen they got, the stronger the scent of coffee became. Carol spied a machine with a full carafe of the filtered variety on the worktop and hoped they'd be offered one. Dave nodded to it and rubbed his hands. Again, Carol had to stifle a laugh.

Lindsey stopped in the middle of the kitchen beside a pile of white washing on the floor. A dark load bumbled around in the machine, its hum quiet. "I don't stand on ceremony, so the cups are in the middle cupboard, the coffee's just there and the milk's in the fridge. I've only got sweetener, and that's by the coffee pot. Help yourselves. I've got the dishes to do."

Carol raised her eyebrows at Dave and shrugged — why wasn't Lindsey more concerned about her friend? Wouldn't housework be the last thing on her mind if the police wanted to chat about her? Or had she spoken to them so much in the past it failed to bother her?

Lindsey turned to plunge her hands into the washing-up bowl, and they got on with serving themselves a drink.

"Shall we wait until your children have gone?" Carol asked.

"Yeah. They'll be off in a minute. It's a fair walk to the primary school, then Tristan's got to double back on himself to go to the secondary."

"How old are they?" Carol stirred her drink then handed Dave the spoon.

"Tristan's sixteen, and Sammy's five. Bit of a gap between them. I wasn't expecting to have two. Sammy was an accident."

Footsteps banged down the stairs, and the accident himself breezed into the kitchen. He poked his tongue out at Dave, grabbed his bookbag off the table and ran to his mother. He punched her backside repeatedly, and Carol had to stop herself from asking him not to do that. Lindsey ignored him. Was this behaviour a regular occurrence?

"Fat bum, fat bum!"

Dave frowned. "That's not a nice thing to say to your mam, and you shouldn't be hitting her either."

"Fuck off," Sammy said.

"Oi!" Lindsey stopped washing a dinner plate and grabbed the tea towel to dry her hands. "These two are the police, so watch your gob."

Sammy didn't seem the slightest bit bothered. "Don't like police."

"Behave or I'll get them to take you away."

"Poo head."

Fuck me . . .

Tristan appeared and gripped Sammy's hand. "Shut up, scrote. School. Now."

The front door closing was the sweetest sound Carol had heard since entering the house. Tristan wasn't kidding when he'd said his brother was a little shit. How Lindsey coped with him was a mystery. Was she having an affair with Geordie's brother so she had something just for herself, a bit of peace and quiet away from the chaos that was clearly her life? What about her husband, if she even had one? Did he contribute to the disharmony?

Thank God it's just me and Dave at home, two middle-aged singletons trundling along together.

"Sorry about Sammy," Lindsey said. "He's . . . difficult to handle."

"Have you asked for help?" Carol sat at the round white table, hoping she didn't come off as condescending. She had no right to talk about how to bring Sammy up, seeing as she didn't have kids and no idea of the pressures they put you under, but the woman seemed harried and might not have considered how to reach out for guidance. She might be too proud or ashamed.

"Nah, they'll only say it's my fault, that I can't control him. Tristan was never like that."

Dave joined Carol at the table. "Don't take this the wrong way, but maybe he needs an assessment. There could be a medical reason he's playing you up, nowt to do with how you're raising him. If Tristan's fine, then it doesn't sound like your fault to me."

Lindsey thought about that. "You could be right actually. Anyroad, he's gone now, thank God, so why are you here about Karen?" She continued with washing up, yesterday's roast dinner things, going by the oily baking tray she held.

Carol decided to hold off on the sad part for now; she didn't intend to tell Lindsey all the ins and outs anyway. "We're investigating Karen Stokes and what went on three years ago. Someone told us she was seeing a man called Geordie. Do you know him?"

Lindsey paused. "Um, yep."

"What's his real name?"

"Lee Ike."

"Have you seen him recently?"

Lindsey gritted her teeth. "Look, if you're really asking whether Karen ran off with Lee, the answer's no. He's still living in Scudderton."

She might not have run off with him, love, but he could have held her somewhere. "We heard you've been seeing his brother."

Lindsey scrubbed at the baking tray with a green-topped sponge. "Fuck, where did you hear that?"

"It doesn't matter."

"It does if people are talking about it. I thought we'd been discreet."

"If there's gossip about you and you haven't heard it, I'd say you're safe and people aren't after getting you into any bother. *Are* you involved with him?"

"Not anymore, so whoever told you I still am is lying. Evan's fucked off to work abroad, comes back every few months for a week. He had his fun with me, then I was dropped like a sack of shit. Good job really, because my old man was getting suspicious when I kept going out. Then *he* left me about a year ago, so I'm up the pub every night, nowt he can do about it, but I still wouldn't want him finding out what I've done. And before you ask, I get a babysitter in for Sammy so Tristan doesn't have to deal with him. She only wants a tenner." She balanced the tray on the draining rack.

Maybe that's why Sammy fucks her about. Parents splitting up, his mam down the boozer, someone else watching him at night.

"It would cause problems if your husband knew?" Carol asked.

"*Ex*-husband. Yeah, although why he'd be interested now is anyone's guess. He's got another woman and a baby. Hardly sees my two. Look, what's this got to do with Karen? Yes, she was seeing Geordie — and I swore I'd never tell anyone about that — but what I got up to and my home life isn't owt to do with her going missing." She snatched a saucepan off the side and attacked it in the water.

"Sorry, we have to ask these things to get a better picture of what was going on back then. Can you elaborate on your nights out with Karen and when she went off with Geordie?"

Lindsey paused and looked out of the window. Bent her head and carried on scrubbing. "She was only allowed out once a week. Craig's a Neanderthal and didn't like her having fun. He's the sort who thinks a woman's got to be chained to the kitchen sink, like my ex does. So we used to go out on a Friday night at the Devil, and about ten, she'd slope off to the woodland beside the pub for an hour with Geordie, then me and her walked home together. Fridays are always packed, disco night, and no one would have noticed her not being there for a bit. It was the only thing she had for herself."

Lindsey appeared shifty, like she was holding information back.

"What aren't you telling us?" Carol watched her closely.

"It's nothing important."

"Okay . . . What about the night she went missing? Did you walk home together then?"

"No, I left earlier than her, and I wish I hadn't now."

"Did Craig ever suspect she was playing around on him?"

Lindsey dumped the pan on the drainer and immersed another dirty one in the suds. "I used to think he'd say she wouldn't have the balls, but . . ."

"But what?"

"You'd have to ask him. I'm not getting involved in that side of things. He could turn on me — he used to knock her around, you know."

"We're aware."

"When she told me she was leaving him, I encouraged it, although I did tell her to take the girls as well. She didn't want to, said she wasn't the mothering sort and they could stay with Craig — he doesn't hit them, by the way. I didn't agree with her wanting to do that, I can't imagine leaving my boys, even if Sammy is a handful, but Karen . . . She didn't want kids."

"Where do you think she would have gone?"

"London, definitely, which is why I was surprised she was seen taking money out of the banks up this way. Why would she stay local if there was a chance of bumping into Craig?"

"So she never went off somewhere and waited for Geordie to join her, then?"

"No, she was just a shag to him, there wasn't owt serious going on, not for him, anyroad — Evan told me. Karen got a bit attached, and despite how it looks, she wasn't stupid. She knew Craig would go ballistic if he found out she'd been messing about with his mate. She had her silly little fantasy of shacking up with Geordie, but I told her it wouldn't work."

"So she said she *wanted* to go off with Geordie?"

"Yep. You know how it is, natters over a cuppa. She had dreams, wondered what it'd be like."

It was time to get to the nitty-gritty, and Carol took a deep breath. "Can you come and sit down for a minute?"

Lindsey stared at the worktop and seemed reluctant to leave the cleaning — or maybe she'd been washing up so she had something to focus on, a way to not show her full face, because where she stood, only her profile was visible. "What's happened?"

Carol got up and took a cup out of the wall cupboard. "Come on, take a seat and I'll make you a brew."

Lindsey frowned, dried her hands and sat opposite Dave while Carol poured coffee. No one spoke, which felt a bit odd, spiky tension growing. Drink placed in front of Lindsey, Carol sat so they formed the points of a triangle.

"Lindsey, I'm sorry to have to tell you this, but a body was found this morning. We believe it's Karen."

The woman's mouth dropped open, and she glanced from Carol to Dave then back again, stunned. "What?"

"Sadly, she was murdered. Do you know of anyone who'd want to harm her? Geordie? Craig? Evan? Someone else?"

Lindsey shook her head, perhaps trying to dislodge the news and kick it out of her mind. "Craig's a prick, but he wouldn't do that. As for the other two, no! I can't believe this . . ." Tears fell, and she left them to do their thing. "What . . . how?"

"She was strangled."

"Oh God. This is . . . This can't be happening. I thought she'd gone, cut all ties, and was finally living a good life."

"So she didn't contact you after she left?"

"No, but I wish she had. We were good mates. At least I *thought* we were. She said she'd let me know where she ended up, then when she didn't get in contact . . . well, I got the arse, didn't I? Called her all the names under the sun for ditching me. I feel bad now."

"Don't. It's a normal reaction. You felt dumped. Craig said Karen was happy with her body shape. Is that true?"

Lindsey's forehead ruffled. "Why are you asking me *that*?"

"It's relevant."

"She put on a lot of weight after having the girls, but it didn't bother her. People called her fat and all sorts, but she just brushed it off."

"So losing weight wasn't on her to-do list?"

"No. Why?"

"She'd lost a lot prior to her death. We're talking around six stone."

"Fucking hell! Maybe she didn't have any money and couldn't afford food?" Lindsey seemed saddened by that. "God, she should have got hold of me, told me, and I'd have helped her out. I haven't got much, but I could have fed her. Has she been in Scudderton all this time?"

"We don't know. Sorry to push that aside, but can you tell me where Geordie lives?"

"You don't think *he* did it, do you?"

Carol smiled in reply and prompted, "His address?"

Lindsey blinked as though still processing the news. "Next door." She pointed to the adjoining wall. "If you're quick, you'll catch him before he goes to work."

Carol stood, thinking about the dangerous game Lindsey had played by seeing Evan when he lived so close. No wonder her ex-husband had grown suspicious. The same went for Karen, being with a man who lived opposite in the same street.

"Can I just ask, when did Evan start working abroad?" *Could he have taken the job to keep out of the way while the police were sniffing around about Karen?*

"About two years ago."

So he was here when Karen went missing and for the aftermath. To make it look like he wasn't involved? "When's he due back again, do you know?"

"Today, as it happens."

Handy, we can speak to him later. "Do you need anyone to come and sit with you?"

Dave rose and gulped his drink down.

"No." Lindsey sipped some coffee. "No, I'll be okay. I just want to be left alone."

Carol picked her cup up and drank some on her way to the sink, thinking she'd need the loo soon. She placed it on the worktop beside a small pan that had a dried-out marrowfat pea in the bottom and geared herself up for confronting Geordie.

Dave pushed his card across the table. "If owt that can help us springs to mind, give us a ring."

Lindsey nodded, spaced out.

Poor woman.

CHAPTER TEN

Kipling Close

Sitting on the stairs, Geordie tied his work boots and stood to grab his rucksack off the coat hook, looking forward to having a McDonald's breakfast. A couple of bacon rolls with brown sauce would go down a treat and help his slight hangover. He'd had one too many last night in the Devil, the darts match going on for longer than usual. He should have come home at ten so he could get a decent amount of kip, but it had been fun, a good atmosphere, and he'd stayed behind for a lock-in.

Dickhead.

He paused at two shadows coming towards the front door. The bell went, and he frowned. He didn't need visitors this morning. His mate would be waiting at the end of the road in five minutes, and if Geordie was late, he'd get a right roasting. Peter had complained a few times last week about Geordie being late, even threatened to stop giving him a lift if he fucked him about again. Geordie hated relying on someone else, but his motor had packed up.

He opened the door, ready to tell whoever it was to sling their hook, but a police ID held towards his face had him buttoning his lips.

"DI Carol Wren and DS Dave Waite. Can we have a word?"

Fuck, it was bound to be about him abandoning his vehicle last Monday when it had broken down. He'd informed the police it was there, and the garage had sworn they'd collected it for repair. Seemed they hadn't. And that was another thing pissing him off. They'd said they couldn't fix it for a month. Something about not being able to get parts until then.

Fucking Brexit.

He sighed. "Look, I'll sort it out later, okay? It was supposed to be moved last Monday afternoon."

"What was, Mr Ike?" the woman asked.

Oh. Not about the car, then. "I broke down. My Jeep was on the hard shoulder."

"We're not here regarding a Jeep," she said. "It's about Karen Stokes."

Ah, fuck it. What do they bloody want now? "What about her?"

"Can you spare us a few minutes, let us in?" the bloke said.

Hang on, I recognise these coppers off the telly. Geordie repeated their names in his head. "Yeah, but I'll have to text my friend. He's picking me up for work and won't be happy."

They stepped inside as if that didn't matter, and Dave closed the door.

Geordie sat on the stairs again and sent a message, telling Peter to come to the house and wait outside, explaining the police were here about Karen.

He should never have shagged her.

Wait, was that why they were here? Had they found out about the affair? What should he do, come clean? Would he be in the shit for not saying anything back then? What was it, perverting the course of justice? Something like that.

He pocketed his phone and stood, gesturing for the police to go into the living room. Thank God he'd cleaned up, ready for Evan coming home. His brother was a stickler for a tidy gaff, and if he walked in later with Geordie's mess everywhere, he'd have a right go at him.

Geordie followed the coppers, uneasy, and went to the window to watch for Peter. "What do you want to know?"

"How long were you seeing Karen for?" Carol asked.

His guts churned. So someone *had* blabbed. It wouldn't be Evan, he hadn't been here for weeks, so who'd opened their mouth? Geordie had thought they'd been really careful, but there were times he'd gone over the road to Karen's, so someone had seen him and put two and two together. Knitty? She was a nosy cow but a good friend of his, and he couldn't imagine her putting him in the shit.

He had a choice: lie and say he'd never slept with Karen . . . or finally tell the truth. It sounded as though they knew for sure, so what was the point in lying? "A few months, can't really remember. Does Craig know?"

"We haven't told him." Carol came to the window. "He seemed unaware when we spoke to him earlier. When did you finish it with her?"

"I didn't. She left Craig, so that was that."

"As we're not up to speed with her case, can you tell us where you were on the night of her disappearance?"

Here we go again. Disappearance. Why won't they get it into their thick heads she walked out of her marriage? She was seen drawing money out, and that should be case closed. "In the Devil with Evan — that's my brother. We stayed for a lock-in until about one, then got a kebab off the van that parks outside on a Friday sometimes. We walked home via the alley with Tom Cubbins."

"Where does he live?"

"Along the road at number two. With his mother."

Dave wrote that down.

Carol stared at Geordie so hard he thought he'd better continue.

"By the time we got back, Craig was out the front and called us over, asking if we'd seen Karen. I hadn't taken any notice of her in the pub, to be honest. I preferred us getting together at hers."

"What about going to the woodland?"

Fucking hell, someone had *really* been talking. Only limited people knew about that. Was it Lindsey telling them his business? "Well, yeah, there's that, but in general, being chatty in the pub would only get people talking, so we had a thing where we left the pub five minutes apart round ten and met down the alley. That night I didn't fancy a bit, so I didn't go outside."

"Was that normal, to not spend time with each other in the pub?"

"Yeah, I didn't want tongues wagging." *Although it sounds like they have been anyroad. Jesus.*

"Why?"

"Isn't it obvious? Craig might have found out."

"All the more reason not to have an affair with her, then," Dave said.

"I couldn't help myself. She's different to other women. Up for it more than the usual, know what I mean?"

"I think I can imagine." Carol's face remained impassive, not one hint of disgust.

So she's not one to judge.

Still, Geordie felt bad for saying more than was required. Karen didn't deserve to be known as a slag, a woman to look down on, loose morals or whatever. She'd sworn she'd only ever done the shit they did together with him, claiming going to bed with Craig was like sharing the mattress with an oaf, an inexperienced one at that. Geordie had felt well chuffed with himself, that she thought of him as good in the sack. Now, it seemed ridiculous, and he saw it for what it was: Karen had been repressed, unable to express herself with her husband. It made sense why she'd said whenever she was with Geordie she'd felt free.

I'm such a bastard.

"Why didn't you admit to the affair back then?" Carol tilted her head. "The police must have asked you if you'd seen her — they'd have spoken to everyone who'd been in the Devil. That was a vital piece of information and could have made all the difference."

"What, like me being the prime suspect? No thanks."

"I can see were you're coming from, but you really should have said something."

"Like I said: Craig. I didn't fancy him laying me out, and he would."

"Was there a reason for the affair? On her part, I mean."

"Yeah. She hated living with Craig and needed an outlet. At first, we just chatted, her moaning about him, asking me if I could help out by having a word with him, get him to see that hitting her wasn't the way to go. I tried, but he just laughed it off. He seemed a bit confused, to be honest, like he didn't get why I thought it was wrong to hurt a woman. Then one day, I nipped round there to drop something off for Craig, a pair of boots that were a bit too small for me, and she was crying. One thing led to another . . . I knew I shouldn't have kissed her, but it's done now, I can't change it. After that first time, Karen was always guffing on about leaving him, and around the night she left, she said she'd be doing it soon, so I just assumed she'd buggered off, which she did, because Craig said coppers had been round to ask him to look at pictures where she'd taken money out of the bank."

"It does seem like she left him, I agree, but there's been a development, so we need to know as much as possible about her. When did you spend the most time with Karen?"

"Over the road when Craig wasn't around, when he was at work, like. We didn't go to the woodland by the alley that night like usual, think I've already told you that."

"Going back to you walking home with Tom and Evan . . ."

"Yeah, so as I was saying, when we got back to the street, we spoke to Craig for a bit. He was waiting by his garden gate, effing and blinding about her being late home and had we seen her. We had, but like I said, I didn't chat to her or owt. We couldn't help him because none of us noticed when she'd left, so Craig went indoors and Tom came here with us and stayed for a few more bevvies. Kipped here, if I remember rightly. His mother, she doesn't like him rolling in drunk."

"Did you love Karen?"

He didn't have to think twice about that. "Nah. I cared about her, and we talked about running off and starting again, but I thought it was just a fantasy of hers. I mean, Craig didn't treat her too well, and I know she wanted to get away from him really badly. The thing is, I was a bit of a wanker and went along with it so I could keep getting in her knickers." That sounded bad, but it was the truth. "Don't get me wrong, Karen was a great laugh and a good . . . well, we got along in the bedroom department, but that was it for me. She wanted more, but I wasn't willing to give it. About three days before she fucked off, she got the gist because I kept stalling about leaving Scudderton with her, so she said she'd go in a few days and find someone who actually gave a shit."

"Were you upset when you found out she'd gone?"

"No, I assumed she'd done what she'd said and left him. It was a relief, if you must know. Keeping it a secret had got a bit much."

"We found a body this morning. We think it's Karen."

The blunt delivery and swift change of subject knocked him for six. "A body?" His skin went cold, and he held his hands up as the cogs whirred and he realised what the coppers might think. "Look, if you're here thinking it's me . . ."

"What were you doing last night and the early hours of this morning?"

Christ, is this really fucking happening? "I was at the Devil, then went to bed. Ask Reg what time I left, he always clocks that sort of thing."

"Can anyone confirm you went to bed?"

"Nope. My brother wasn't home. Fuck, how did Craig take it?"

"Probably how you might think."

"Will he be told about me and Karen?"

"Not at the moment. We don't want to give him another blow to deal with, but it might well have to come out later down the line. It depends where our investigation leads us."

"Shite."

"Play with fire and you end up getting burned," Dave said.

Don't I know it, but no need to rub it in, pal. What was it with this bloke? He clearly had an issue with people having affairs. "What . . . what happened to her?"

"She was murdered," Carol said.

"Jesus Christ."

"Don't leave the country, Mr Ike." She smiled tightly. "We might need to speak to you again once we've reviewed Karen's file."

"I'm telling you, it bloody wasn't me."

She shrugged. "We'll soon find out if it isn't. We know your brother works abroad. What time is he due back? We'll need to speak to him, too."

"About three, but it wasn't him either, he was with me and Tom the night Karen walked out on Craig."

"Okay. Have a good day at work."

They left, and he sagged onto the sofa. Karen, dead? How had she been murdered? Why was she even back in Scudderton? Had Craig tracked her down and killed her?

A car horn tooted, and Geordie got back up to look outside. Peter glared through the driver's-side window. Geordie contemplated telling him he couldn't go to work now, but maybe it was best if he wasn't here when those coppers came to speak to Evan. Besides, work would keep him occupied. Thinking about Karen being dead wasn't something he wanted to do. If he hadn't strung her along, made her think he'd run away with her, she might still be alive.

A pit opened up in his stomach.

Guilt burned holes.

CHAPTER ELEVEN

Kipling Close

Carol stood on the pavement and contemplated getting a uniform down to chat to all the neighbours to see if anyone had seen anything going on last night, specifically Geordie and Craig acting oddly, but by the time an officer arrived, many residents would have gone to work.

She didn't believe everyone on this end of the estate claimed benefits like the rumours said. People could be wicked like that, casting aspersions. She'd grown up poor and understood exactly what it was like to want nice things, how you scrimped on food to get them or left one bill for another month. Circumstances and life were cruel, and many had to look on while the rich flashed the cash. Being out of work didn't equal laziness in most cases. The lack of jobs around here meant those willing to work couldn't.

She told Dave her thoughts on them doing door-to-door enquiries. "So we could do it together, split up. There's only sixteen houses to cover, and we've already spoken to four of the residents, although we should double-check with Lindsey as to whether Geordie was in the pub last night."

"Okay, you take this side, I'll do the other — Julia Bolton lives in number fourteen, so I'll sound her out regarding the night Karen went missing."

Carol nodded. "Odd that Craig isn't aware she lives down the road from him."

"Maybe he knows but wanted to play with us."

"Dick."

Carol walked up Lindsey's path. She hated to bother her again so soon after they'd left, but needs must.

She tapped on the glass and waited.

Lindsey opened the door. "What *now*?"

It was clear she'd been crying. Her mascara no longer had perfect wings but rested at the edges of her eyes, splodges, one of them smeared downwards to flirt with her cheekbone. The eyes themselves, red-rimmed, spoke loudly of a woman who mourned her friend, and perhaps a sense of guilt had brought on extra tears. That was the thing with life. Assuming things were all well and good and you knew all the facts, but when the truth became apparent, it bit hard with razor-sharp teeth, throwing everything into confusion.

Carol felt for her, but she had a job to do. "Sorry, just one more question. You were at the Devil last night, yes?"

"Yeah . . ."

"Was Geordie there?"

Lindsey nodded. "Darts was on. He's always there for that."

"Did you see him leave?"

"Yep, he walked home just ahead of me about twelve."

"And he went into his house?"

"Yes."

"Okay, thanks. Did you see owt going on in the close when you got back?"

"Like what?"

"Any neighbours coming and going?"

"No, it was all quiet."

Carol had one last shot. "Maybe the babysitter saw something."

Lindsey bit her bottom lip. "I doubt it."

"I'd like to speak with her all the same. Can you give me her details?"

Lindsey appeared to want to scream. "For God's *sake*. Hang on while I get my phone." She strutted into the kitchen and returned, holding her screen out.

Carol took her notebook from her pocket and wrote down the name "Hayley" and a phone number. "That's brilliant. Where does she live?"

"Number two."

So why didn't she just say that? "Oh, so she's a Cubbins?"

"Yeah, Tom's daughter. His wife died of cancer a couple of years ago, so him and her moved back in with his mam."

"Right, well, thanks again."

Intrigued as to why Lindsey had seemed reluctant to involve the babysitter, Carol left her and made her way towards number two. A black-haired man with grey at his temples came out just as she got to the end of the garden path, and he paused in the process of closing the door, leaving it open and staring at her.

"Mr Cubbins? Tom?" she asked.

"Yeah, who's asking?" His blue suit looked the worse for wear, his white shirt grubby on the collar, and he held a briefcase. His red tie hadn't been knotted and hung limply around his neck.

She took her ID out and held it up, then put it away. "DI Carol Wren."

"What's the problem? I'm going to be late for work. I've got to be in Liverpool by lunchtime. If I don't set off now, the roads will be chocka."

Carol thought about Karen's wounds. While butchers didn't tend to wear suits, she'd ask anyway. "What do you do for a living?"

I'm a salesman. Listen, if it's all the same to you, I'll be off."

"That's fine by me because I'm here to speak to your daughter, anyroad. Hayley?"

That stalled him, and he scowled. "She's in bed, and what d'you want her for?"

"Were you home when she got in from Lindsey's?"

"Just about."

"Where had you been?"

"At the Devil."

"What time did you arrive here?"

"Can't remember, but it was after last orders." He gave her a shifty look.

"If you're worried about mentioning a lock-in, don't be. I'm not interested in that. Were Lee Ike and Lindsey there last night?"

"Geordie? Yep." He frowned.

"And what about on the night Karen Stokes went missing? Tell me about that."

"What's this *really* about?"

She wanted an answer. "Were you with Lee?"

"Yes! I kipped at his and Evan's, why?"

"We're investigating Karen's case."

"So what's Hayley got to do with owt?"

"How old is your daughter?"

"Eighteen."

"Then I don't need to tell you what I want to talk to her about." She walked up the path and stood beside him, knocked on the open door and called out, "Hello?"

"Fuck's sake, you're going to upset Mam by shouting. She gets lairy about noise. Hang on." Tom walked inside and went upstairs.

A grey-haired woman with pinched features poked her head around the kitchen door, a pinny covering her pleated skirt and white, short-sleeved blouse. "What's going on? Why all the racket? Oh. Who are you?"

Carol took her ID out again and introduced herself. "I wonder if you and Hayley can help me."

"What with?" The lady approached, seeming eager to have a chat now.

"Can I have your name first, please?"

"Sherry Cubbins."

"Thanks. Did you see owt going on in the street last night?" She didn't want to influence her and mention Craig — Carol didn't think Geordie had done anything to Karen, but she couldn't trust her instincts on it yet. She'd had egg on her face for doing that in the past. Geordie could have killed her later, once the street had gone to sleep. With Karen's death between midnight and 3 a.m., it was a plausible theory.

"Like what?" Sherry asked.

"People out and about late."

"The only bloody people I noticed was my son and that Geordie singing as they walked along the sodding road. I tell you, if it wasn't for our Hayley, I wouldn't have let Tom live with me. He was only meant to be here for a while until he got a place from the council, but they said he was adequately housed at mine and blew him off. Why he can't rent somewhere private is beyond me, because he pays me fuck all for his keep. I reckon he's got savings." She sniffed. "Mind you, he's always at that ruddy pub, so maybe not."

"The Devil?"

"Yes."

"So did you look out of your window and see them?"

"No, I was in bed and heard them. Cringed, I did. They could have woken the neighbours up, and I don't know about you, but I don't like upsetting them."

Tom appeared at the top of the stairs and came down, tie flapping, followed by a blonde with beach waves. He gave Carol an evil look and brushed past her, muttering about traffic jams, and stomped up the road to a blue car.

Hayley stood beside her nan at the door. She had the same beetles above her eyes as Lindsey. Carol thought her *Beauty and the Beast* pyjamas were cute.

"She wants to know if you saw owt." Sherry nudged her granddaughter. "Last night."

Hayley frowned. "I was at Lindsey's, so what am I meant to have seen?"

Carol smiled. "I need to know of owt you might have spotted while you were there and on your way home. In the street."

Hayley shook her head. "I saw nowt."

"So no one was out when you came home?"

"No."

Satisfied with that, Carol left them to it. She knocked at the rest of the houses on her side. No one had seen anything dodgy going on. All had been in bed by midnight and hadn't even heard the men singing.

She turned to find Dave, who was coming away from Knitty's house. She met him by the car. "Got owt?"

"Yep. Julia Bolton confirmed what we already know about the night Karen went missing. Julia hung around with her until Karen left."

"Did Karen tell her she was leaving Craig?"

"No. Then there's Knitty — she seems to know a lot about the people around here. She saw Geordie and Tom Cubbins, they'd woken her up by singing 'Eye of the Tiger'."

"Fucking hell. Nice."

"I know. Tom went into number two, Geordie to his house. Lindsey came along a minute or so later, then Tom's daughter, the babysitter, left Lindsey's."

"That marries with what I've been told." A thought struck Carol. "Apart from Lindsey not telling us Geordie was with Tom when she followed him home. I wonder why she didn't mention that. Shit, I'm going to have to piss her off again."

"What's the problem?"

"She wasn't happy when I went back there just now. I can't blame her."

She sighed and walked down the close to Lindsey's. She knocked, and when the woman answered this time, her eyebrow beetles got into a fight, heads butting.

"For crying out loud . . ." Lindsey rolled her eyes.

"Apologies again. Was Tom Cubbins with Geordie when you followed him home?"

A flush broke through the yellow make-up. "Yes."

"Why didn't you say so?"

Lindsey sagged against the doorframe, folding her arms. "Because I didn't want to talk about him."

"Why?"

"Do I have to say?"

"I'd rather you did."

"Look, I'm shagging him, all right?"

So? "Why is that something to hide?"

"Sherry. She'd have a fit and kick him out, and I'm not ready for him to move in here yet, *okay*?"

"Why would she have a fit?"

"Because I'm not the sort of woman she'd want for her son. Too common, according to her."

"Fair enough. Sorry again for troubling you. I really am going to leave you in peace now."

Carol strode away and got in the car where Dave waited.

"Get owt interesting?" he asked and plugged in his seat belt.

"Only that Lindsey's seeing Tom Cubbins."

"Right. So what's next?"

"We'll come back later to speak to Evan, but in the meantime, we'll nip to the station and get together with Michael and Katherine. Something might come to light from Karen's misper file."

"We can but hope."

Carol started the engine and drove out of Kipling Close, only marginally further forward than when she'd first entered it.

Bollocks.

CHAPTER TWELVE

The Incident Room

Back in the incident room, Carol went to the whiteboard, writing out all the information she and Dave had gathered. A picture of Karen from three years ago, printed off from her missing person's file most likely, sat at the top, and it was clear someone had been cropped out of it. A cheek rested against hers, male because of the stubble, and she reckoned it was Craig. Karen wasn't smiling. She appeared agitated, uncomfortable, so apart from standing so close to a man she'd detested, maybe she hadn't liked being in front of the camera. So it felt wrong that she'd had a SOCO photographer taking image after image this morning, nothing she could do about it.

Death took away all rights to what happened to you afterwards.

A sobering thought.

Carol sighed. The starvation angle was bothering her — *was* it anorexia like Rib had suggested? Had Karen really left her husband and gone into hiding, wanting to lose weight to snag herself a new man and taken it too far? Maybe she'd met someone and he'd ended up abusing her, killing her. Or had she been abducted? Only no one had witnessed it, plus she'd been seen, so therefore, there was no abduction in the eyes of whoever had dealt with the case.

If she's been kept somewhere against her will all this time . . .

Carol shuddered. The idea of that didn't sit well. Three years was a long time to be incarcerated. To be abused with lit cigarettes. It was torture of the most sadistic kind — whoever had done it must have gained pleasure from it. Satisfaction. To have administered so many, they surely liked doing it.

Her mind went to Craig and what Knitty had implied. *Could* he have been the one to burn his wife? Lindsey hadn't thought so, but if he'd hit Karen a lot, if he'd found out she'd had a fling with Geordie, then the burns could be a punishment.

So why hasn't he gone after Geordie, then?

And why strangle her? Why cut off the baggy skin? Had Karen done something to tip the killer over the edge? And where had she been? All things they needed to discover.

Carol reviewed the board again. Michael had added information about the pay-as-you-go phone used to call the police last night about Karen's body. It had been purchased at the big Tesco, and the manager, a Mr Bolton — any relation to Julia? — was going through the data to establish what time it had been bought and how the person had paid for it, cash or card. Bolton was also sorting CCTV so they could see who it was.

Carol ran a check. The manager was Julia's father. Small world.

She wrote that down then moved to Michael's desk and bent over, her hands either side of a notepad, supporting her weight. "Can you play the nine-nine-nine call, please?"

He clicked out of a window he'd been working on, accessed the file and pressed play. She listened to the opening speech from a woman at the call centre, then waited for what the other person had to say.

"There's a dead woman down by Buns 'n' Bread."

A chill went down Carol's spine. It was a man, talking in an American accent. Southern. Was he from Texas or something? Or had he disguised his voice?

"*Can you say that again that, sir?*"

"*There's a dead woman down by Buns 'n' Bread. Better get down there before Jolene finds it.*"

Jolene? Who was that?

"*Jolene? Can you give me her second name?*"

Laughter from him. "*Just a little joke.*"

No talking.

"*Sir, are you still there?*"

Silence.

"That's it," Michael said. "Weird isn't the word."

"You're not wrong there."

"I did a search for a Jolene. No one of that name around here, although there are over five thousand of them in the UK. The main Google reference was the Dolly Parton song."

"Do we take it that's what he was referring to? Where does Dolly come from?"

Michael peered over her arm at his notebook. "She was born in Tennessee, so the accent makes sense. It's odd, but it's a link."

"Hmm."

"I looked up the lyrics. It's to do with a woman taking someone else's man."

Carol went cold all over. "I wonder if Geordie had a girlfriend when he was seeing Karen. Karen would have taken someone's man then . . ." She thought about phoning Lindsey to find out but scrapped that — she didn't fancy an ear-bashing. Knitty would be the best bet, more receptive to talking, plus she seemed up to date with gossip. "Give me a second." She turned. "Dave, did you find out Knitty's phone number yet?"

"Yep."

He rattled it off, and she prodded the number into her mobile.

It rang three times.

"Hello?" A hoover or something droned in the background.

"Hi, Knitty, it's DI Carol Wren from earlier."

"I know. I put your number in my phone. Hang on, let me switch this machine off. I'm at a client's, and they like their floors buffed." The noise stopped. "What can I do for you?"

"Geordie. Was he seeing anyone else at the same time as Karen?"

"Of course he was. He likes sowing his oats, that one."

"Can you remember who it was?"

"No idea, he had a few on the go, although he denied it when she asked him."

"How do you know?"

"Didn't you hear me when I told you about the glass?"

Christ, the woman must have listened to Karen's conversations at every opportunity. Those walls had to be thin too, if she'd picked up so much.

"Okay, thanks for your help. Oh, one more thing. Do you know a Jolene?"

"Only the song."

"Right, I'll let you go, then."

Carol ended the call and popped her phone away. She sat on the edge of Michael's desk, her energy depleting because they'd been up since what-the-fuck o'clock. "What time did the triple-nine call take place?"

"Four forty-five a.m. PCs Lloyd and Kenner went out there, thought it was a hoax — I spoke to Kenner as he was going off shift earlier. They discovered the body and called it in. I've had someone looking into where the call was made. The last ping on it was the local mast, so did the caller phone straight after they'd dumped her? A bit risky, if you ask me. Officers could have been patrolling the area and spotted them."

"Maybe the killer likes living on the edge."

"Or they're deranged, possibly even a bit dim to not have thought of that. Also, was the caller even the killer? It could have been someone else."

"Maybe. Okay, any Jolenes will need crossing off the list regardless of where they live — as in, we want to know if they've got any ties to Scudderton and the general area. It could be a wild goose chase, but get hold of Richard Prince and ask him if he can spare a few uniforms to deal with that for you."

"Will do."

Carol had to move on to the next issue. Katherine had been at work for half an hour prior to Carol and Dave rolling in, so she'd only managed to skim Karen's missing person's file, although "skim" to Katherine meant she'd have taken in all the relevant information anyway — her mind was amazing at retaining things. They'd discuss her findings in a minute.

Dave sat at his desk, his feet up on it, a coffee cup in hand.

"You're going to be bloody buzzing if you're not careful," Carol said to him. "All that caffeine."

"I could do with the pick-me-up."

She smiled. They'd gone to the Lord in their village yesterday for a roast beef dinner, then just happened to have a few bevvies, leaving around eight to go home and scoff cheese toasties to soak up the alcohol. It was curry night on a Monday, so they planned to eat in the Lord again later, work permitting — masala, rice, naan and a poppadom for six quid wasn't to be sniffed at.

Carol clapped to signal their briefing needed to get underway. "Okay, we'll go back to the beginning. Katherine, what have you got for us?"

Katherine explained everything Carol already knew, then said, "Right, three years ago. No one saw Karen getting into a vehicle. She wasn't even seen after she left the pub. If I was her, I'd have gone down the alley at the side, because that leads to the Coldwater estate. It's the quickest route there."

"As we don't know which scenario is the right one, this is tricky," Carol said. "She could have been abducted, or she could have arranged for someone to take her somewhere and they've kept it quiet, knowing how Craig would react."

"There were no busses or trains running around the time she left the Devil." Katherine tapped her pen on her pad.

"The last time for either of those was ten p.m. or thereabouts, so it would have been by other means. A car, van or motorbike, unless she walked to wherever she wanted to go."

"What else did you dig up?"

"Craig didn't report her missing until the morning. Eight a.m. He thought she'd got drunk and slept at someone else's house. Asked whether that was a regular occurrence, he said no. He thought she'd be home to sort the kids for school." She flipped open a file. "I've got the transcript of his interview here. Next he was asked why he'd think she'd slept elsewhere if she didn't usually, and he said it was all he could think of."

"It's more likely he thought she wouldn't dare not come home, so staying overnight at a friend's place was the logical conclusion, although I'd imagine he'd have expected a phone call from her at least."

"I've got her mobile records to go through," Katherine said. "All the messages and whatnot, but the main file says there's nowt untoward, all calls and messages are the same as your average person's."

Michael cleared his throat. "I did a search on any abuse. She never once complained about him to the police. We weren't called out to any domestic disturbances. The only times we've gone to the house were about Karen's disappearance and the Stokes girls, a chat about whether they're the ones doing the muggings and robbing lately. The latter was PC Mulholland."

"So she was either ashamed of what Craig did to her and didn't want to report it, or she was afraid he'd hit her again if he found out."

"If that's the case, why chance having an affair?" Katherine asked. "It makes no sense to me at all. If I was scared of my husband, you can bet I wouldn't do owt to set him off. An affair is a big thing. A man handy with his fists would get arsey over it."

"Maybe she'd gone past caring," Carol said. "She knew she was leaving him, had done for years if she was saving up money, so what was a quick fling with Geordie when she was leaving Craig anyroad?"

Katherine snorted. "Even worse that she went with one of Craig's friends. It's like she was goading him. If she'd stayed and the affair had continued, surely Craig would have suspected something in the end."

"But she *didn't* stay," Dave said, "so that's by the by, and he told us he'd have given her a black eye if she'd been fucking about."

"Well, she did," Katherine said, "and d'you know what? I admire her for grabbing what she wanted. It must have been hell living with him, not to mention those girls of hers. Imagine not wanting kids and feeling like you had to have them, then when they arrived, you had no feelings for them — I read the board about what Knitty said. Karen must have felt so trapped."

"And it took years for her to get up the courage to leave," Michael added. "Then when she did, things went wrong."

Carol nodded. "What are your thoughts on what went down, *how* it went down? Abduction or something else?"

"It's pointing to something else," Katherine said. "She left then maybe met someone up the coast and everything went pear-shaped."

"It does look that way," Michael agreed, "but what if *Craig*'s the one we're after?"

"He was with his daughters while Karen went to the pub." Carol stood and paced. "Knitty — Nora Patten, the next-door neighbour — seems to think he's capable of getting someone else to kill her, and she said she heard his telly on that night."

"Doesn't mean he was indoors watching it, though," Katherine said. "He might have put it on to make his girls think he was home, then slipped out and waylaid Karen when she walked home from the pub. On the board it says Geordie, Evan and Tom saw him at his gate when they arrived in Kipling Close. What if he'd just got back from taking her somewhere and had to make out he was annoyed she wasn't back yet for appearance's sake?"

It was a good theory, Carol couldn't deny that. "What exactly does the file say he was doing that night?"

"At home babysitting the kids."

Carol grimaced. "I hate that word when it comes to fathers. Does it actually use that term in the file?"

"Yep."

"Fuck's sake. Fathers don't babysit. As if they're doing the mother a favour by being with their own kids."

"Step off your soapbox," Dave said. "I don't fancy spending the rest of the day with you wound up."

Carol saw his point, and he knew her too well. Sometimes, she let herself get annoyed with one little detail and it ruined her mood. "Fair enough. What else, Katherine?"

"It's all basically what you already know, but I'll get back to it in a sec and see if there's owt else."

Carol turned to Michael. "Owt on the Freddo yet?"

"The details on the wrapper are being traced. Someone will get back to us on which shop it was delivered to."

"That will be a big help, as is knowing the phone was bought from Tesco. Saying that, the shop might have been chosen on purpose, away from where the killer lives."

A ping sounded from Michael's computer.

"Talking of Tesco —" he opened an email — "Mr Bolton's written something." He peered to read it. "The phone was bought with cash at 6.04 p.m. on June fifteenth this year, a Wednesday. Bolton says the cashier remembers the purchaser because they looked so odd. Also, outside CCTV was checked, and the person left Tesco and walked down an alley, so there's no car involved, although they may have parked behind and been caught on any cameras there. I'll chase that up. Oh, and there's an image attached."

Carol went over to him and stood by his chair. Michael opened the photo, and it filled the screen. What the fuck? Someone with a blonde wig, a life-like mask and big boobs stood in line at the checkout. Going by the build and height it was a man; there was no waist as such, the red dress he had on hanging straight off the breasts instead of moulding to curves.

"Fuck me," Dave said over Carol's shoulder. "That looks like Dolly Parton."

A shiver sped through Carol. So Jolene *was* relevant. Did that mean the affair angle in the song was, too? *Were* they looking at Craig Stokes for this? Or was there a woman scorned in the equation? Someone Geordie had been with who'd taken umbrage as well as taking Karen?

No, the image on the screen was a fella, she was sure of it. So had a woman got him to do her dirty work?

"This is so bloody *strange*," she said.

Katherine came over to Michael's other side. "What's stranger is two more women went missing around the time Karen did. I've just done a quick check."

"What?" Carol's heart thudded too hard.

"A month after Karen, a lady called Lesley Johnson disappeared. A month after that, Teresa Fett. And guess what's even stranger than that?" Katherine paused. "All of the women were classed as overweight and had blonde curly hair."

"Jesus Christ." Carol spun away from the desk and walked in a circle. "Were their cases closed as well?"

Katherine nodded. "Afraid so. No leads, except they'd all been in the Devil on the nights they'd vanished."

Carol glanced at Dave. "We're going to have to go down there and speak to Reg."

Dave nodded. "Right."

Carol moved to the door. "Katherine, look into Lesley and Teresa. See if there's a link to Karen, Craig, Geordie or Evan. I want you poking into the social media of all three women — they might even have been friends. Has anyone found out yet whether Karen's parents are definitely dead? I know Knitty said they were, but I want to be sure."

Michael nodded. "Both deceased, unfortunately."

"All the more reason for Craig to have such a hold on her. No one to oversee what was going on. Any siblings?"

"No, and her only uncle killed himself."

"Christ. Then check whether Lesley's and Teresa's family are still around. If they are, go and speak to them."

"Okay." Michael opened up the police search engine and got to work.

Carol walked out.

This had turned into a fucking nightmare.

CHAPTER THIRTEEN

Truth-Hunt Cottage

Grim had left the New Me Clinic earlier than expected. His client's operation had gone smoothly, and she'd come round from the anaesthetic quickly, soon perking up. He'd done the paperwork regarding her operation and returned home, glad to be the boss, no one telling him he had to put in a full day.

He'd checked the internet prior to leaving. Someone must have tipped off the local journalist from The *Scudderton Star*, as it was front-page news on the website along with a photo of forensic officers bending to inspect something outside Buns 'n' Bread. That wouldn't do them any good, Grim hadn't even been out the front, and he'd laughed at them wasting their time. What wouldn't be funny, though, was if they found something of him in the alley, but he'd had a forensic suit on, so maybe not.

Foregoing a nap for now, he got on with cleaning out number one on Guilt-Ridden for the next arrival. It was a bit whiffy from where Karen had shit the bed when he'd stormed in and strangled her, and the mess she'd left behind had gone hard. He picked it up with tissue in his pink-Marigold hands and dropped it in the portable toilet, attacking the plastic mattress with disinfectant spray and a cloth. He mopped and used a hard scrubbing brush on the tiled walls, stripped the blanket and pillow off the bed for washing, and smirked at the mattress they had to sleep on. They didn't deserve a bottom sheet or a quilt. This was prison, a place of reform, and they had to suffer with the minimum in home comforts in order to want to tell the truth and agree to make a go of their future relationships, then be set free.

Shame it hadn't worked out like that in Karen's case.

You're full of shit. Admit what you're really doing.

He laughed off the voice in his head and got on with sorting the caravan toilet, then used spray and a squeegee to wash the Perspex wall, removing all of Karen's fingerprints. She'd had a horrible habit of placing her palms to it, leaving sweaty smears. His last job was mopping then spraying the floor and walls with Zoflora so the next guest at least had a nice smell to walk into.

He left number one open to air it out and exited Guilt-Ridden to wash his gloves and collect the meal trolley. For Lesley, he'd made a sandwich with Marmite — she *hated* that — and as her enticement to talk, her favourite thing, a red velvet cupcake. For Teresa, he'd chosen her most hated filling, corned beef and piccalilli, and on the other side of the scale, *her* favourite thing was a crossword book and a pencil.

They ate the bad and could be rewarded with the good — *if* they played ball. Grim reckoned if he was in their shoes, he'd admit to an affair, be remorseful about it, and then he could have the prize.

What would his favourite thing be?

A faithful wife.

No chance of that. Emma was currently on her third bloke after leaving him. She couldn't seem to hold down a relationship, although the first failure with Shark hadn't been her fault.

He'd think about that later when he set the bilge pump to work.

In the bedroom, he put on his Queen outfit and opted for a sapphire brooch surrounded by diamonds instead of the pearl necklace — both had belonged to his mother. He slipped the mask on and tucked the neck piece beneath his blouse, then did the buttons up. The wig came next, and he caught sight of his reflection in the mirror. The mask looked so much like Mam it never failed to startle him. He missed her, but like Emma, she'd left him. At death's hand, admittedly, but still, he'd been discarded.

That was what he couldn't handle. Three women had abandoned him, so was it Grim who was at fault, not them? He was the common denominator after all.

Angry with himself for taking the blame when *he'd* been the wronged party, he stomped downstairs in bare feet, not bothering with his queenly, American tan tights, and grabbed the meal trolley from the kitchen. The women had better watch themselves because he was in a bad mood now.

He walked to Guilt-Ridden and pushed the trolley up Lesley's path. He had an apology to make. Since he'd worked out who he needed to snatch tonight, he'd realised Lesley hadn't been lying. It *was* someone else who'd had an affair, not Lesley. But how could he save face? How could he let her go now? Yes, he could still threaten to kill her parents, but he wouldn't touch her mother. She'd been one of his patients, so she was safe. One of his precious people. But would Lesley's anger at him not believing her all these years override her fear of him harming those she loved? She could very well tell the police, who would whisk her mam and dad to a secure location while others turned up at Truth-Hunt Cottage and arrested him.

It was time to stop fooling himself and admit what was really going on here. He'd *never* intended on letting any of them go. How daft would that be? No one in their right mind would believe his threats. He'd kept them so no woman could leave him ever again.

Shit.

He lifted the cow knocker and let it drop, squinting through Lesley's "window" and not seeing her inside. He laughed. Of course he wouldn't bloody see her, it was a painting but, as always, he loved to pretend.

His mother dying, Emma divorcing him and the ex-girlfriend casting him aside had really twisted his melons. Not enough that he couldn't acknowledge it, though. He knew exactly how insane he'd become but had so far managed to live a double life. Esteemed surgeon on one side, jailer on the other.

No, not a jailer. Someone desperate to be loved.

He used the key and pulled the door outwards and, as usual, propped it open with the trolley. He stepped inside and looked at Lesley, her hair shorn so she reminded him of the Emma from years ago. Her naked body was similar to when he'd first begun a sexual relationship with his ex-wife — Emma had piled on the pounds after their marriage — and the short hair was just like she'd had as a teenager, when she'd loved him the most, going through her pixie phase.

I want to go back to that time, when everything was okay.

He stared at Lesley and said in his best clipped British accent, "Good day to you, dear. How are you?"

Lesley clutched at her stomach. "Hungry."

"Then it's a good job I've brought you a sandwich."

She winced, knowing full well what it would contain, it was the same each time he made them. "There's a red velvet cupcake, too."

A flicker of spite flashed in her eyes. "Why do you bother bringing it? I never get to have any."

"Ah, today is different."

Hope lit her up, the fool. "Why?"

"Because you've been telling me the truth, haven't you? It *was* someone else playing around, not you."

She cried. Relief?

He ignored her irritating noises and opened the hatch, pushed the tray down, and went outside to collect the food. All of it. She could enjoy her cake, but then he had the unfortunate job of telling her she couldn't live here anymore. He didn't need to ask himself why he wanted them to stay just for him to decide to get rid of them anyway. It was because *he* was the one severing the relationship, not the woman. *He* was the one in control.

Thoughts collided in his mind. He was a jumble of contradictions. Maybe he should accept that there didn't need to be a reason why he was doing this apart from it being his way of hurting Emma, even though he wasn't actually doing it to her. These women represented her, and that should be good enough for him. If he came to terms with that, it would save him staring at his ceiling every night worrying about it.

Lesley got off the bed and took the food, placing the sandwich and drink on her nightstand. She sat, holding the paper plate under her chin, and scoffed the cake, an animal desperate to fill her belly.

He didn't like that. It reminded him of Emma always eating cake, a pig on the sofa, mess all around her where she hadn't cleaned.

"Slow down," he barked. "You'll make yourself sick."

She did as he'd asked immediately.

"Good girl. I need to clean the toilet."

She nodded and got up, red crumbs attached to her lips, and used her foot to push the toilet towards the space at the bottom of the Perspex. Locking the hatch, he left the blue front door open so she could enjoy the mural on the back wall while he went off to clean the loo out.

Back on Guilt-Ridden, he placed the toilet on the floor and scooted it under the dividing screen.

Lesley had finished her cake and sandwich and returned to her bed. He sat on the wooden chair inside number two.

"Can I go home, then?" she asked.

Her hope was so bright it disgusted him. She wanted to leave him.

He smiled indulgently, hiding his internal agony. "I'm afraid not. I've been lying to you *and* myself. It's time I was honest. You leaving was never an option, I have to face that now." He didn't bother adding that he'd enjoyed killing Karen, how he'd imagined it was Emma, and he wanted to do it again. He wouldn't tell her his other thoughts either, that during the murder he'd felt alive for the first time in years, he'd had a purpose — to purge those hateful emotions Emma had inspired, to make himself feel better.

It was his new drug, overtaking his previous one, which was imprisoning the women.

"What?" Her eyes filled with tears.

"I'll be kind and cook you whatever you like for your final meal, though. I can't say fairer than that."

She sobbed, throwing herself back so her head hit the wall, then she got up on the bed, screeching, and clawed at the fan, getting her fingers caught up in the slatted cover. What did she think, she could escape out of that little hole?

Silly cow.

"What would you like for dinner?" he shouted above her din.

She didn't answer.

Oh well, she could go without.

He locked her inside, excited at the prospect of doing to her what he'd done to Karen. He chuckled and pushed the trolley down Lesley's path then up Teresa's. Should he tell her the good news today too, or wait?

Grim knocked on the pink door and once again peered through the "window". He slid the key in the lock, propped the door with the trolley and got on with sorting the hatch. Sandwich and drink placed on it, he held the crossword book and pencil up.

"Look what you can have." He waggled them.

Teresa slapped a hand over her mouth then dropped it to her lap. "Really?" She sounded wary, like she didn't believe him.

"Really." He placed it on the hatch tray.

She raced over and took it all, going back to bed. "Thank you."

Well, he hadn't expected that, and he almost changed his mind about killing her. Teresa had always been pleasant once she'd got into the swing of things. Maybe he'd keep her for a while longer. She was the one who looked the most like Emma, so perhaps he should be kinder to her, then she might let him into her bed. They could play at being a married couple.

"Toilet," he said.

She mimicked Lesley's actions, and he closed the hatch and carried the loo away. After he'd cleaned it, he sat on the chair inside her home.

"You've got some time to get all the crosswords done, but not long." He'd made his mind up. Teresa had to go to make way for new blood. She would never be Emma.

She frowned. "Why?"

He smiled. "You'll see."

CHAPTER FOURTEEN

The Leisure Centre

Grim greeted Shark with a friendly slap on the back, much as it tore his heart into pieces to do so. He'd made a plan, and acting as though they were still pals was the best way to go.

"I have to be honest, I thought you wouldn't come," Shark said.

Honest? Shark wasn't capable of it after this deception.

Grim acted surprised. "Why? We made a promise as kids to always be mates no matter what, so Nymph leaving me doesn't change that."

"Thank God. I thought you'd go mental."

"Nah, me and Emma have been on the skids for a couple of years now. She deserves happiness, and I can't give it to her, simple as that. Come on, we've got a match to play."

On the court, Grim resisted hitting violent lobs at Shark — he so badly wanted to hurt him, but now wasn't the time. Shark won, further exacerbating Grim's anger — he'd already won his wife, so to take the game too was adding insult to injury.

They had a drink in the leisure centre café, hot chocolate, Grim wanting people to see them there together. Their chatter was the same as always, except Shark avoided any mention of Emma.

Grim changed that.

"So are you planning on staying in the caravan, or does Emma want yet another dream cottage?" Grim rolled his eyes to make out he was on Shark's side.

"Staying put for now. I don't earn as much as you, remember, and I'm shit at saving, so if she wants a deposit for a new place, she'll have a long wait."

Grim laughed. "Good luck with that."

"She said you didn't fancy having kids."

That stalled Grim's smile. Why had she discussed their private things with this dickhead? "No, it was never on the cards, and she knew that from the beginning." He hadn't wanted children taking up all her time and attention. "Why, has she been griping about it?"

"Not griping as such, it just came out in conversation when . . . Doesn't matter."

"When what?"

"When we were discussing what we wanted out of life."

"Ah, 'the chat'. Sensible."

"She actually wants a nipper."

Grim stifled his anger. This was news to him. "She never said."

"A couple of years ago, she started getting clucky."

"So around the time we were going off the rails?" This was a lie. As far as Grim was concerned, they'd been right on track, but he'd say whatever he could to get information out of Shark.

"Yeah."

"Shame. Still, if she'd have told me she'd changed her mind, it wouldn't have changed mine, so she's better off with someone who wants them."

"See, that's the thing. I don't."

Grim frowned. "What?"

"Listen, this is going to sound bad, but I didn't even want her to leave you. It was a fling, nowt more, but somehow it's come to this."

Grim couldn't believe this. Emma had left him for a bloke who didn't really want her? She'd crushed his heart for no reason? "Fuck me, I pity you trying to get out of this one." He laughed, but not unkindly, more of a matey, conspiratorial chuckle. "What are you going to do?"

"I don't know, but having her make-up and shit all over the place is doing my head in, and she's only been there one night."

Grim didn't say, "Tough!" He didn't say, "Serves yourself fucking right for stealing my wife." Instead, he shook his head. "She's left it all out, hasn't she? The make-up, the clothes."

"Yeah, and I had my caravan nice and tidy. I don't like mess."

"That's what you'll get with Emma. She's lazy. I did make jokes about it whenever the group met up."

"I know, but I didn't realise it was that bad. She left all her clothes on the floor last night, just stripped for a shower and walked away from them."

Grim cringed at the image of Emma taking her clothes off for this man. "I had to clean the cottage yesterday after she left. I got rid of all her clutter and mess. I have to say, actually being able to see surfaces is pretty nice. Oh, and I threw out all of her convenience food. That'll be another thing that gets on your nerves. She doesn't cook from scratch and enjoys pigging out on the sofa."

"Bastard. Rub it in, why don't you?"

"You reap what you sow, pal. Fancy going for a beer at the Devil?"

"Yeah, can do. I'll meet you there, seeing as we're both driving."

"Park down the Backstreet?"

"Yep, living dangerously."

They parted ways, and Grim followed him to the Backstreet, a road opposite the marina, the backs of warehouses either side. Parking wasn't allowed, there was a sign up saying so, and during the day, it was a favourite haunt of a ticket inspector. Sod following the rules, not tonight, although Grim didn't plan on being there for long.

He parked a metre or so behind Shark's crappy run-around, put gloves on and reached into the passenger footwell for the crowbar. The bloke wasn't going to get away with this lightly. A whack to the head would do the trick, teach him a lesson.

He got out of the car and kept the bar behind him, approaching Shark, who bent into his boot, fishing for a coat and putting it on. Grim raised the crowbar with one gloved hand and brought it down on Shark's back first. Shark shouted in pain and slumped, the top half of his body folded over into the boot. His position was off, so Grim gripped his jacket with his free hand and yanked him out a bit, the head now within striking distance. He bashed Shark's skull, only intending to do it once, but anger reared up and pushed him to do it again.

Time skipped, and Grim stared down at the bloodied mass that had once been a head. He slung the crowbar in the boot and folded Shark's body into the confined space, closing the lid. The crowbar had been a new one — still in the packet — that Grim had been meaning to use for a job at the cottage, and he'd rested it on a piece of plastic in his car so no carpet fibres attached.

He rushed to his own boot and, using his other gloved hand, opened the wet wipes and washed as much off himself as he could, thankful he had black clothing on. He placed the discarded wipes in an open carrier bag he'd put in there earlier, then sat on his plastic-covered seat and drove to Tesco, going down every aisle, walking slowly, wanting to be seen. Back at the cottage, he burned the wipes, his clothes and his shoes in the gas barbecue, leaving it to do its thing while he put the shopping away, then had a shower.

Later, he took the ashes and poured them in a bucket, then put the carrier bag and plastic from the seat in the barbecue. It turned into a strange shape, curling in on itself, much like he'd done last night in bed. Once it went cold, he sprinkled the ashes on the moors a mile beyond his garden, burying the misshapen plastic and parts of his shoes that hadn't disintegrated, using his hands as spades, the earth sodden from the recent rain.

The walk had done him good, given him time to think and go over what he'd done. As far as anyone was aware, Grim had gone shopping after tennis. The route to the Backstreet didn't have any cameras as far as he knew, and besides, if it came to it, he could say he'd changed his mind about having a pint and left Shark to it in the Backstreet. A flimsy alibi, but he didn't care. He was glad about what he'd done, and spending time in prison would be worth it.

Back at home, he sat in his now sterile, mercifully clutter-free living room and smiled.

Emma would return to him now, but there would be rules.

No more mess.

CHAPTER FIFTEEN

Undisclosed Location

Police had been in the street, scaring him. Bones wasn't sure what to do, because on his weekday morning walk, things had churned up in his mind, everything clamouring for his attention. Each time he saw a police officer, he went funny. When that Mulholland bloke had turned up a while back, Bones had thought the copper had come for *him*, but he'd asked questions about the Stokes girls instead. Even if Bones saw a uniform in town or on the pier, he crapped it.

Paranoid, that's what he was.

Once, he'd convinced himself they were following him, waiting for him to get his phone out and take pictures or videos. Catching him in the act. They'd ask to look at his mobile, then see the pictures, and they'd have him bang to rights on withholding important information regarding missing women, the muggings, and other stuff Bones had videoed.

One of the stars of his films was dead now. The rapist. Mr William "Butterfly" King, a copper's grandad. Bones had met him at a dominoes tournament in the town hall, and Butterfly had gone on about his grandson while showing Bones how to play.

Bones had filmed him running up to a young woman from behind in the dark, hitting her on the head and dragging her into someone's front garden behind a long hedge. Bones had been out later than usual, it was gone midnight, he knew that much, and he'd followed them, creeping up the path, his heart going ten to the dozen.

* * *

What he saw frightened him and excited him at the same time. He hadn't wanted to be excited, it had just happened down there. *At first, his sights went to two pairs of feet, high-heeled shoes on the outside, men's soft-soles in the middle. Then his attention scooted up to the heads. Butterfly had tucked his next to hers, mumbling something, and she had her eyes closed, his hand over her mouth.*

The phone camera came out without Bones really thinking about it, and he viewed it through the screen instead of for real, light from a lamppost shining enough to see. It was better watching this way, as if it wasn't really happening.

Butterfly took what he wanted, did what he wanted, grunting, the woman unresponsive. Bones couldn't stand it anymore, so he shut off the camera and tiptoed across the street, hiding behind someone's bushes.

Butterfly came out, and Bones stood from his hiding place and snapped a picture, his flash going off. Fuck. *He dipped down, spying through the gaps in the leaves, and Butterfly paused, turning to see where the light had come from. Then he ran.*

Bones should go into the other garden, where the girl was, but he was too afraid. He thought she might be dead, seeing as she hadn't moved when Butterfly had been . . .

She staggered out onto the pavement, crying, pulling her skirt down.

She'd lost one of her shoes.

Phone the police, phone the police, phone the police . . .

She didn't. Bones didn't, but he took a picture of her beneath the lamppost as she leaned against it and shut her eyes.

Oh God, it's that woman who goes to the library, the one who carries the pink rucksack.

She stumbled in the opposite direction to Butterfly, and Bones went home. His foot scraped loudly on the back fence on the climb over, and he paused, waiting, a lump in his throat. Emotions. Fear of being caught. Disgust at what he'd seen and how he'd reacted to it. The idea of the Bully catching him, giving him a beating.

He was a bad, bad person for not doing the right thing.

Bad.

* * *

Bones scuffed his shoe on the floor, the noise around him too much, too loud, people chattering and laughing. He couldn't get away from them either. If he walked out now, he'd be right in the shit.

He gathered his things together, preparing for the time to leave. He'd be allowed out soon.

His mind wandered while someone droned on and on about this and that.

Earlier this morning, those coppers had been asking about Karen. Maybe it was only a matter of time before they found out what had happened to her. He wouldn't have the continual, nagging dilemma of whether to show them his phone then. They could dig deeper, find out Lesley and Teresa were linked. And Mulholland was going to catch the Stokes girls at it, so that would solve things there, too. Butterfly was dead, and the *other* person Bones had filmed deserved to be caught, so did it *matter* what he'd done anymore?

He didn't know, and that question, along with many others, followed him to his next destination.

CHAPTER SIXTEEN

The Little Devil

Carol sat at a small round table with Dave, another coffee in front of them courtesy of Reg, the landlord, who'd gone off to put through someone's breakfast order. The customer had collared him just as he'd been about to sit, and because the barman was busy, Reg said he'd deal with it himself. That could be to give him time to make up a story — they'd told him why they were there — but Carol doubted it. Reg was a nice bloke and had always been helpful in the past.

She should pull him up on the lock-ins really, even though they hadn't caused any hassle. If he ignored her in the future, that was up to him, but at least she'd have given him a warning, done her duty.

Some things just weren't worth pushing for. She dealt with much worse crimes, and in her book, people sipping a quiet drink after hours wasn't one of them.

"Reckon he'll remember something from so long ago?" Dave asked.

"When it involves missing women, wouldn't you? That sort of thing sticks in the mind. And anyroad, this is Reg we're talking about. He's got a good memory when he *wants* to tell the truth. Let's hope he fancies opening up to us today." Her heart did a strange blip. The coffee here and at Lindsey's was the strong type, and her body wasn't used to the excessive caffeine. "Christ, this is my last coffee. It's sending me jittery."

Dave nodded. "Same."

They sat and observed the patrons for a while. Some might find it odd that Carol had chosen to discuss things in earshot of other people, but her view was that if anyone overheard, they might be able to offer further insight.

What was keeping Reg?

She was about to get up and find him.

Dave jerked his head. "Ay up, he's coming back."

Reg sat, placing doorstep bacon sandwiches in front of them, and sighed the sigh of someone who'd already been rushed off his feet, and it was only just eleven o'clock. "Get those down you."

"Cheers." Dave snapped up one half of his immediately.

"Thanks," Carol said, thinking she'd eat hers in the car. "So, like I said when we came in, we're on Karen Stokes's case and have discovered two more women went missing around the same time."

"I remember the police coming here. I was surprised you weren't one of them to be honest, but then again, you were on that big case, weren't you?"

She nodded. "Poor Richard and Oliver dealt with the brunt of other cases during that time. What do you remember from back then?"

"It's in your files, I'm sure. I gave statements all three times. Not much to tell really. All the women were in here and left like you normally would, which is why I didn't pick up on owt odd. They'd had a few. I mean, Karen was weaving drunk, but then that's not unusual. I think she boozed it up to forget about her life at home. Everyone knows about Craig and his fists. She'd come in with a black eye, making out she'd bumped into something, but after a while that starts to sound like a lie, doesn't it? People aren't stupid, they know what's what. When you've got bruises on your face, the mind automatically goes to the partner getting a bit lairy."

"What kind of people are Lesley and Teresa?"

"Lesley's a good woman. She wouldn't do owt wrong. She likes a laugh, I've seen that for myself in here, but she hasn't got a spiteful bone in her body. And Teresa, she's one of the gentlest people, the type who enjoys a drink but doesn't get loud. She's the sort to stand on the sidelines while her friends do all the noisy stuff."

"The opposite to Karen."

Reg laughed. "You've got that right. A law unto herself. Gobby, nosy, pushy, you name it. I often wondered if that was why Craig hit her. You know, to take her down a peg or two, shut her up. Whatever his reasons, I told him it was wrong, but he didn't seem to think so." He paused, scrubbing his chin. "The newspapers got hold of what's going on down by the bakery, then."

Shit. Carol hadn't checked online when she'd been at the station. "What's been said?"

"That there's a woman's body down there."

"We really don't need that." She drank some coffee, felt sick and thought she'd better leave the stuff alone.

"Other news, by way of gossip, is that it's Karen." Reg shook his head. "Bloody sad."

It was bound to happen, people in Scudderton talked, and Carol's only concern was that a police officer had leaked the information. Or maybe someone had overheard a conversation going on inside the boundaries of the outer cordon. She thought about doing a press release, but for now, what was the point? Word would spread anyway, and if anyone knew anything, they'd come forward. Still, she might have to do one regardless if they didn't get anywhere.

She may as well confirm it. "Yes, initial identification shows it's her."

"Marty, my barman, said the body was taken away about half an hour ago," Reg went on. "Poor cow, eh?"

Maybe we'll have more answers by the end of the day if Rib cracks on with the post-mortem.

"Were there any strangers in here on the nights in question three years ago?" Carol asked.

"We're talking off-season, so no, all locals and regulars."

That took a weight off. No tourists to track down. She hadn't thought to ask Katherine when the women had actually gone missing and kicked herself for it. "What month?"

"Are you testing me?" Reg nudged her in the side and chuckled.

"Might be." She'd never admit she wasn't up to speed.

"Well, I've got a memory like an elephant for stuff like this, so if you think I've forgotten, think again. Two thousand and nineteen, it was. October for Karen, the week before Halloween, Friday the twenty-fifth. Then November for Lesley — a Sunday, and I remember that because it's darts night. Third weekend of the month, the seventeenth. December for Teresa. We had a Christmas fancy-dress party, and she'd come as Mrs Claus. That was Friday the twentieth."

Did he go and look that up while the bacon sandwiches were being made?

"Blimey, Reg. Ever thought of becoming a copper?" Dave had finished his sandwich and wrote the dates down. "We could do with someone like you on our team."

Reg laughed. "Nah, I like running this place too much, and I'm getting on a bit now, anyroad."

"What do you recall about Lesley's and Teresa's relationship status? Did they meet men here?" Carol eyed her sandwich. It was calling to her. Sod it. She took a bite.

"There was a conversation. Not on the night Lesley went missing, but a week or so before. Marriages, that's what it was about, and Lesley said she'd end up on the shelf at this rate and she hadn't had a boyfriend for years — she'd been raped around then, see, and didn't trust men. I shouldn't have been listening and wished I hadn't when I heard that bit."

Rape? Does that change things? "Bloody hell, poor sod. So you don't think she'd have got into a car with a man, then?"

Were they looking for a woman? Females who killed were rare, so data collectors would have you believe, but in the Smith case, a woman had been doing all the murdering. Could they have another one on their hands now, like Carol had thought earlier? A woman scorned?

"Maybe," Reg said. "Her friends kept telling her to report it to the police, but Lesley said no, she couldn't cope with the questions. I hope she ended up reporting it, though. As for Teresa, well, she was having it away with some bloke from out of town. He's from up the coast a bit — married, by all accounts. They met in here every week on a Tuesday for quiz night. I asked her once, when she was on her own, who he was, and she told me about him. Anyroad, I passed it on to Richard, and he interviewed the fella. He must have had an alibi, because as far as I know, nowt was done about him."

Another affair. "We'll go down and speak to Rich about it," she said to Dave.

"Who the fuck did this?" Reg whispered, glancing around at the nearby tables. "I always thought it was off that three had gone missing and nowt seemed to come of it. Okay, with Karen, I get it, she was leaving Craig anyroad, but the other two? From what I know of them, they wouldn't just fuck off."

"We hope to find out." *But if they're linked, will their bodies turn up like Karen's?* Why would that be, though? Was the killer bored of keeping them captive? Had all three been taken by the same person, or was it just a coincidence? The seesawing between abduction and leaving of their own free will wore Carol down. "Do you remember owt else that could help us?"

Reg pondered, elbow on the table, his hand to his mouth. He shook his head. "Only listening to people afterwards, you know, when the police had spoken to everyone who'd been in here on those nights. I'd remembered most of the customers, gave Richard a list, but with the place packed out, I might have missed a few. Anyroad, people were speculating as to what could have happened, and most thought it was dodgy. When it was in the paper that all the cases had been closed, we couldn't believe it."

Carol couldn't either, and she was surprised Richard hadn't mentioned Lesley and Teresa when he'd informed her about Karen going missing. But what if the other two cases were similar to Karen's in that both women had expressed the need to move away? No, Carol couldn't get on board with that. Three women didn't just walk out of town weeks apart and not contact their families.

So why had the cases been shut down?

Maybe the leads went dry. We can't look for someone indefinitely.

Or maybe . . . What if they were also caught on camera withdrawing money?

The idea of that sent a shiver through her. It meant there was a pattern, one that had possibly been missed, and she felt guilty. She and Dave had been so caught up in that other big case at the time that they'd been unavailable to work on other local ones. Richard wasn't a detective, and while he was a damn good copper, he would have been stressed to the max trying to do her job. Oliver Havers, another sergeant, would have been the same. Too much work on, not enough time to breathe, to sit and really think about things.

She sent Dave one of her looks: *Oh fuck, something's been missed.*

He raised his eyebrows and stood. Patted Reg on the shoulder. "Cheers for breakfast, but we have to get going."

Carol stood, too. "Thanks for everything."

Reg smiled. "Anytime. I hope you find whoever did this."

"So do we, pal," Dave said.

Carol picked up the rest of her sandwich. "Just a warning, Reg, so I've done my bit. The lock-ins have come to our attention."

"Right, I'll knock them on the head, then." He winked and struck up a conversation with Dave about the merits of using a greenhouse for growing the veg the pub served on the roast dinners.

Carol smiled and walked outside, eating along the way. She stared at all the boats in the marina while she chewed. An unsettling thought crept in. Lesley had been raped. Was she one of William King's victims? If she was, this was going to bring everything up for Michael again. It had been hard going for her to persuade him to remain in his job once he'd found out what his grandad had done. Recently, he'd sworn he was fine coping with that sort of thing at work, but what if this brought on a relapse for him?

Carol ate the last of her sandwich and took a deep breath. People were shits, and in her line of work, she unfortunately saw that side of folks more than others did, but Michael wasn't his grandad, and if people were pathetic enough to treat him differently because of something he'd known nothing about, then they needed their heads testing.

No one around here would have thought the domino-playing pensioner was capable of what he'd done. *No one.*

Dave came out and stood beside her. "What did the cogs in your head throw up?"

She smiled at how in sync they were. "Number one, did William King rape Lesley? Number two, I need to get Katherine on something — Michael's probably out visiting Lesley's and Teresa's parents, so he can't do it. What if they were also caught on ATM cameras withdrawing money?"

"Shit."

"Hmm. If they were . . ."

"We could be looking at one person taking them all."

"Yep. We'll drive down to Buns 'n' Bread. Rich is probably still there."

Carol sent a message to Katherine and Michael about Lesley's rape to keep them in the loop. Plus, it would give Michael time to process the news before he returned to the station.

* * *

The Outer Cordon

Richard closed his eyes briefly, perhaps recalling the past.

"I did flag that," he said, "but with nowt else to go on, the withdrawals being the only link, what else could we do when everything else had gone cold? I should have mentioned Lesley and Teresa when we were discussing Karen, so I apologise for not doing that. Stupid of me, because what if the other women turn up dead now?"

"You had too much going on up top," Carol said. "It happens to us all, but yes, that's my concern, that if they *were* taken by the same person, they might be killed. What about CCTV in the areas of the ATMs? Was that checked?"

"Yes, and I should have told you this, too. Each woman walked off afterwards as if they were okay. They didn't meet with anyone, just left the high street. After that there were no cameras, so we couldn't see where they'd gone. Shit, this is going to play on my mind now. I dropped the ball in not telling you."

"It doesn't matter," Carol said. "What does is that we know *now*, and remember, we're all human. This morning you were controlling a scene, had a lot to deal with, so don't beat yourself up. Reg mentioned Teresa was seeing some bloke up the coast. What happened there?"

"He was at a work function that night. Solid alibi, because he stayed until last knockings, some party or other, and he shared a room with a male colleague who confirmed that. The hotel has cameras back, front and sides, and neither of them were captured leaving until the morning. Oliver checked on ANPR, and Teresa's bloke's car was clocked on his way to the function then again when he left, heading towards Sandsend where he lives. It wasn't him."

"Okay, so we don't need to revisit that." Carol sighed, her gaze on the mouth of the alley. "Karen's been removed, then."

Richard looked over his shoulder then back to her. "Yes, and I'm frustrated because no bugger saw or heard owt during the night. All house-to-house enquiries have come up blank. According to Todd, his team haven't found owt either apart from the usual. Fag butts, litter, that sort of thing."

"Maybe something will come of that when it's processed." Carol didn't think there was much they could do here. Standing around didn't accomplish anything. "We'll head back to the station and check in with Katherine. Have a look at Lesley's and Teresa's files, see if owt clicks."

Richard smiled. "If anyone can see something me and Oliver didn't, it'll be you."

She appreciated the compliment, but it was an awful lot of pressure to live up to.

* * *

The Incident Room

Katherine was already a step ahead. She'd dug up the ATM lead while Carol and Dave had been out. "So, while there's a link with the ATMs, I can see why the cases stalled and it isn't Richard's or Oliver's fault. We've been in that situation plenty of times, haven't we, where there's nowhere else to go. No one has the time to devote to these cases years down the line, and as there was proof of life, why would anyone still look for them anyroad?"

Carol agreed. "I'm determined to solve this."

"So am I now I know Lesley was raped."

"She's had a rough time of it. Violated then possibly abducted, although it does make me wonder if she went off somewhere to lick her wounds after being attacked and just didn't bother telling anyone. Her head must have been messed up. What does the file have on her?"

"Unfortunately, she waited over a fortnight to report it, so any evidence was long gone. She'd burned her clothes too, but one of her shoes had been found in the garden where it happened. A neighbour had put it in their bin. Luckily, it hadn't been emptied, but unluckily, nowt of the attacker was found on it by the lab."

Carol winced, but she understood why Lesley had kept quiet. Shame. Embarrassment. Fear. "Why didn't she come forward immediately?"

"Too frightened her attacker knew who she was, where she lived, because he raped her in her own street, ten houses down from her front door."

"Oh God, that's bloody awful. She was so close to home."

"I know, sickening, isn't it?" Katherine let out a long breath. "She'd been to a book club at the library and was on her way back. He hit her with something hard on the head—she still had a yellow bruise, and the hospital checked her out in case her skull had been damaged. It hadn't. He dragged her into someone's front garden, did the deed, then ran off."

"Did she see his face?"

"No, she kept her eyes closed once he threw her onto the grass and she knew what was coming. She thought it was better to let him do it, for her to remain still rather than fight and anger him. She was scared he'd kill her."

"I can imagine. What made her go to the police in the end?"

"Someone else got raped two weeks later, and it was on the local news. She felt guilty for keeping it quiet, because she thought if she'd spoken up, he might not have attacked the other woman. Oh, and he'd spoken to her. Local accent."

"What did he say?"

"'*You've got your legs open, asking me for it. You're a tease. You want it, you know you do.*'"

Carol's eyes burned. "Bastard. Could it have been him who took them all?"

Or *was* the rapist Michael's grandad, now deceased? The fact William King had killed himself and revealed in a note app he'd been preying on women for decades had been a massive blow to her DC.

Thank God Michael isn't here at the minute.

Dave frowned. "William killed himself last autumn. Is he our abductor and the women have been stuck wherever he took them ever since? That would explain Karen being so thin. She'd been starving, maybe eking out whatever provisions were left."

"That doesn't explain the botched surgery," said Carol, "or how Karen got dumped."

"William could still have raped Lesley, though," Katherine said, "then someone else abducted her. A bloody shitty set of cards to be dealt, granted, but weirder things have happened."

Carol hoped Michael was okay since she'd sent the message. The thought of him upset, trying to cope with the news, tugged at her heart. "Should I check if Michael's okay?"

Katherine shook her head. "Leave him. He's better off digesting it by himself."

"That's what I thought." Carol flapped the neckline of her top to get some air. It was hot despite the fans whirring. "What about Lesley's and Teresa's phone records. Owt weird going on there?"

"No, they're the same as Karen's, your everyday calls and messages. Absolutely nowt sinister going on."

"What are your thoughts on the other two women?"

"That they were taken by the same person, had to have been. Karen didn't walk out on Craig, someone grabbed her before she could do that."

Dave nodded. "I have to agree. The state of Karen points to her being held somewhere."

"*Where*, though?" Carol sat back in Michael's chair. "Keeping three women quiet for years is a bloody big job. A detached house, definitely not a terrace, unless there's a cellar."

"Think about the garage in the Smith case," Katherine said. "It'd been soundproofed."

Carol groaned. "So the place could be anywhere. Was Craig's searched when Karen disappeared? It bloody better have been."

"Yes, all three women's residences were. Nowt untoward." Katherine drummed her fingers on her desk. "You've already heard from Richard about Teresa's fella, and I've got nowt to report there. He's clean, and his wife wasn't spoken to, so he got away with the affair."

"Bet he was relieved." Dave sounded sarcastic and disgusted.

"I noticed you were arsey earlier at Geordie's," Carol said to him. "Are you okay?"

"It just grates on me, that's all, but I get why Karen was seeing Geordie. Living with Craig would send anybody into someone else's arms."

Dave's ex-wife had done the dirty on him and recently had a child with the man she'd been seeing behind his back. She'd gone into labour two weeks early and had given birth to a girl. Dave coped well for the most part, but his heart was clearly still sore.

"Nowt I can't handle," he said. "At work, I mean."

"Okay. Do you think we should get a medical opinion on Karen's surgery?" Carol asked. She looked at Dave and tried to convey she didn't want to speak to any surgeons herself.

He got the gist. "I'll contact the hospital and see if someone can nip here and have a gander at some photos. I don't fancy sending them via email."

"Thanks." Relieved, Carol said, "You two review these files, see if owt else sticks out. I've got something else to do, then we'll need to go and see Evan Ike. We should be done here by the time he turns up at his house.

It annoyed Carol that she was bound to a desk for the next three hours, but being a detective didn't mean haring around everywhere all the time. Often, it was picking through files or online information that brought the breaks.

She just had to hope this time was one of them.

* * *

An hour later, Dave went downstairs to speak to the surgeon, who'd popped by on his way home. He knew full well why Carol didn't want to do it, though she wouldn't speak about it in front of Katherine or Michael, and Dave didn't plan on bringing it out into the open. Carol would likely prefer to keep many things to herself or only for Dave's ears.

The chat proved fruitful in a way but didn't reveal anything Dave hadn't already thought of — that a proper surgeon wouldn't have made such a hash of it. The bloke felt the cuts were made by someone who didn't know what they were doing, but . . .

"It's weight-loss surgery," he said. "All the wounds you describe other than in the photos I've seen are to remove excess skin, so whoever it is has knowledge, but then again, we can all search owt on Google."

Dave was inclined to agree. "So, the cuts themselves. Ragged. Wouldn't anyone be able to slice in a straight line?"

"You would think so, wouldn't you?"

Maybe they'd enjoyed cutting her so haphazardly.

It was one of those questions that would only be answered if the offender gave it to them when they were caught.

And they will be, but they might not explain things.

Dave sighed. The downside of his job.

CHAPTER SEVENTEEN

Medina Gardens

Michael preferred being in the incident room, but sometimes he needed to help out and leave his beloved desk. Today, he was glad, considering the text Carol had sent. Last year, when Grandad had killed himself by jumping off a cliff, Michael had contemplated giving up his job and doing something different, more in a mental health capacity, to help people with multiple personalities like Grandad must have had, but Carol had helped him through it, showing him he was needed, valued, and what his grandad had done wasn't a reflection on him.

No, it *wasn't* a reflection on him. Michael didn't go around raping women, and if he'd known his what his grandad had been doing, he'd have dobbed him in, no matter how much he'd loved him. Did he still love him? That was the thing in a situation like this. The person Michael and his family had known didn't match who he'd been at night when he'd stalked women and violated them, for too many years to count. Michael loved the man he'd thought his grandad had been — nice, kind, gentle — not the monster he'd become on the quiet.

All those women. That was what Michael couldn't get over. Some had reported the rapes, others had only come forward once the revelation of the rapist's name and death had hit the news. All were receiving counselling, and for the more recent cases where DNA had been taken, the samples had been matched to his grandad.

The shame had been crippling.

Most people around these parts hadn't blamed the family, hadn't tarred them all with the same hideous brush, but a few seemed to think if it was in the blood, the lot of them would be tainted. That was ridiculous, but it didn't stop the sharp sting when people shouted shit at Michael and every other male in the family.

"The apple doesn't fall far from the tree!"

Uncle Zeb had taken it badly. He'd been best friends with Grandad as well as them being related. He couldn't get to grips with how he hadn't picked anything up over the years, and the guilt weighed heavy. As for Mam, Grandad had been her father, and knowing she had a half-brother who was also a criminal . . . Mason Ingram from the last big case had been the product of a rape, DNA had proved Grandad was his father. Mason had killed people, and Mam refused to have anything to do with him while he rotted in a prison cell. Michael didn't want anything to do with him either.

Mam had gone into her shell, revolted by Grandad, feeling sorry for her late mother for being married to him. Feeling sorry for every one of them who'd been duped by his perfect, gentlemanly behaviour, his shining eyes, his outwardly good nature. And not being able to ask him *why*, that was a kick to the gut. Had Mason's mam been the first victim, or had there been more before her?

Carol had saved Michael. They'd formed a bond during those chats, become closer than they'd ever been, and he'd forever be grateful she'd persuaded him to stay. The embarrassment of the whole episode had been swept under the carpet by his other colleagues, and he suspected Carol had a hand in that, telling them Michael was Michael, he wasn't

Mr William "Butterfly" King, so whatever had happened wasn't his fault.

The one thing Michael still couldn't deal with was the Jekyll and Hyde aspect. How could someone who presented as so loving be such a beast? How had Grandad managed to hide who he really was? The team dealt with people like that on occasion, but never had he thought someone he'd looked up to would turn out to be such a vile creature.

He flung those thoughts out of his head and stared out of the windscreen at the next house he had to visit. He'd already been to see Lesley's parents, who were convinced her rapist had kidnapped her. His immediate thoughts had gone to whether Grandad had done it, and he'd felt so sorry for her mam and dad, left to live without closure, worrying where their daughter was, whether she was alive or dead. They'd asked about what they'd seen on the internet earlier, was the body Lesley's or someone else's, and the relief in their eyes when he'd said it wasn't their child had torn at his heart.

How awful to be glad someone else was dead if it meant it wasn't your loved one. It was a natural response, though, wasn't it? Almost as natural as Michael wishing someone else's grandad had been a deviant.

He just had to see Teresa's mam now — her father was dead. Wicked as it sounded, he couldn't wait to get back to the station. Seeing raw emotions was hard to handle these days, and he preferred hearing it second-hand from Carol and Dave, although that was also difficult to process. He was already bottling up his tears from being with the Johnsons — sitting with his mother after Grandad had died, watching her crumple, had opened up a new way of feeling for Michael. He'd always been sensitive, but dealing with his grief and anger, not to mention that of his family members, had shown him how stripped away you became when someone close to you was no longer there. How debilitating it was when you discovered they were a disgusting human being.

The cremation had been family only, held early in the morning, the hearse leaving from the funeral director's instead of Mam's house. The shame of it all had been too much to announce a funeral, to have others attend. The thought of someone turning up and shouting the odds while they'd laid him to rest — in Hell, Michael hoped — would have tipped their grieving over the edge.

It was a lot to process.

He sighed and got out of the car, making his way up a gravel path to the front door. A pretty bouquet of flowers sat in a pot on the step. Ruining someone's day by regurgitating the past wasn't fun, but as Lesley's parents had stated, all three disappearances could be linked. Michael was beginning to lean that way too, as the Johnsons said Lesley had been captured on CCTV withdrawing money. Katherine had sent him a message saying the same thing.

It was definitely fishy.

He raised the knocker and let it clatter back down. Yvonne Fett opened the door, the hope in her eyes too much to witness, so Michael concentrated on her forehead and held up his ID.

"DC Michael King. I rang earlier?"

"Come in," she said. "I've got tea in the pot."

He followed her down the hallway, sliding his ID away, telling himself he *had* to make eye contact with her or she might think things were off. She sat at a table, gesturing for him to join her, and poured tea from a pot with the spout poking out of a yellow cosy with cartoon sheep all over it.

Tea and milk sorted, she challenged his mettle by looking him straight in the eye. "What do you need to know?"

"We've reopened your daughter's case."

Her eyes misted. "It's to do with that body by the bakery. Val, Mrs Johnson, she phoned and told me after you'd left hers."

"Yes, during our investigation, we discovered three women went missing around the same time. Clearly, we're concerned that if the same person took them, Lesley and Teresa may be in danger."

She laughed bitterly. "They've been in danger since the day they were taken, son, but no one listened to us, going on about having proof of life because of the withdrawals. That's all well and good, but what if they were forced to take the money out? What if whoever took them wanted the police to check the banks and see them alive?"

"It's possible."

"I know damn well it is. My husband died of a heart attack, you know, a month after Teresa was abducted — and I say abducted, because a mother knows when something's wrong. She's alive, I can feel it." She patted her chest. "In here. I'd know if she was dead. My girl is breathing. All that needs to happen is for you lot to find her."

"I can promise you, we're doing everything we can to make sure that happens. As you're in contact with the Johnsons, are you also keeping in touch with Craig Stokes? I know Karen's parents are dead, but I thought—"

"No, we don't have owt to do with Craig. We tried to reach out and band together so we could keep searching for them ourselves, but he wasn't interested. I did think it was him once upon a time, but why would he take Teresa and Lesley as well, and where the hell would he put them?"

The conversation continued with Michael asking all about Teresa and what she was like. Yvonne went into the past, recalling happy memories, happier times, and her smile made it appear she wasn't a grieving woman. She mentioned a man Teresa had been seeing, but he'd been cleared of any involvement.

"I hated the fact he had a wife and had conned Teresa into thinking he'd leave the missus for her. I told her that was highly unlikely, but she was in love with the cheating bastard. I was disappointed in her, for seeing him when he had children, when his family could be broken up because of her, but once she went missing, I knew I'd forgive her everything if I could see her again."

A tear fell down her cheek, and it choked Michael up. He reached out a hand, and she grabbed it, him the lifeline, her drowning once again, begging him with her eyes to bring her little girl home.

Michael cried, too.

CHAPTER EIGHTEEN

The Incident Room

Michael had returned and passed on all the information he'd picked up from the Johnsons and Mrs Fett. Carol chugged it all through her mind, and she had to agree with them. One person was responsible for the disappearances. The ATM lark alone was too much of a coincidence for her, and she believed whoever had abducted them had forced them to withdraw the money.

She'd left Katherine and Dave poring over the cold cases and had viewed the evidence footage of the women walking away from the cashpoints. She had to agree with Rich, they seemed okay, casual, no furtive glances or jerky movements. At each ATM, the pattern was the same, and it hurt Carol to see Karen so healthy in size compared to how she'd been found in death. She could only hope Lesley and Teresa were alive and could be rescued.

"Proof of life in this case has turned out not to be the case in the sense we'd usually take it," she said to Michael at his desk. She'd pulled a spare chair over to chat with him and her team. "As in, yes, the footage is proof they were alive, they appear well, but something sinister was going on behind the scenes. Can you *imagine* what that must have been like to go to a cashpoint among all those people, knowing you couldn't ask for help? They must have been threatened."

"Them or their family members," Dave said.

"If I wasn't bound by certain laws, I'd string this fucker up when we get hold of him." Carol clenched her fists then stretched her fingers. "I've been racking my brains on the location, so as well as the big Tesco being a factor regarding the pay-as-you-go, after I viewed the cashpoint footage, I did a map and geographic profiling to see if we can work out where the person lives, as well as going over offender hunting behaviour and target selection."

"So, for whatever reason, you think they're fixated on a specific type?" Michael said.

"Right. I'm willing to bet it's someone important to them," Carol said. "We've seen this time and time again. Target selection . . . the location that ties them all together is the Little Devil. Tesco is the thing that's throwing me, as that's on the other side of town out of the way. Michael, can you check if owt's come through about that Freddo?"

He opened up his emails. "One came in while I was out."

He opened it, and Carol leaned forward to read: *Sent from factory on Friday 8 July to Sainsbury's, Scudderton.*

Carol smiled. "So it's not an old chocolate bar Karen had in her bag from when she went missing. That's exactly what I was hoping for. Michael, get hold of Sainsbury's. What's the betting we have another Dolly Parton as our purchaser."

She sniffed her disgust at whoever they were after, then walked to the map to add Sainsbury's. She tied red wool around each pin for the pub, Tesco and Sainsbury's. "A triangle at last." She pointed to it. "Nearby one of those points is where our offender lives. How far out or in, I don't know yet, but you can bet they live closer to either the pub or the two supermarkets."

"Feels like we're getting somewhere," Dave said.

"We are. I want a list drawn up of all homes near those three points. There are going to be a lot because of not only the Coldwater estate by Tesco but the other one by Sainsbury's, not to mention people who live near the marina by the Devil. We'll get uniforms to help on the estates now — big job, could take days — and two others can visit the outlying houses. Michael, can you get that organised for me, please?" She caught the time on the wall clock. "Shit, Dave, we'd better get to Kipling Close and speak to Evan. If we're not back by five, you two, go home and get some rest. There's only so much we can do in one day."

"Hang on a sec," Michael said. "Just had another email. Craig's vest was pushed through for a quick result. Barbeque sauce."

Carol nodded. "Okay, and that reminds me to check in with Whitney." More than ever, she understood Rich's slip-up earlier. *She* had a lot going on up top, too. "I'll go and check my emails first, though."

She jogged to her office and booted up her computer.

Rib had sent his preliminary findings, but he hadn't finished the post-mortem yet and estimated he wouldn't be done before six, as he had the painstaking task of cataloguing every cigarette burn. What she found interesting, which Rib likely knew she would, was that Karen had possibly had more than two children. Michael had gained permission to view her medical files earlier, and there was no mention of a third or more pregnancies. Rib stated parturition scars, and the depth, plus the amount of them, could indicate more children. However, he'd prefaced that by saying studies had shown that many women who'd never given birth had such striations, too.

He'd also written:

I'm not kicking you when you're down, Bird, because there's hope. Of all the female post-mortems I've done, I've been spot-on with the amount of pregnancies I've predicted. A lot of people in my profession will pooh-pooh it, but I've seen what I've seen, so they can think what they like. Now, the only reason I've mentioned it is because it may well be relevant to the case. It isn't clear yet if or when Karen had another child, I'm only going by my own experience, but if she did, what happened to it?

On another note, she's had several bones broken, old injuries — her arm and her nose. None of them appear to have been set by a medical practitioner, so I can only assume she walked around in pain until they knitted together on their own. They're old.

Anyway, I'll leave you to get on. I'll send you my proper report once I'm finished, but you'll likely be in the pub by then. Might catch you there later, depends on how I go.

Carol wondered the same thing as Rib and hoped they weren't on the hunt for a child as well as the women. Maybe they ought to pop in on Craig before they went to Evan's and put feelers out.

Her phone rang, and Whitney's name came up on the screen.

Carol answered it. "Hi, how's it going?"

"We're going to need a police excavation team down here."

Carol's guts rolled. "Why?"

"Craig's just broken down and admitted something. I warned him the house could be searched again, even the garden. One of the girls stared at me, and I knew something was wrong. I took her into the kitchen and asked."

"What did she say?"

"There's a baby buried out the back."

"*What?*" Carol shot up and paced, adrenaline flowing, all the air going out of her. "Rib's just mentioned pelvic bone scars, and I was thinking she'd been forced to have a baby in captivity. Jesus Christ, what the fuck happened?"

"He hit her one time too many while she was pregnant about six years ago, gave her a shove, and Karen fell down the stairs."

Carol recalled him saying about a shove. "The bastard never said a word to us."

"I know, he said he hadn't. The girls witnessed it — and Karen giving birth. She lost the baby. He buried it."

Christ alive, that would have been traumatic. "Hadn't she been to see a doctor before that, about the pregnancy?"

"No."

"Bloody hell, that's why there are no records. Okay, I'll action a team. You organise somewhere for the girls to stay; try Lindsey's over the road if Craig hasn't got any family."

"He does, but they live in Wales and he doesn't want owt to do with them. His daughters have never met them."

"Right. I'll send someone down to collect him for questioning, but me and Dave are on the way anyroad. We have to see Evan Ike. Does Craig look like he's going to bolt? Can you handle him alone until someone gets there?"

"He's fine. Crying."

"So he should be. Bastard. Hang tight. We won't be long."

Carol phoned for two officers to go to Craig's then arranged for an excavation team. She walked into the incident room, weary, flabbergasted at the turn this case had taken.

She related the latest to her team.

"Fuck me," Dave said. "He's something else, he is."

"Those poor girls," Katherine said. "To have known. What a horrible secret for them to keep. No wonder they've gone off the rails."

Michael dropped his face into his hands. "This is a bloody nightmare."

Carol couldn't agree more. "I know, yet when we discussed pregnancy with him regarding her abdomen wound and there was a suggestion that someone had cut a child out of her, he said even he wouldn't stoop that low. Yet he's admitted he caused her baby's death? If he's capable of killing an unborn child and putting it in the ground, what *else* is he capable of?"

* * *

Much as Carol wanted to read Craig the riot act, she didn't. He appeared devastated by what he'd done — or was that to throw her off? She supposed the relief of unburdening himself had been immense. It still didn't make everything okay, though. A baby had died because of him, and two girls and their mother had to keep the secret, tormenting themselves with knowing a child lay beneath the mud and fearing it would be discovered. Carol understood a lot about psychology, and she pondered whether the girls had subconsciously been mugging and robbing in the hope they'd actually get caught, then they could blurt out the truth. Them denying being thieves when Mulholland had questioned them could be a last-minute, knee-jerk reaction, the secret rearing up in their minds and the consequences of revealing the truth stopping them from doing it.

No wonder they didn't do anything their father said. They had leverage against him. If he tried to get them in line, all they had to do was remind him about what he did.

The girls were now with Lindsey, who'd agreed to look after them until Carol knew what was happening with Craig at the station. They'd receive help at some point, to talk through their experience and how it had affected them. A social worker would be assigned.

Carol allowed the uniforms to take Craig in, and she asked Michael and Katherine to do the initial interview. If it was just about the baby and nothing more came to light, Carol would speak to him in the morning.

She had Evan to deal with now.

She crossed the road with Dave as the excavation team arrived from one of the bigger divisions.

"He's sorry," Dave said.

"I know, but I'm so fucking angry about how his girls were forced to hide it. No child should have to keep a secret like that. They'll need therapy, and what if the CPS don't want Craig released? What about his daughters then? What, do they go to Wales, to family they don't even know? Why the *fuck* don't people think about what they're doing and how it affects others? He's a selfish prick, and I don't like speaking ill of the dead except for my father and William King, but Karen's no better. She went along with it all."

She stomped up Evan's garden path.

Dave stood beside her. "Deep breath, all right?"

"I know." She composed herself, unable to get the image out of her mind of a tiny baby under the mud. It was a boy, and he'd been wrapped in a blanket then put inside a black bag, according to Craig. She'd never forget this for as long as she lived. Never.

An elusive memory prodded her, but she couldn't grasp it.

The door opened, and an older version of Geordie stood there.

"Evan Ike?" Carol held up her ID. "DI Carol Wren and DS Dave Waite. Can we have a word?"

"What about?"

"Didn't your brother get hold of you, then?" She cocked her head.

"Nope." He stepped back so they could enter.

They gathered in the hallway, the front door ajar. Carol shut it and went through the usual questions for an hour, dying to sit on the stairs to rest her legs. It seemed Evan wasn't going to offer them a seat in the living room.

His story matched everyone else's. His reason for taking work abroad had been to get away from Lindsey, who'd been talking about kicking her then husband out so they could be together. Odd, then, that she "wasn't ready" to let Tom Cubbins move in now.

"Her and Karen were the bloody same, leeches, trying to get me and Geordie to stay with them. I didn't want any part of it, although it was a bit of a punch to the gut when Karen went missing. I saw your lot taking Craig off. Was it him?"

"He's been arrested on another matter. Well, thanks for your time and for being so honest."

She left the house, Dave following, and veered towards Craig's instead of the car.

"What are you doing?" Dave asked.

"I want to see that poor little boy being found."

Dave stopped her on the opposite path, a hand on her arm. "No, love. No. It'll wreck you. If you don't need to see it, don't."

"But I feel like I need to do something. Be there. Give a shit."

"The team in the garden will give a shit."

She deflated. He was right, but the gnawing in her belly wouldn't go away, nor would the questions. Had the baby taken a breath? Was it stillborn? Had Karen been glad she'd lost him?

Carol would get her answers soon, because she was about to butt in on Craig's interview. She wanted to look into his eyes when he told her about his son's last moments.

* * *

Interview Room Two

She wished she hadn't bothered. Craig's account hurt Carol's heart so much she had a physical pain. The baby had been born dead at five months gestation, and Karen had lost a lot of blood, weak for days afterwards. He hadn't even phoned for a doctor, and neither had she. She'd remained in bed while Craig had buried the child later that night, getting his daughters to help with the digging. That part had Carol wanting to punch his lights out, especially when he admitted he'd told them they could go to a reform centre for doing it.

"You're actually disgusting," she said, not giving a shit that what she'd said was on tape. "Those poor girls."

"I know, it was rotten, but I was scared, see. Where are they?"

"With Lindsey."

"When can I go home?"

"I doubt you can. Your place is a crime scene. If the Crime Prosecution Service feel you should remain in custody, if there's enough evidence to keep you, we'll have to arrange for your girls to be taken care of. By your family. If not, they'll go into the care system."

"Fuck, I don't like my mother."

"She lives in Wales, yes?"

"Yeah."

"What's so wrong with her that she can't look after your kids?"

"Nowt, she wouldn't hurt them, but me and her don't get on."

"Is she better than care?"

"Well, yeah, but—"

"Then that's all you should be concerned about. *Their* welfare, not the fact you're not on speaking terms with your mam. Not only have they had to keep this horrible secret about the baby, they've also been through three years with not knowing where their mother is, and now they've found out she's dead. That's *a lot* for children to cope with."

Carol hoped, despite the mud, the weather over the years and the general damage insects created, that some form of evidence was on the black bag, the blanket and the remains of the baby. Sometimes, despite the severity of a crime, people were allowed out on bail if they weren't a danger to society or wouldn't repeat the same crime. In this case, she couldn't see Craig killing another baby. The red tape sickened her. He'd admitted it and shouldn't be out on the streets, but there was the other side of the coin to consider. Too many people had been convicted for crimes they hadn't committed. For all they knew, Karen could have done it and in some weird sense of loyalty, Craig and his daughters could be taking the blame.

"Did you know Karen didn't want children?" she asked.

"Yeah, she said it enough, but I *did* want them, so that's what happened." He rubbed his red eyes. "I'd always wanted a boy."

"Shame you killed him, then," she snapped.

Dave kicked her foot under the table.

She'd gone too far but didn't regret it. "You refused a solicitor. Why?"

Craig sniffed. "Because I did it. A solicitor will tell me to go not guilty."

"So you're prepared to go to prison without a trial? Why now? Why not back then?"

"I got scared. Shit myself when Whitney said about another search. When Karen went missing, they looked in the garden but didn't dig. This time they might have. It was better to come clean."

"Karen's dead, you could have blamed it all on her. Threatened your daughters to say the same."

He laughed, an unpleasant sound that set Carol's teeth on edge.

"*They* were the ones threatening *me* earlier. They heard what Whitney said, and they told me if I didn't tell her, they would. And you've said yourself. There'll be evidence of me on the stuff I buried. It's over. Fucking over. I'm done for."

"You are, Mr Stokes, and I hope you get put away for a long time. Interview suspended at 5.16 p.m."

CHAPTER NINETEEN

The Lord — Mollengate

What a fucking day. It had gone on forever, and Carol was shattered. She'd sent Michael and Katherine home after she'd nipped into the incident room to check whether any news had come in yet about the Jolenes in the country, plus the footage from Sainsbury's showing who'd bought the Freddo. Nowt had arrived, and nothing new had come in from Rib or Todd, so that was it, time to leave. Tomorrow was another day, and they could hit the ground running then.

Carol's masala had been lovely, and she was currently washing it down with a well-earned glass of white wine — only a small one in case they got called back to work. Dave had opted for half a lager, and he was doing well, three-quarters still left.

"Do you want to talk about today?" he asked.

She tucked hair behind her ear. "Do you?"

"Nope."

"Me neither. It's been too much. I'm worried I won't sleep tonight."

"The baby."

"Hmm."

Dave clapped. "Okay, we'll play 'I Spy'."

She laughed. "What the fuck?"

Dave smiled. "I spy with my little eye, something beginning with C."

"Me?"

"Very funny. No, look around."

She did, and her attention landed on her ex. "Oh, the creep, or is the word more like 'See You Next Tuesday'?"

"Yep, he just came in. What's the betting he comes over again, talking about more storage boxes."

Carol rolled her eyes. She'd laugh if he didn't get on her wick so much. Her ex-lover was obsessively tidy — so much so, whenever she'd been over at his place to scratch an itch, she'd been scared to touch anything bar the bed. She'd been messy once upon a time but had seen the error of her ways, how clutter in the home also cluttered the mind, and she'd grown to enjoy living in a clean home — nothing to do with him, though. His kitchen, however, was too much, and when he'd pressed her to move their relationship to more than just fucking, she'd thought about his tendencies with a bottle of disinfectant spray and a cloth and declined. He still insisted on speaking to her in the Lord, but at least he'd stopped bugging her via the phone since a restraining order had been mentioned.

"Christ alive, he's coming over *again*," she said. "I don't give a fiddler's fuck about his bloody boxes."

Dave scowled. "I'm going to warn him off. I've had enough. This is harassment."

"What's the point? He'll just say he's being friendly. There are plenty of witnesses to back him up."

He stopped by their table and grinned down at her. "Carol! So nice to see you."

"Err, okay, but I don't want to see you. I don't know how many times I have to say that before you get the message."

"But there's something I want to tell you about."

"New storage boxes?"

"Yes, and they're three ninety-nine in Home Bargains at the moment, so you need to go and get some for your cottage."

People have been talking if he knows I've moved out of the flat. "I've got cupboards, I don't need boxes."

"But . . ."

Dave stood. "Have you ever been arrested, pal?"

Her ex jerked his head back in shock. "No!"

"Do you want to be?" Dave canted his head.

"Of course not!"

"Look, fuck off out of it before I get a shit on. Come anywhere near Carol again, and I'll have you for harassment, pestering, whatever charge I can make stick. She doesn't want you. It's over. Deal with it."

The ex-lover stared at her. "Are you two together?"

Carol shrugged. "If we are, it's none of your bloody business."

He stalked away to the bar, and Dave retook his seat.

"What a fucking clown," he muttered.

"You can say that again."

"What a fucking cl—"

"Pack it in." She laughed, catching the ex's eye; he'd turned around just as she'd glanced his way.

He didn't look happy, but she'd been honest with him from the start. Sex, nothing more. It wasn't her fault he'd caught feelings she didn't reciprocate.

CHAPTER TWENTY

Truth-Hunt Cottage

Knitty had known her final client of the day since they were kids. Grim paid her to go over to his cottage, but she didn't need to. It always sparkled and, a complete turnaround from when his wife had lived here, it was sterile, had no heart to it, and didn't feel like a home at all.

Still, she'd do it anyway. Use his steam mop, polish, and wipe all the kitchen surfaces, including the cupboard doors.

She got on with it, her last room the lounge. It always gave her the creeps in there, like someone watched, or the walls were alive, breathing, but that was silly. Maybe Grim had hidden cameras to see if she actually cleaned anything. She wouldn't put it past him and was surprised he'd even requested her for the job, seeing as he'd had a massive go at her that time after Emma had left him.

Shark had been murdered around then — and wasn't that a shock and a half? Everyone's emotions were understandably raw. They'd got together at their usual pub by the park and talked about Shark, remembering him, although it hadn't been as nice at it could have been because of the tension between Grim and Nymph, who'd outright accused him of bumping Shark off out of jealousy. Well, that was bloody daft, as Grim had already said in front of everyone that their marriage was dead in the water, so why would he care if Nymph went with Shark?

Then Grim had announced his only peeve was the rest of the group keeping the affair quiet. He'd zeroed in on Knitty and ripped her a new one, and she'd shot back that she hadn't even *known* about any affair, so he could go and do one, knob-rot. She honestly had no clue, it had been kept from her too, and she suspected it was because she was known as a gossip and would have run straight to Grim and let the cat out of the bag.

He hadn't believed her.

The group had met up without him after that. A couple of years passed, then he'd rung Constant Cleaning to book someone. As usual, her boss gave out a list of names, and he'd picked her. She was instructed to only go there once a week when he wasn't in — he'd leave a key under the back doormat — and she'd been so anxious earlier about being late because of having the police round this morning, she'd worried he'd be in by the time she arrived.

So she'd had to text him, and he'd said fine, he'd go out and get some dinner and be back for seven: *Make sure you're gone before then.*

"Whatever, dick-splash," she said then giggled in case there *were* cameras watching her.

A knock on the front door had her pausing. Who the hell would be out this way if it wasn't Grim forgetting his key? Why didn't he just use the one under the mat? She left the room and went down the hallway, opening the door, still clutching her yellow duster. A police car sat on the drive. First they were at Craig's, now at Grim's. What was going on around here?

Only one uniform stood there. It'd said on the telly that more and more officers were riding solo because of the cuts. Dangerous for them, she reckoned. What if an offender turned nasty?

Well, he was safe with her.

"Can I help you?"

"Hello." He introduced himself. "I just need a quick word about where you were last night."

She frowned. Could this be to do with Karen? "At home."

"And what's your name?"

"Nora Patten. I don't live here, I'm just the cleaner."

"Ah, okay. Do you know when the homeowner will be back?"

"No idea. He's gone out for dinner." She told him Grim's proper name. "If this is about Karen Stokes, I've already spoken to a man and a lady. Them coppers off the telly. Carol and Dave."

"That's brilliant. I'll leave you be, then."

She waved him off, curious as to why the police had come out here. Maybe they were speaking to all residents in the area. Although intrigued, she shrugged and returned indoors.

Job done, the hoover and everything else put away just how Grim liked it, she took his payment in the envelope off the kitchen worktop and opened it. Not only was there money inside but a note. He wanted her to come again tomorrow, five o'clock, because as well as her cleaning all of his kitchen appliances inside and out, he mainly wanted her to sort his washing machine. Something about the rubber door seal being mouldy. She had an easy solution for that, involving bleach on kitchen roll pressed inside the seal, and she could get on with it now to be honest, but no, she could do with the extra money he was offering for tomorrow. Besides, she wanted her dinner.

She got on her moped and rode back to Scudderton. She stopped off at the pier and walked to the end where June's Chippy stood. It had been a fight to get through the crowds — sodding holidaymakers — and the chip shop was roasting inside, the air scented with oil and vinegar. In the queue, she was sweating in no time, and one of the young lads served her the usual, cod and chips with a side of mushy peas.

She struggled through the crowd again, her dinner package clutched tight, and stepped off the pier onto the pavement, glad she was going home. Dinner in the box on the back of her moped, she drove home, coming to a stop, puzzled by a big van outside Craig's.

What was all that about? She got off her moped and pushed it into her front garden, parking it on the patio slabs she'd had laid for it. Indoors, she filled the kettle at the sink in front of the window, dying for a cuppa, and glimpsed a flash of white through a knothole in the dividing fence. Intrigued, she went outside and crept up to the wooden slats, peering through a bigger hole.

A forensic tent had been erected.

"Oh my fucking God," she whispered, the past crawling into her mind and scaring her silly. She jumped at the distant sound of someone knocking on her front door and rushed through the house, the smell of her vinegar-dampened chip wrapper reminding her she had yet to eat. She opened up, jolted by a copper standing there in uniform.

"Sergeant Oliver Havers," he said. "Can I come in and have a word?"

Of course he bloody could. She hadn't had this much excitement in ages. Then again . . . what if he'd come for *her*?

They sat at the table, cups of tea in hand, and he asked her whether she'd seen Karen pregnant after she'd had her girls.

"No, but she always had a big belly, so I couldn't really tell . . ." She felt mean for saying that. Maybe she should have kept it to herself. But it might be important. If he was talking of another baby, where was it? With Karen's tummy the size it was, she could have carried it without anyone knowing.

"Did you notice any suspicious activity in 2016?" he asked.

"That's too far back. I'd need specifics." *I need to know what's really going on.*

He told her just enough for her to realise she'd been lied to, just enough for her to link the question about the baby to an event that had happened six years ago. Craig and his daughters hadn't been burying a new puppy at all but a baby. She'd watched the burial from her bedroom window and asked Karen about it the moment she'd next seen her. She'd believed the story, although now she came to think of it, she'd never heard a puppy yowling at night, and they usually did that at first while they settled in.

A baby. A poor little scrap who'd been thrown away like rubbish.

Knitty didn't want her dinner anymore.

CHAPTER TWENTY-ONE

The Little Devil

Grim sat in his SUV at the mouth of a street close to the woodland opposite the Coldwater estate. His target had walked by earlier on her way to the pub, and she hadn't come back this way since. He'd prepared himself to wait hours, and his gritty eyes stung where he'd stared ahead in the building minutes. He wouldn't have to wait long now. Last orders would have been called, so unless she hung around for a lock-in, she'd appear soon.

His mind wandered. Knitty had cleaned satisfactorily. He'd come back from having dinner and inspected everything. He didn't need her, but he liked knowing a woman worked for him, a woman was doing everything Lazy Emma hadn't, and it was especially satisfying that it happened to be Knitty. She and the others owed him for keeping the affair quiet. He couldn't wait to hurt them. Knitty, Blitz and Thunder. He'd show them the pain he'd been going through. Killing Karen had released something in him, and he'd left Knitty a note about his kitchen appliances for tomorrow to lure her to his cottage. She always had loved getting extra money.

For tonight, he'd focus on his new guest. He hadn't had time lately to watch her as much as he had with the other three, but he knew her basic movements.

He concentrated on the alley ahead, the one beside the Little Devil. People had come and gone all night, his heart leaping every time, Grim lowering himself in his seat if they came too close.

He should have worn one of his disguises. Too late now.

The shape of a bloke ambled down the alley, heading towards the estate, hands in his pockets, attention on the path. Grim clenched his teeth. There were bound to be others walking through here to get home from the pub, but it still annoyed him. All he wanted to see was *her*. She was like Emma had been years ago, nice and slim, not like the others he'd taken. At least he wouldn't have to perform surgery on her.

The man, who Grim thought of as a pest, came into proper view, and then he didn't seem such a pest at all.

Well, well, well. Look who we have here.

Should I combine the two jobs together?

Rage answered him when the fella reached the end of the alley and stood on the pavement to check for traffic. Unlikely any drivers would be around at this time of night, but it was ingrained in you, wasn't it, to look both ways no matter where you were. He glanced right and left, then right again, and put one foot out onto the road. He stopped, peering back over his shoulder, and Grim stared that way, too.

Fuck. The new subject was coming, waving at the man, tottering along on her high heels.

This wasn't supposed to happen. Grim had envisaged it in his head, her coming along alone, but his plans had gone out of the window.

Blitz. This had to be kismet.

Blitz faced the road again and carried on, clearly ignoring Subject, who was catching up to him. What was she saying? Her mouth moved, so she was calling something.

I'm going to do it. Sort him while I have the chance.

Grim started the engine, his headlights illuminating the tarmac, lighting Blitz up. Car in gear, foot down on the pedal, Grim shot forward, speeding out of the residential street and swerving onto the road ahead. He ploughed into Blitz. Grim wasn't going fast enough to really hurt him, but the body landed on his bonnet all the same, Blitz staring at him through the windscreen, a mixture of anger and bewilderment on his face, then recognition. Grim reversed quickly, the body falling off and hitting the ground, Subject standing there with her phone out, finger poised over the screen.

Shit. She could fuck this up.

Grim gunned it forward and stopped short in front of Blitz. He got out, the picture of worry, and ran to kneel and check for a pulse.

Thank God he'd already put gloves on.

"Get the fuck off me, you lunatic." Blitz must have banged his head. Blood oozed from the side, his hair matted with it, and his cheek had bleeding grazes.

Grim didn't like his attitude. Emma had called him a lunatic when he'd gone up to Shark's caravan a week after he'd killed him and asked her to come home.

Subject rushed over and knelt, the phone in her hand forgotten, the bright screen displaying a keypad where she'd been about to phone for help.

"What the fuck happened?" she said, her voice slightly slurred.

"I don't know." Grim sounded distraught. "My foot slipped on the pedal."

"Why did you reverse with me on the fucking bonnet, then?" Blitz tried to get up and groaned. "Is this your way of getting back at me?"

Subject frowned. "What are you on about?"

Grim should have known Blitz wouldn't be receptive. "I put it in the wrong gear. It was meant to be in neutral. I'm so sorry. Let me take you to the hospital, get you seen to."

"That's the least you can fucking do, but I don't want to get in your motor if you can't even drive it properly."

"Come to mine," Subject said. "I'll ring for a doctor or something."

"Let me drop you home, pal." Grim needed to regain control, but with two of them here, it might prove difficult. Blitz had always been unstable, one wrong word away from erupting.

"Are you mental?" Blitz grimaced. "You were the one who wanted nowt to do with me, with us, yet you want to take me home? You don't even know where I live anymore or what's been happening in my life." He sucked in a breath. "Fuck, my left thigh is banging."

"Do you two know each other?" Subject asked.

"Something like that," Blitz said.

"Look, let's just take him up on his offer," she said. "He said his foot slipped. If he was a nutter, he'd have driven off, not offered us a lift."

"Fuck's sake, you have no idea what he's capable of. I do." Blitz gave Grim a filthy look.

"Can I borrow your phone?" Grim asked the woman. "I haven't got mine on me, I only nipped to the shop for a pint of milk."

"What d'you need it for?" Subject eyed him funny.

"To let my girlfriend know why I'll be late," Grim lied. "She'll worry."

Blitz trumpeted out a laugh. "So you've got a girlfriend now, have you? Finally got over Nymph?"

Subject sighed. "I don't know what you two are guffing on about, but I'm going to sit in the car."

Much to Grim's surprise, she handed her phone over then strutted off to get in the passenger seat.

Grim had to think on his feet. He put the phone down low and pressed the side to switch it off. "Stay there, you might have broken something. I *am* a doctor, or had you forgotten?"

"Not the kind of doctor I need," Blitz grumbled. "Last I heard you were a fucking plastic surgeon."

Grim smiled. "Whatever, pal, I still know what I'm doing. I'll check you over. Do you hurt anywhere?"

"The tops of my legs where you fucking ran into me."

"Shit, I really am sorry. Hang on, I'll go and get my bag."

Grim got up and ran to his boot, conscious how close they were to the surrounding houses, and that someone else could come down the alley at any minute. He slung Subject's phone inside and grabbed a heavy-ended tyre iron from his emergency car kit. It would have to do. Annoyed the headlights were still on and Subject might see, he returned to Blitz and crouched, glancing back to check what she was doing.

The light from a lamppost gave her a sepia effect. She had her eyes shut, her head against the seat.

Fate was playing him a blinding hand.

Should he abandon ship? Call the police himself and admit to colliding with Blitz? But it'd mean waiting to capture Subject again, and he wanted *this* Emma to suffer *now*. She had a lot of cigarette burns in her future, more than the others. Plus, he might not get another easy opportunity with Blitz if he phoned for help.

See it through.

While Subject was snoozing, Grim slapped a hand tight over Blitz's mouth to tone down any noise, then walloped him on the top of the head, the tyre iron creating a sickening crunch, the muffled scream hot against his palm, teeth scraping it. Grim shifted his thumb up to cover the nose as well. Blood trickled out of a small hole in the skull.

He once again checked on Subject.

Eyes still shut.

Blitz drummed his heels on the road, scrabbling at Grim's arm with his clawed hands, trying to get him off. The bloke was usually a force to be reckoned with, so the car hitting him, not the mention the iron, must have knocked a lot of wind out of his "I'm a gobby wanker" sails.

Grim checked their surroundings. No one else was around, and because of the position of the car and the houses with no windows on their sides for anyone to look out of, he was safe.

He pressed his body weight onto his hand, but Blitz wasn't giving up easily.

"For fuck's sake! Die, will you?" Grim whispered.

He smacked him twice more with the iron, widening the hole he'd already made, and the skull cracked further, blood rushing now. Incensed he'd lost the plot on this one and that Subject could have woken up and witnessed this part, Grim got up and spied on her again.

She must have fallen right asleep. Her mouth hung open.

Grim got on his knees to continue using the iron until there were no signs of life. Blitz was an inconvenience, a traitor, and he'd deserved to die for getting in the way, for lying, for keeping the secret.

"Serves yourself right, pal."

Grim got in the car, slung the iron in the rear footwell behind the passenger seat and yanked into reverse gear. The grinding noise woke Subject.

Shit, why didn't I drug her first?

Am I off my game?

It was seeing him *that did it. I didn't expect it.*

"Fucking hell, that scared me." She laughed a drunkard's laugh and peered into the back seat. "Where is he?"

"Decided to go home on his own." *Please don't look out the front and see him.*

"On his own? What a numpty. Have you got my phone?"

Grim kept eye contact with her and slowly flipped the centre console open. He took out the syringe.

"On his own? What a numpty. Have you got my phone?" She held her hand out for it.

He clunked the childproof locks so she couldn't escape.

"Oi, what the fuck's going on?" She struggled to unlock her seat belt, staring at him with anger in her eyes, not fear.

So, she was feisty. He'd have fun taming her.

Grim elbowed her in the face, once, twice. The sound of her nose bone breaking was nothing new. It had happened the last three times, too. She screamed, lashing out at him, her nails finding a home in his scalp for a second or two. It fucking hurt. Irate, he batted her hands away with one hand while stabbing her thigh with the needle in the other. He depressed the plunger, staring at her face, and her eyes grew wide.

"What the . . . ? You just . . . What . . . ? Fucking hell, fucking hell, let me out." She tugged at the door lever, panic overtaking her.

Grim smiled. In a few more seconds, she'd be out for the count.

She slumped towards the door, her forehead donking on the window, and he put the syringe away, clambered up on his knees, reached over the far side of her, and pulled the lever, lowering the back of her seat.

He quickly assessed the area. Free as a bird, he reversed around two hundred metres then gunned it, screaming in jubilation as he drove over Blitz, the car rising like it did on speed bumps.

One final act to ensure Blitz was really dead.

Grim had sailed too close to the wind for his liking. Things hadn't panned out as he'd expected, and there were so many reasons why he could get caught this time.

A way ahead where there were no lampposts, he looked in the rear-view mirror. Someone stood at the end of the alley. They were too far away to see his number plate and for Grim to know who it was. They glanced in his direction, probably clocking his rear red lights, then rushed into the road, their attention on the dead fuck who'd been a liar, a bad friend, one of Emma's allies.

I'll have to get rid of my car.

He turned at the end of the road and drove past the edge of the Coldwater estate to his right, where many houses stood in darkness, people tucked up in bed. The bright lights of

Tesco shone in the distance on the left. He took the lonely road parallel to it, the one with the high bushes and trees either side, and let out a relieved breath. Home wasn't far away, which meant the box Subject would spend the rest her life in wasn't far away either.

He smiled despite an uneasy feeling in his gut. He had another Emma, and that was what mattered. How would he dispose of his car without it being noticed, though? He lived out in the sticks, true, but a fire in his garden would still attract attention. Grim had his run-around too, the one he used for drives farther down the coast, his little red convertible he'd bought after Emma had left him, hoping she'd see his new wealth and want to come home. He could use that for future abductions. It wasn't ideal, too noticeable, too small, so maybe he ought to call it a day. Yes, Subject would be his last one, then he'd concentrate on Knitty and Thunder.

It would be easier than snatching people off the streets.

Or running them over.

He laughed at that and pulled into his driveway, parking around the back.

The voices in his head piped up, telling him he'd get caught this time, and as he placed her on the bed inside number one with the red front door, he almost believed them.

CHAPTER TWENTY-TWO

The Woodland

Bones videoed the man in the SUV knocking the other bloke over. He'd started the camera rolling as soon as the headlights splashed on, but he'd been anticipating a kidnap, not that! Freaked out, he shut the camera off, turned and scarpered farther into the woodland, away from the accident site, too afraid to remain. He'd been bored until he'd spotted the SUV parking up. He'd seen it there from about eight and had known in his gut the driver was back to steal another person. Why did he want to do that after all this time? And what about the woman who'd come out of the alley just before the collision? Bones hadn't filmed her, he'd seen her in his peripheral, and besides, she'd been too far away from him to make out who it was.

Bones stopped in the shelter of trees down by where there were no lampposts and hid behind a large trunk closest to the road. The SUV came past. Bones squinted to see, but only the surgeon was inside it as far as he could make out. He'd studied his profile on the photos for a long time so knew the shadowed face well. Had he decided it was better not to take the woman, if *she'd even been the one he was after? And what had he done with the man?*

Bones legged it back the way he'd come but kept himself hidden. Close enough to watch without using his phone camera on zoom, but far enough away that he wouldn't be noticed. Someone was in the road with the run-over fella, and they had a phone to their ear.

Bones wondered what he should do. How he'd get out of the woodland and down the alley without being spotted. He'd bet the police and an ambulance would be here soon.

Shit.

He retraced his path, jogging away from the scene towards the thicker trees. It would bring him out on the edge of the estate, but at least he could cross the main road in darkness. A detour, but one he had to take. He needed to go home, wait behind the garden fence until all the lights had gone off, then climb over.

His limbs felt weird. Heavy, too loose, like the accident had turned his muscles into mush. He thought about his reasons for keeping quiet, and they were stupid when he measured them against the crimes he'd filmed. But while he'd get an ear-bashing from one of the people he lived with for being out past curfew, it was the Bully he feared most. He'd get a kicking, and no one wanted one of those.

I wish I had the guts to come clean, but I don't.

Bones trudged on, his head dipped, his attention on his feet as he put them one in front of the other.

Maybe he should stop sneaking out.

Maybe he should climb over the fence as soon as he got home and hope no one had seen he'd snuck out earlier — and didn't see him coming back in.

And maybe he should delete everything off his phone, his laptop, and stop being such a weirdo creeper.

* * *

Bones made it home and walked down the back alley at the bottom of the gardens. He leaned against a fence and took a deep breath to steady his nerves. He'd witnessed so many bad things, was it any wonder he was quiet and stayed inside his own head? People commented on it, how he didn't interact much, how he was there in body but not in spirit. He had so many things going on in his life as well as the videos and photos that sometimes he wanted to curl up into a ball, go to sleep and never wake up.

Having bad memories of the Bully also rolled around in his brain from time to time. The slaps, the kicks, the woman screaming, Bones silent, because he'd been taught from an early age if he made a noise it'd make things worse. *She* hadn't quite got the memo on that, and she'd made a lot of racket every time the punches came. So much so that one night, the next-door neighbour had come round to see what all the fuss was about.

It was a lot for Bones to cope with.

He peeked through a knothole in his fence. The kitchen light was off to the left, but a cream glow seeping out around the curtains to the right meant someone was up in the living room. He wasn't surprised.

He checked the back bedrooms.

Darkness.

A quick scoot over the fence, and he was in the garden. With no security light flicking on, he walked slowly up the path, ducking under one of the rotary washing line arms. If he hadn't, he'd have hit it and the pegs would have rattled out that horrible sound he didn't like. It reminded him of clacking monster teeth.

He slid the key in the lock. Turned it. Pushed the door open and stepped into the kitchen. Held his breath.

Voices filtered in from the living room.

"Do you want to go to bed?"

"No, I'm fine."

"Come and sit down. I'll make you a hot chocolate if you like."

Bones's heart thundered. *Fuck, they might come in here.*

He got upstairs without anyone spotting him and sat on his bed to watch tonight's footage again. He loaded it from his phone to his laptop so he could see things better. Earlier, viewing it as he'd recorded it, he hadn't taken that much in apart from the car hitting that bloke.

He popped his earbuds in and pressed play.

Bones enlarged the screen and concentrated to make out who'd been run over, and his heart thumped harder, his stomach doing a mad flip.

He recognised him.

He clicked stop and wondered what impact this would have. How it would affect people. The frame had paused on the body in the road. Was he dead? Had the surgeon stuffed him in the boot of the SUV when Bones had run away?

To calm himself, he clicked out of that file and into another. It was the woodland again, but this time, Karen and Geordie were at it against a tree, and Bones got excited. He didn't mean to, and he wished his body wouldn't respond.

Maybe he ought to stop lying to himself.

He loved the videos like this one.

CHAPTER TWENTY-THREE

Rosebush Cottage

The ringing work phone pulled Carol away from the film she and Dave were watching. The jarring sound prodded at her irritation gene. While she was well aware that when on a murder case they could be called in at any time, she'd been enjoying the evening, apart from the shitshow of an ex turning up.

"Ay up, duty calls," Dave said from the recliner by the window. "I just put my bloody pyjamas on an' all."

"We might not have to go in." Carol grabbed her phone from beside her on the sofa and looked at the screen. Alton Sinclair's name stared boldly back at her. The night-time station sergeant.

Carol swiped. "Hello, pal."

"Sorry to bother you . . ."

Bless him. "You wouldn't have done it if it wasn't important. What's up?"

"About an hour ago, a call came in for assistance needed on the Coldwater estate. The main road by the woodland. Ambulance required. Lloyd and Kenner took it and have reported back in. A hit-and-run, no witnesses as of yet. The bloke was deceased upon their arrival. A wallet in his pocket had identification." He told her who the victim was.

"Oh fuck." Carol now understood why she'd been phoned. "You saw a search had been done on him by my team, yes?"

"Yeah, so I thought you'd need to know."

"I do, although I don't know how he fits into this yet."

"Officers are at the Little Devil in case he'd come from there — no word from them yet. He *could* have been drunk and stepped out into the road, but the thing is, the head injuries don't match being run over. It's as if he's been bashed with a weapon. The EMTs let Lloyd know it looks suspect, so Rib's been called in."

"That changes things dramatically. Okay, thanks for letting me know. We'll pop down there now."

"Like I said, uniforms are dealing with questioning people still at the pub. The usual is being done to find the vehicle involved, and some officers have been called back in to do door-to-door enquiries close by where it happened. Oliver's the scene sergeant tonight."

"Brilliant, that saves me the job of sorting it all out. We'll go straight to the woodland."

"Sorry again, Carol."

"Not a problem." She ended the call and stared over at Dave. "Unless you want to go to work in your jim-jams, you'd best get dressed. Tom Cubbins is dead."

* * *

The Woodland

Protective gear on over her clothes in this sort of muggy weather was uncomfortable. Carol's clammy skin had her wanting a lukewarm shower.

Cordons had been set up across streets coming off the scene, plus at each end of the main road along the top of the estate. The offender could have gone down any one of them as an escape route. One direction led to the big Tesco, and the other to town. She'd bet they'd gone the Tesco route. Less chance of being spotted — town meant going by Buns 'n' Bread, and they might not have wanted to risk coppers still hanging around down there, and haring through the estate would have brought noses pressed to windows.

On the way over, Dave had mentioned the geographical profile map Carol had done earlier. She'd checked her emails on her phone, and no officers had reported anything suspicious during their house-to-house, but as with the Smith case, the offenders had been spoken to by officers and had appeared nice and friendly, no one to set off blips on the radar, yet they'd been monsters.

What if that had happened this time, too?

She'd nip to the station in a bit and look at the pages of residents Michael would have compiled earlier. As usual, he'd have attached them to the whiteboard. She could check the officers' reports against the residents' names and see what was what.

For now, she had to concentrate on what was before her.

SOCO milled about doing their thing. A tent had been erected, and Carol had parked behind Rib's vehicle at the town end of the cordon, then walked up to the scene, Dave musing he'd been dozing off watching a film and now, here they were, and wasn't life weird how it flipped on you in an instant.

She approached Oliver Havers. "Hi, Ollie."

"All right, Carol?" He gestured around them. "Not something I expected after going back to the station from Kipling Close."

"Oh, did you get owt there?"

He took his notebook out and found the correct page. "Nora Patten next door to Craig had something interesting to say — I sent you notes not long before I got called out to this. She was told they'd buried a dog in the garden — Karen said that to her a couple of weeks after the burial, although Nora couldn't recall exactly when that was. She was pretty distraught to work out it was a baby."

"I bet. So she didn't hear owt around that time?"

"She said there was always some noise or other from next door, although you'd think if someone had fallen down the stairs, that would have made a din. She reckoned she was probably at work when it happened."

"Okay. Any other neighbours come up with owt?"

"No." He slid his book away.

"What about the baby. Is he . . . ?"

"He's been removed. Rib has him, so he's in safe hands now."

"God. It's been on my mind all evening."

"Horrible business. And as for this . . ." Oliver wafted a hand again and explained what his officers were doing, then continued with, "News back from the Devil is Tom had been in there and must have been knocked over fairly soon after he'd left. Evan Ike found him and called it in."

"Hmm, his name crops up again. Was Geordie in the pub, too? Did he not walk home with his brother, then?"

"Lee stayed for a lock-in."

Carol had known Reg would continue to hold them so wasn't surprised. "What's the general consensus? That Tom was knocked over then struck with a weapon, or struck *then* run over?"

"I don't know. I haven't had a chance to speak to Rib yet."

"Have you had owt back from people in these houses?" She indicated the ones closest to them.

"Most of them were in bed, but those who weren't said they didn't hear owt. That surprised me, because you'd think they would. Surely the deceased screamed after being hit — either by the car or the weapon."

"With no CCTV, we'll probably never know exactly how it went down. Okay, we'll go and speak to Rib."

At the tent, she switched her booties out for clean ones, depositing the old into the designated bag, put her mask up, then stepped inside. Ben Asher, Todd's second-in-command, stood with Rib beside the body, which lay with his head to her left, his feet to her right. Carol avoided giving Tom a closer inspection.

Dave came in and stood next to her.

"Nice to see you, Bird," Rib said. "Did you get pulled out of the Lord?"

She smiled, hoping her eyes crinkled enough to see. "We were at home actually, so bog off. What have you got for me?"

"Someone who's had a battering. Blunt force trauma, maybe a metal bar. He's also been run over — and I mean that literally."

Carol still didn't inspect Tom. A broken skull was bad enough, but whatever the weight of a car rolling over a body had done wasn't something she wanted to see. "So, do you reckon he was attacked first?"

"I think he was knocked down, *then* the driver attacked — there's a scrape on the cheek where he likely hit the ground from the impact of the vehicle, plus a mark on the side of the head that indicates *he* struck the tarmac, not that something struck him. But the other wounds . . . He was alive when he was hit with the weapon. Lots of blood."

Ben folded his arms. "I hear he's something to do with your current case."

Carol nodded. "He is, but he was a peripheral character, as in, he was questioned when Karen Stokes went missing because he'd been in the pub that night, then had spoken to Craig, her husband, once he'd got to Kipling Close. Tom was basically an alibi for Lee 'Geordie' Ike and his brother, Evan, and vice versa. This could either be a coincidence or his killer is also Karen's."

Dave stared at the body. "A coincidence is all well and good, but this stinks of someone knowing Tom would come this way, surely."

Carol agreed. "So did Tom have more to do with Karen than he let on? He might not be the actual kidnapper, but does that mean he'd also known about Lesley and Teresa and where they'd been taken? Or, conversely, was *Tom* their abductor and whoever killed him had found out? Think of Ortun in the Mason Ingram case. He murdered someone because he thought they'd killed his sister. Is this a similar situation? Do we have a vigilante? We can't blame Craig Stokes for going off on one about Karen's kidnap and death because he's in the nick."

Ben scratched his forehead with the back of his gloved hand. "That hurt my brain."

Carol laughed. "It's hurting mine. If Tom hadn't come up in the missing women case, it would be a damn sight easier, but he's involved, however lightly, so we have to take that into account. Has his NOK been informed? His wife died of cancer, and he moved into his mother's with his daughter."

"I was waiting for you to get here before anyone was sent to inform his mam," Ben said.

"Okay, then that's our next stop, although with Hayley being eighteen, she'd be the NOK. I'm inclined to tell his mam first, to be honest, and let her tell the daughter."

Carol didn't relish it. Sherry Cubbins had seemed to have two sides to her when Carol had spoken to her before: arsey and gossipy.

She knew which one she'd encounter when they knocked on her door. It had been clear she didn't like being woken up.

* * *

Kipling Close

The excavation team's van stood outside Craig's. Carol supposed they were still working under the tent, sifting through the soil, bagging it, doing whatever they did when a body was unearthed. She resisted going over there to ask about the baby. What she wanted to hear was that he *had* been in a blanket and not stuffed directly into the black bag. What she wanted was for his death to have never occurred.

At Sherry's door, she took a deep breath and knocked. From what Sherry had said about being woken up by Tom and Geordie singing, Carol and Dave weren't going to get a nice reception, and it would get worse once the woman found out why they'd come calling.

A bedroom window flashed open, and Sherry stuck her head out.

"Did you forget your key again, Tom?" she whisper-shouted.

Carol stepped back from beneath the porch roof. "It's us, Sherry."

"What the bloody hell do *you* want?"

"We need to come in, I'm afraid."

"Sodding hell. Hang on."

The window thumped shut, and idly, Carol mused that earlier, Sherry had mentioned not wanting to bother her neighbours with noise, yet she wasn't fussed about it tonight.

The hallway light flicked on, then came the faint thud of footsteps on the stairs. A chain scraped across, and Sherry opened the door in pink fleece pyjamas.

Fleece, in this weather?

Maybe the older woman had dodgy circulation.

"Get in, then." Sherry stalked off to the kitchen.

Carol glanced at Dave, made an *eek* face, then entered the house, following Sherry, who stood with her back to the sink, a cigarette in one hand and a lighter in the other. She lit up and peered around Carol at Dave.

"If this is about that Karen business again, I don't know owt, and if it's about whatever's buried in the garden over the road, I don't know owt about that either. I said so to the copper who came earlier."

"Is Hayley home?" Carol asked.

"No, she's down at Lindsey's, as usual."

"Have you been in all night?" Carol hated asking that when she didn't think Sherry had killed her son, but she needed it on record.

"Yes."

"Okay. I think it's best if we take a seat."

Sherry appeared alarmed. "Why, what's happened?"

"Let's just sit for a minute, okay?" Carol went to a chair and took a load off.

Dave guided Sherry by the elbow. They sat, and Carol steadied herself to give the bad news.

"I'm telling you first and not Hayley because I think you'd be the best one to inform her. It's Tom. There's been an incident."

"What?"

"He was run over on his way back from the pub."

Sherry choked on the smoke she'd inhaled, spluttering and coughing. Once she got control of herself, she whispered, "*My* Tom?"

"Sadly, there's more."

Tears rolled down Sherry's cheeks, and she swiped at them, the glowing end of her cigarette too close to her hair. "What is it?"

"He died, love. I'm afraid it's murder, as he has injuries to that effect."

"Injuries? What do you mean?" Sherry shook her head in disbelief.

Carol imagined this must be a surreal moment, where Sherry couldn't work out if it was happening or if she was dreaming.

Dave held her hand. "Someone struck him with a weapon."

Sherry let out a groan, a long cow *moo* that seemed to come from her soul, and it just about did Carol in. Grief so raw like this was heartbreaking to witness, and she swallowed the lump in her throat. Sherry sobbed so hard she dropped her fag on the table. Dave stood and bent over, hugging Sherry, and Carol rescued the cigarette, stubbing it out in the ashtray.

It was going to be a long night. Hayley should be here to sit with her nan, the young woman would be gutted about her father, but if she wasn't back yet, that meant Lindsey was still at the pub for the lock-in.

Carol held her mobile up to Dave to indicate she'd be making a call and left the room. She found the lounge and shut the door, phoning Whitney.

"Hi, Carol."

"Hi. Are you okay with watching all the kids without Hayley there until Lindsey gets home?"

"Yep. Has something happened?"

Carol explained, then finished with, "I don't want to leave Tom's mam by herself."

"Okay. They're all asleep anyroad."

"How have the Stokes girls been?"

"Moody. Nowt I didn't expect. They've got a lot to cope with. Lindsey didn't mention staying out later than eleven, so I'll give her a ring now."

"Thanks. Send Hayley along. I'll go out the front and wait so she's not out there alone." Who knew if the killer was lurking.

Carol put her phone away and went outside, waiting at the bottom of the garden path. Hayley left Lindsey's, walking towards Carol with a carefree air about her, one that would be smashed to pieces when Carol told the poor thing her father was never coming home again.

Some aspects of Carol's job really were shit.

CHAPTER TWENTY-FOUR

The Incident Room

An hour later, having left Sherry and Hayley consoling each other, their refusal of having a FLO in attendance vehemently voiced, Carol and Dave sat at his desk side by side and went through the printed list of residents near the geographical triangle. It took a while. Carol was about to give up and leave the rest for the morning — until a name caught her eye.

She pointed at it and shuddered. "I didn't even think of involving him. Mind you, I wouldn't have spoken to him if I could help it, but you could have, you know, when you had a chat with a surgeon from the hospital. Then again, he doesn't work there now, does he? He's got his own clinic. Maybe that's why he didn't enter my head."

Dave snorted. "I would have avoided him anyroad, he'd be the last one I'd consult. You know my feelings about him."

Dave disliked Carol's ex as much as she did, and it annoyed her that Mr Storage Box himself had appeared in their investigation, albeit only as someone who still needed to be eliminated from their enquiries. The ex-lover was a pest who couldn't take "get lost" for an answer, but a killer? She didn't think so. She'd been to his cottage on numerous occasions, and while she hadn't poked around — she'd just gone straight up to the bedroom bar one time she'd seen his kitchen — the place didn't strike her as somewhere women would be held hostage. For a start, she couldn't imagine he'd want anyone else in his home, messing it up.

"It says here he was out when the officer called at his cottage, and Nora Patten was there, cleaning," she said.

"So? She told us she does the clients farther out of town." Dave laughed. "There's him, bleating on at you about how to keep a clean home, when he's got someone else doing it for him. What a hypocrite."

"Hmm. Do we need to worry about him? I mean, he *is* odd."

"But we didn't think so when you first started seeing him. Okay, to be brutally honest, I didn't have him down as your type, but as it was just for sex, I didn't say owt. We could have had our view tainted because he went iffy after you told him you didn't want a serious relationship, pestering you and coming off as a creep."

"That's true." But she was curious about who she'd been to bed with now. "I didn't look him up in the database when I got together with him because we're not supposed to, but . . ."

"You can now, you have a legitimate reason because his name's cropped up in our investigation," Dave said. "Want me to do it?"

Carol nodded.

Dave accessed the database and put in a search. "Oh, bugger me, he's on file."

Carol's stomach muscles clenched, and she stared at the wall ahead, not the screen, worried she'd been dating a secret lawbreaker — but surely you had to have a clean record for his line of work, didn't you? "What's he down for?"

"An altercation with his ex-wife and friends at the Castle pub."

"What was it about?"

"It was a wake of sorts, that's what the report says, for another friend of theirs who'd been murdered. The body was still with us, so no funeral at that point. Those two detectives from one of the other divisions came and dealt with it, remember?"

"I vaguely recall that. What happened at the Castle?"

"Your ex got lairy and had a go at them all."

"Why?"

"For keeping a secret from him to do with his wife and another member of the group. An affair. It got out of hand when he threw a punch, and the landlord phoned the police. There's a note here that says they all have nicknames, and they kept referring to each other as those instead of their normal ones when interviewed."

"Weird. Mind you, it's no different to 'Geordie'. Who are the friends? Do we know them?"

"There's your 'See You Next Tuesday', Noel Bartlett, aka Grim Reaper." Dave cracked up. "What the fuck? Did you know he was called that?"

"No! He's the least Grim Reaperish person I've ever come across. He's such a wet blanket."

"I don't disagree. His ex-wife is Emma Bartlett, that's what she was called at the time, anyroad. Her nickname is Nymph. Ever seen her about?"

"Not that I'm aware of. He told me she'd left him for a friend of theirs but didn't go into specifics. As you know, I didn't want to go down the 'sharing our pasts' route because that wasn't the sort of relationship I was after. Who's next?"

"Shark, deceased, Joseph Viticci. Knitty — as we know, that's Nora Patten. Another fella, Thunder. Oh fuck. Look at who that is."

Carol read the screen. "Bloody hell! I don't know what to think."

"Me neither."

"Who's the other one?"

"Blitz, Tom Cubbins."

Carol tried to make sense of it all. Four of these names had come up in this case already, but did that mean any of them were involved with Karen's death and the missing women? Just because they were friends, it didn't make them criminals. She laughed at her mind going in that direction. Ridiculous.

Wasn't it?

"The murder," she said. "The Shark bloke. What's it say about that?"

Dave accessed the file and started reading. "Give me a few."

Carol got up to make them a cup of tea, thinking about Noel and whether she'd missed something about him. Whether he had any traits she should have spotted. But she'd only wanted him for sex, she'd left his bed as soon as it had been over, and she hadn't spent any quality time with him in order to get to know him. Their conversations had revolved around keeping his home spotless and expressing his love for those bloody storage boxes.

Regardless of whether she actually suspected him for any of this, he would have to be looked into. She thought back to earlier in the Lord. He'd ordered a meal and had left shortly after. Carol and Dave had stayed on for another hour then headed home.

She finished the teas and took the cups over to Dave.

"Cheers." He popped his on a coaster.

Carol sat. "Come on, then, what's it say?"

"Okay, Joseph had gone to play tennis after work with Noel/Grim — I'm still chuckling about that. The match was the night after Emma had left Noel. She'd confessed she was having it away with Joseph, which makes me wonder why Noel would even want to meet a friend who'd been shagging his wife."

"I can imagine wanting to have a go at him, but playing tennis, no."

"I thought the same. After the match, according to Noel, Joseph had said he was going for a pint at the Devil. He parked in the Backstreet. Someone waylaid him there, attacked him from behind with a crowbar, which was left in his boot along with his body. His head was a mess. No fingerprints anywhere."

"Blunt force trauma to the skull, same as with Tom Cubbins. Coincidence?"

"Many people have used the same weapon and method, so I'm on the fence about that one."

"Where does it say Noel went after tennis?" Carol asked.

"Tesco then home. He was in the supermarket around the time of the murder, CCTV there proved that, but with no witnesses in the Backstreet, no cameras around the area, and no exact time of death as Shark wasn't found until the next afternoon . . . It says here Noel was ruled out."

"Joseph was found a day later? That sounds strange when you think of Mr Traffic Warden and how he prowls that street during the day."

"Oh, he spotted the car, but like I said, Joseph was in the boot. The warden issued a ticket in the morning, and when the car was still there in the afternoon, he called it in to be towed. As we know, the Backstreet needs to be kept clear. Easy access for the lifeboat crew. They're the only ones allowed to park there while they're on a shout. Everyone else does it expecting to get a ticket, and there are a few of them, because I've seen many a vehicle down there. Granted, they're usually holidaymakers, but still."

"Hang on. If Emma had left Noel for Joseph, didn't she wonder where Joseph was all that time? I assume they shacked up together."

"Two secs." Dave clicked through the file. "Emma gave her address as one of the caravans on the cliff. She'd moved in with Joseph."

"So why didn't she report him missing?"

Dave clicked again. "She did, just as the car had been taken to the police compound."

"But that was hours after he would have been due home."

"Maybe she knew nowt would be done for twenty-four hours so waited until closer to that time."

"The boot was checked, then?"

"Yes, opened by an officer, and Joseph was discovered."

"So the last person to see him alive was Noel?"

"Appears so."

Carol blew out a long breath. "Can *you* see Noel killing anyone?"

"Not really. He's a drip."

"But then he knows all about weight-loss surgery. If you were a surgeon, wouldn't *you* botch things to throw people off?" She couldn't believe she'd actually said that. "Noel is an oddball, but not like *that*."

"No, he doesn't seem the type, but we've said that before . . . We're going to have to speak to Noel, anyroad. *Both* of us."

Carol nodded. "I'll put my differences with him aside. Do we go now or wait until the morning? Go and visit him at his clinic?"

"The morning. It's almost two, and we could do with getting some sleep."

Carol agreed, her mind whizzing.

Something was off, they just had to work out what it was. Especially because Thunder was Geordie bloody Ike.

CHAPTER TWENTY-FIVE

Truth-Hunt Cottage

She woke, groggy, just like she'd been when she'd come round from having her appendix out. Her whole body was heavy, as if it had sunk into the mattress, glued there by some form of paralysis, but she lifted her arm, so she was able to move well enough. Her dry mouth screamed out for a drink, so she glanced to her left. A bedside cabinet like the ones in hospital held a Styrofoam cup and a bendy-stemmed white lamp. A shower area, a weird toilet, a transparent screen, a wooden chair on the other side of it . . . *Was* this a hospital? Had she had an accident? The screen had what she assumed was a hatch, so would she get fed through there? Was this some modern way of keeping doctors and nurses safe from infection? So many shops had Perspex up, so it could be that.

No, this doesn't feel right.

She glanced down at herself to check for one of those gowns they put you in when you had an operation.

She was naked.

Embarrassment filtered through her. Someone must have taken her clothes off! They'd have seen her bits, could have done anything to her and she wouldn't know.

Why am I here, why am I here, why am I—

It came back to her. Going down the alley after Tom, calling to him, her wanting to have a sex in the woods then someone to walk home with. The accident, that bloke who'd knocked Tom over. The memories skipped to the horror of when she'd realised something was off. Him elbowing her in the face. The stab on her thigh. Losing consciousness.

Fuck. Had he *abducted* her?

She winced, and pain erupted in her cheeks. He must have broken her nose. Her top lip felt swollen too, and now she came to think of it, the taste of blood sat heavy and stale on her tongue.

Slowly, and with much effort, she sat up, her head weighing a ton, the strange little room spinning. She closed her eyes to centre herself, and soon, the whirling sensation stopped. Eyes cracked open again, she stared through the screen at a door. It had a letterbox but no glass panels.

That wasn't right either.

She jolted as it opened, and a scream built in her chest and lodged there as if too afraid to emerge from her mouth. Someone tall stood there in a blonde wig and mask, a red dress, heeled shoes, and whoever it was had massive boobs. It was so surreal and terrifying, she couldn't make a sound.

"Ah, you're awake."

It was that man's voice, the one who'd taken her. Why was he dressed like that?

Fuck, fuck, please, don't hurt me.

He propped the door open and stepped inside, sitting on the wooden chair. She stared ahead at a mural of a street. What? She opened her mouth to shout at him, to demand why she was there, but nothing came out. Every part of her tensed, and it *hurt.*

"Welcome to the Guilt-Ridden Estate."

She didn't know what the *fuck* he was on about.

"There are rules." He crossed his hairy legs. One of the shoes came loose and dangled from his toes. "I am Dolly tonight, but sometimes you'll meet Queen and Carol. I'll care for you as much as you deserve."

She blinked. Carol?

Does he mean that copper?

"Are you struck dumb?" he asked.

She tried to make a noise, anything would do, but she couldn't.

"Hmm. Scared into silence, are we? Then maybe you should have thought about your actions. You wouldn't be here if you had."

What actions? What had she done?

"There's a fan above your bed. You must *not* look or talk through it." His eyes behind the mask widened. "If I catch you doing it, I'll switch it off so you'll bake in your box. Women should be placed in boxes, they belong there so they do as they're told, so they don't hurt you. A box with a pretty bow on it is everything."

She shook her head, fear rippling through her. He was a nutter, and she was in here with him, stuck.

"You'll be fed if I feel like it, although you can drink the shower water if I haven't brought you owt for a while. Sometimes I do forget, I'm a very busy man, but I won't apologise for it. I need to earn more money so Emma comes back."

Emma? Is that Geordie's friend?

"Or maybe it will win Carol over. You *will* tell me the truth when I ask you questions — and believe me, I'll know if you're lying. You *will* be sorry."

Sorry, for what? And what if he forgets me for so long I die?

"I'm on the hunt for the truth," he said. "You're in Truth-Hunt Cottage, and this is where I'll clean you."

She shivered. What did he mean, clean her? Was he going to wash her or something? The idea of him touching her brought on a retch.

"Stop doing that, you silly cow."

She swallowed; she'd wet herself if she wasn't careful, but his voice had been so loud and mean. There was the toilet, but she wouldn't go in front of him. She had *some* dignity.

"That's better," he said, gentler now. "You'll apologise for what you've done — and mean it. You'll learn how your actions have affected others because I'll tell you what it feels like to be cheated on, to be left, to have to rebuild your life."

"I'm not having an affair," she managed, her words elongated.

What did he inject me with?

She shook, terror settling in properly, the knowledge that she'd been kidnapped, that she might not get food, might not ever be released from here. Was this who'd taken Karen, Lesley and Teresa? Would he kill her?

"But you have in the past." His mask lifted at the cheeks.

Was he *smiling* under it, smug that he'd caught her out? And what had he been doing, spying on her? The thought of being watched without knowing it creeped her out. She hadn't seen anyone lurking.

"What?" She sounded so odd, her tongue too thick.

"Thunder!" he shouted.

Frightened by his outburst and confused as to why he'd say that, she stuffed a knuckle in her mouth and bit it. Her bladder distended.

No, please, no . . .

"You played with Thunder behind your husband's back."

"I-I don't know w-what you're on a-about."

"Geordie."

She blinked. "Loads of people have been with Geordie, but I bloody well haven't. I was with his brother, Evan."

He blinked, appearing confused. "Are you lying to me?"

"No! I swear, I was with Evan, so why pick me?"

A glaze came over his eyes. "Because you were married, Lindsey. You cheated. You've got some punishments to take, more than the others, because I took a woman who shouldn't even be here, and that's because of you. You can have all of the pain she's already been through plus your own."

Others? Oh God, he is *the one . . .*

He tilted his head, and the curls on the wig swayed. "Someone was gossiping, saying Lesley was seeing him, but they got it wrong, they meant *Lindsey*. It was *you* all along. She told me, but I wouldn't listen. I *must* learn to listen in future. To believe." He frowned. "*Did* I mishear the name?"

She didn't think he'd meant to say that out loud.

He stood, took a key out of a pocket in his dress and unlocked a door in the screen — she hadn't noticed it before. Lindsey backed up on the bed, into the corner, feeling so cumbersome, and watched him. He stepped inside and locked the door again, his gaze on her, not what he was doing. If he came close, she'd kick out, hit him where it hurt and get that key. Run away. Where was Truth-Hunt Cottage? Were there any neighbours who'd help her?

He slid the key in his pocket.

Lindsey's body tensed, her muscles pinching, spasming, her chest tight with utter terror. "Keep away from me."

"You don't get to call the shots anymore, cheater. You'll do as I say — you'll learn it's pointless to fight me."

He lunged towards her, kneeling on the bed and gripping her wrists. He took a pair of cuffs from his pocket and clipped them in place, then produced another pair and snapped them on her ankles. Lindsey wanted to fight, but her limbs were still so heavy, and shock had pinned her in place.

He got off the bed and stood, yanking her down the mattress so she lay on her back. He stepped away, pulling a packet of cigarettes and a small box from the other pocket. And smiled.

"Time to light a match."

When the glowing end of the cigarette met with her face, she finally released that trapped scream.

* * *

She had wailed. A lot. Grim had loved the sound — it was Emma, begging him not to do it anymore — but he'd been conscious of the minutes ticking by and what he had to do next. Lesley. It was time for her to meet her end, and while stuffing her in the boot of his sports car wasn't a problem — she was so skinny now — he couldn't afford for the vehicle to be seen when so many coppers would be floating around the woodland and town. He'd have to leave her somewhere else.

He uncuffed Lindsey and left her bawling, going upstairs to change into his forensic suit, then walked back to Guilt-Ridden and entered number two. Lesley shot up from the bed, her eyes red where she'd perhaps been crying. She'd likely been listening to Lindsey's screeching through the fan and knew what had been happening.

"It's time to leave," he said and unlocked the Perspex door.

"Home?"

"Some call it that, yes."

She frowned but let him guide her by the elbow into his operating theatre by the kitchen. She balked, pressing her toes to the floor, and he snatched her wrist, squeezing it tight.

"No annoying me." He pulled her over to the bed. "I apologise for not listening to you, for not believing you, but I can't let you go."

Fear stained her irises. "Please, no . . ."

He gripped her around the throat with his free hand and propelled her backwards to the bed. Her eyes bugged, and she used her spare hand to slap at his face as she fought for breath. She kicked out, her foot going between his legs, the strike just glancing his balls, and his patience snapped. This was nasty Emma, the one at the caravan who'd threatened him. He squeezed harder, wanting to obliterate her, to stop her looking at him as if he were a devil. She gurgled, and he had to turn away — this wasn't Emma, this was an innocent woman.

"Shit," he said through gritted teeth, the two sides of him warring with each other. "I'm sorry. I'm really sorry."

Her last utterance was a garbled growl.

Then nothing.

* * *

Lindsey's skin felt burnt all over. Every bit of her seemed on fire, and she sat on the cold floor facing the Perspex screen, only able to stand something touching one part of her. If she got on the bed, that would mean her back, thighs and shoulders would come into contact with the mattress, and it was too much.

A thud had sounded not long ago, behind her in the distance, but she didn't have any energy to care what it was. He'd been brutal, using cigarette after cigarette, and at one point had stabbed a burning match into her ear and one on the bow of her lips.

Tears fell, their salty heat crawling into the burns on her cheeks, and she winced, unable to stop crying. He'd even scalded her palms, so she couldn't place them on the floor and brace her weight on them.

"Can you hear me?"

It was faint, that voice, and stuttered, but yes, she'd heard it.

"Hello?" Lindsey shouted, her word coming out hoarse.

"The fan. Talk there."

Lindsey frowned, remembering what he'd said. Should she ignore him and speak to the woman? She got up — shit, the soles of her feet hurt — and climbed on the bed, clenching her teeth through the pain. Every movement stretched the burns and increased the heat. The smell of her make-up sizzling was still in her nose, the foundation she'd applied for her night out. She stared through the whirring fan blades. A living room! So she was in a house. Oh God.

"Hello?" she said.

"Have you been burned?"

"Yes."

"Under the bed will be some salve. I didn't know that until Lesley told me. He finds it funny to play tricks."

"Lesley Johnson?"

"Yes. I'm Teresa. Teresa Fett."

Oh my God. She didn't sound the same. They knew each other from the pub.

"Lesley!" Teresa called.

No reply.

"Shit. Lesley!" Teresa shouted.

Lindsey swallowed. Maybe she'd been drugged.

"I think he's taken her away," Teresa said. "Fuck!" She screamed the last word.

More tears pricked Lindsey's eyes. If he *had* taken Lesley, it meant she'd end up like Karen, didn't it?

The room spun, and Lindsey pressed her forehead to the cool wall beside the fan unit, closing her eyes.

Her kids. They'd find her gone come the morning. Would Whitney know something was off and get the police out looking? What if Lindsey never made it back? What if her bastard ex had to take the boys? He'd have full control again. She couldn't let that happen.

But who's going to stop him?

She cried along with Teresa, whose fan-garbled sobs came filtering in along with thumping sounds, her maybe punching the wall. Lindsey's wounds flared, so hot, so prickly, and she dreaded what else he had in store for her.

This had to be a nightmare. She'd gone home, fallen asleep, and would wake up in the morning finding she'd just had a dream.

But no, it was all too real.

She hiccupped a sob.

What had he done with Tom?

CHAPTER TWENTY-SIX

The New Me Clinic

The morning was a bright, hot one, the sky a lovely clear blue, not even a breeze stirring Carol's hair. At eight o'clock, she and Dave sat in the car outside the New Me Clinic, and nerves bit into her at the thought of seeing Noel. Her interactions with him had been reduced to his annoying interruptions at the Lord, so to have to deal with him without snark, to follow the rules and be polite, would be a test for her.

"You can take the lead," she told Dave. "I'll do the notes."

"I was going to suggest the same, save you being uncomfortable, plus the records will show you took a step back because of your association with him."

"I wouldn't say me using him for sex would cause an issue at work. He's no one to me, wasn't even important when I *was* seeing him."

A silver car pulled in and parked beside the other six already there. A woman got out, clicked her key fob and entered the clinic carrying a leopard-print overnight bag.

"Someone coming for an op?" Dave said.

"Looks like it. We'll get in there now, then."

They'd already seen the staff arriving from seven onwards, and Noel's red sports car had been there when Carol had parked behind it, blocking it in. There was always the risk that if he *was* the bloke they were after, he'd make a run for it. She still wasn't convinced he had it in him to kidnap and kill, but best to cover all bases.

She led the way and walked inside the clinic into a waiting area that was more like a living room. Sofas, chairs, coffee tables, soft music playing. The only thing crushing that illusion was the curved reception desk directly in front of the glass front doors. The lady from the car park stood there signing a form, and a woman behind the desk, dolled up to the nines, black hair long and lush, had similar make-up to Lindsey. Her eyebrows were from the same lagoon.

"Can I help you?"

Carol spotted her nametag. Isla.

ID held up, Carol introduced them. "Can we have a word with Noel Bartlett, please?"

"Um, he'll be prepping for surgery."

Prickly that Noel was calling the shots without even knowing it, Carol said tightly, "It's urgent, so surgery will have to wait."

The lady with the form placed the pen down and narrowed her eyes. "I have a schedule."

"So do we." Carol smiled and looked at Isla. "The more we argue the toss, the longer he'll be delayed."

Isla used her desk phone and explained a policewoman called Carol was here. Carol's anxiety spiked at having to see her ex any minute. She couldn't stand him anymore, but he seemed oblivious to her snideness, no matter how thick she laid it on, although he always took offence at Dave shooing him away.

Noel breezed through a door at the back, beaming a smile and heading for her, as if he had tunnel vision. Carol's revulsion joined the anxiety, and she couldn't believe she'd ever found him attractive. He might still be good-looking, but his behaviour since she'd ended things was downright ugly. His many voicemails and messages had riled her up, begging her to give him another chance as though she'd been the love of his life and not just someone to go to bed with.

Dave straightened to his full height beside her.

Noel stopped short upon seeing him, as if he'd thought Carol was here on her own. What, had he imagined she'd come to her senses and wanted to start seeing him again?

Fuck me . . .

"Carol! What a lovely surprise. Come on through." He kept his smile in place, swivelled and returned to the door, holding it open.

Carol went first — she didn't want Noel touching her or doing anything inappropriate behind Dave's back. She squeezed past Noel and entered a corridor. On the left, a row of windows with open Venetian blinds, and behind them, staff in scrubs doing various things in the large operating theatre. On the right, a row of doors which she assumed were private rooms for the patients. She walked along and waited outside the one at the end that had Noel's name on a plaque. She turned and kept her sights on Dave as the two men approached.

"Let's go inside and chat." Noel opened his office door and strode in, no holding the door for them this time. He sat behind a glass desk, the only thing on it a laptop and a silver phone in a dock.

As she'd expected, the room had no soul, just the desk, a chair behind, two in front. He didn't even display his diplomas or medical certificates.

She chose not to sit, and neither did Dave.

"How can I help you, Carol?" Noel smiled at her, completely blanking Dave.

What an arsehole. She took her notebook and pen out.

His face fell. "Oh, is this an official visit?"

She didn't answer.

Dave broadened his shoulders. "Where were you last night between ten o'clock and midnight?"

Noel smiled at Carol. "At home. Why on earth would you need to know that?"

"What about the night before, between midnight and five?"

"Again, at home. In bed." He sent Carol a creepy leer.

She held back a shudder.

"Can anyone corroborate that?" Dave asked.

"As you know, Carol, I live alone, so no."

She couldn't stand his smug look and how he was ignoring Dave, so she bent her head to write in her notebook: *What a prick.* She showed it to Dave as though passing on work information then stared at the closed laptop.

Dave coughed. "What were you doing on the night Joseph Viticci was murdered?"

Noel's eyebrows quivered, but other than that, he didn't appear bothered about the change of direction. "I'm sure if you checked your files, you'd see I was in Tesco."

"How long have you known Tom Cubbins?"

Noel's eye twitched, but that didn't mean anything. It had often done that when Carol had been in his company.

"Since I was about nine. Why?"

"What about Lee Ike, Geordie?" Dave pressed.

"The same. He moved here from Newcastle around then."

"Nora Patten? Your cleaner?"

Noel's face paled, the first dent in his poised facade. "How do you know she's my cleaner?"

"We're the police, we know many things. An officer called at your house in relation to a case we're working on. Didn't she tell you?" Dave sighed.

"Err, no, she didn't. What case?"

"The abduction and murder of Karen Stokes."

Carol watched Noel for signs of guilt, but his reaction was like any innocent person's would be. A frown of confusion. She dipped her head again, his eye contact with her too much.

Noel blurted out a laugh. "What has that got to do with me?"

"That's why we're here," Dave said. "To see if it *does* have owt to do with you."

Carol itched to observe him again. While she didn't want to, she was playing Dave's usual role of monitoring. She raised her eyes. Noel still stared straight at her. Why wouldn't he look at Dave?

"Of course it doesn't," Noel blustered. "I don't even know a Karen Stokes. When was she murdered?"

"The night before last. Someone performed weight-loss surgery on her. *Badly.*"

Noel smiled wide. "Well, then, that wouldn't be *me.*" He prodded a finger at his chest. "I have so many five-star reviews on my website it isn't funny. I'll show you if you like, Carol."

Again, she didn't respond. She didn't want to give him the chance to brag. The boasting about his storage boxes was bad enough, thanks.

"How do you know it was weight-loss surgery?" Noel linked his fingers on his desk, his expression giving away what he was likely thinking: *How does a mere policeman have any idea about my job?*

Carol glanced at Dave. His smug expression told her he had a jibe lined up, and she couldn't wait to hear what it was. Noel needed putting in his place.

Dave said, "I spoke to an esteemed surgeon at the hospital, the best around."

Noel laughed too loudly to cover his disbelief that Dave had dared to say such a thing, but he still wouldn't look at Dave. "That's not true, because *I'm* the best."

"That's a matter of opinion." Dave straightened his tie. "Do you drive a vehicle other than the red car out the front?"

"I don't have another vehicle."

Liar. I've seen it, and we ran a check on you earlier.

"What about your SUV?" Dave asked.

"Oh, *that.*" Noel flicked his hand in the air. "I sold it."

"When?"

"Last week sometime."

"Who to?"

"I don't know, I didn't ask his name. The buyer was a traveller passing through. He saw the 'For Sale' sign in the car window when he drove past my cottage and knocked on my door. It was only fit for scrap, so I didn't see a problem with not informing anyone I'd sold it, although I'm sure the DVLA will have something to say about that if you have anything to do with it."

"*Scrap*?" Carol blurted, annoyed with herself for butting in. "That was a luxury four-by-four."

Noel smiled indulgently. "You know next to nowt about cars, my love. What may appear well put together on the outside could be broken inside. Just because you don't see the damage, just because you don't bother lifting the bonnet, doesn't mean it isn't there."

Was that a jab at her? If he was broken, she was bloody glad she'd ended it.

"Is that in reference to your ex-wife?" Dave asked.

Noel inhaled through his nose, the kind of action that said Dave was boring him. "No."

Dave tapped his foot. "She left you for Joseph Viticci, who just happened to be murdered after you played a tennis match with him."

Noel laughed as if Dave was a thicko, and kept his attention on Carol. "I gave my blessing to Emma. I was fine about those two moving in together. I told Joseph that when we went to the leisure centre. Our marriage had been dead for some time. If it wasn't, I wouldn't have gone with *you*, Carol. I'm loyal. I don't cheat."

Is he implying I do?

Dave sniffed. "So why did you assault Geordie at the Castle if you were okay with everything that was going on?"

"Ah, didn't you *listen*? It doesn't seem like you did. Not a good trait for a police officer. I said I was fine about Emma and Joseph. I *wasn't* fine about my friends knowing they'd been having an affair and none of them told me. I'm sure you can understand that, *Mr* Waite."

Dickhead.

Noel flicked his focus to Dave at last and gave him a spiteful smile. "You were also the last one to know."

That was a low blow, bringing Dave's personal life into things. Who the fuck had been talking about him? How had Noel found out? Carol had the strong urge to poke him in his nasty little eyes and demand he reveal his source. The idea of people gossiping about her partner had her seeing red.

Dave ignored the taunt — because he wouldn't want to give Noel the satisfaction of seeing him blow up. "Don't go anywhere, *Mr* Bartlett. We may need to speak to you again."

Noel leaned back, relaxed, his elbow on the chair arm, his finger beneath his bottom lip. "By all means, but I have two clients today back to back and won't be finished until about nine tonight, so you'll have to wait in line. My patients come first." He stood and walked around the desk to open the door. "If that's all . . ."

He strutted out, his footsteps tapping. Carol looked at Dave and made the "wanker" sign, and Dave smiled through his irritation at Noel. She left the room and disregarded Noel standing with the other door open, refusing to thank him for his cooperation.

Glad to be in reception, although she sensed Noel's eyes on her back, she thanked Isla and strode out of the clinic, never happier to be away from the man.

She made her mind up. She'd get a restraining order against him. They'd be able to eat and drink in the Lord uninterrupted. He wouldn't be allowed in if they were there.

Fuck you, pal.

CHAPTER TWENTY-SEVEN

Sunshine Caravan Park

On the most popular caravan site in the area, Carol stood by an outdoor swimming pool that was bursting at the seams with holidaymakers, mainly kids jumping in, splashing bathers and letting out shrieks of happiness. It was just gone 9 a.m., yet you'd think it was later, what with everyone out catching some sun.

They'd already phoned ahead to speak to Emma, who'd reverted to her maiden name of North. She'd said she'd go into work later so they could speak with her now. A quick check into her before they'd gone home in the early hours had shown she'd taken over renting Joseph's caravan after his murder. The vans formed several horseshoes around the swimming pool and clubhouse, grass between each section for people to eat outside or kids to play ball. Emma's was in the second row.

Carol climbed the three metal steps and tapped on the glass, stepping back down again just as the door opened outwards.

Emma stood there, taking Carol aback.

She had long blonde curly hair.

Carol had trouble processing that Noel could be the man they were looking for. Was it because she'd known him personally? She thought of Michael and how he'd struggled to accept his grandad had raped those women. What you knew someone to be didn't necessarily make up all they were. People had secrets, things they kept hidden, sides of themselves they didn't show the world.

Was Emma looking like the other women something to worry about?

"DS Dave Waite and DI Carol Wren," Dave said, his ID held up.

Carol must have taken a longer time to think than she'd realised, and Dave had filled the awkward gap. By way of an apology, Carol smiled at Emma, who beckoned them inside.

"Would you like a cold drink?" Emma walked to the fridge in the compact, open-plan kitchen, her floaty, flower-patterned dress wafting around her calves.

Carol glanced around at the mess. It was just as bad as the Stokes house. Did she want to risk drinking from a glass? Would it even be clean? Some stood upside down on the drainer, cloudy, not washed properly. "Um, what have you got?"

"Can of Fanta?"

Carol's favourite. "Yes, please." She looked around for somewhere to sit on the built-in seating and gave up — too many clothes and whatnot.

Dave remained by the open door, probably to air the van out as it didn't smell too healthy. A hint of mould and a lot of rotting vegetables. The bin beside the fridge overflowed, a lettuce leaf hanging out, a limp green tongue. Emma handed the orange drinks out and, thanks given, Carol pulled the tab. She took a long slug, savouring the cool fizz on such a hot day. Dave reluctantly closed the door so no one outside would hear their conversation, and the air immediately turned rancid again, thick from the summer heat and cloying from the stench.

Emma swiped a pile of clothes off a fixed chair onto the floor and sat at a two-person dining table. "What do you want to know about Grim? Err, Noel."

Is he a psychopath? would be a good start, but it wasn't very PC.

Carol wondered where to begin. *From the start.* "Tell me how you got to know him and what your marriage was like — if that's okay. We just want to build a picture of him at the moment." *I want to know who he really is, whether he's not the person he showed me.*

Emma eyed her. "Is he a suspect for owt?"

Is this visit not a surprise to her? Has she been waiting for this day? "His name has come up in an investigation, so we have to cover all avenues. He may well not have owt to do with it, but we like to check anyroad."

"I get you. Okay, where shall I start? I've known him since I was nine. School, going round in a little group, you know the sort of thing."

Carol didn't. She'd been a bit of a loner when little, especially after Mam had gone, too afraid to make friends in case it popped out that her father hit her, something he'd warned her to keep to herself. As a teen she'd had a few mates but never hung around after school with them. "That's you, Grim, Shark, Thunder, Blitz and Knitty, yes?"

"That's right, although Thunder came along after we'd formed the group. He moved here from Newcastle. We all got along, stayed friends up until I left Noel. *I'm* still friends with them all, but Grim isn't."

"Was Craig Stokes a part of the group, too?"

"No, but he's one of Geordie's friends."

"We heard about the altercation in the Castle."

Emma rolled her eyes. "It was bad of me to mess around with Shark behind Grim's back, I do understand that, but only Thunder and Blitz knew. Knitty was oblivious. Grim was convinced she'd been told, but honestly, the poor cow was clueless. So he took it out on Thunder — Geordie — and punched him. At the time, I was gutted about Shark's murder so wasn't really listening to the argument, I had to tune Grim out by then because the sound of his voice had my skin crawling. Sorry, do you need me to talk about them with their real names?"

"That would help, yes."

"Okay, so Joseph had been killed the night after I left Noel — do you know about that?"

"Yes, and about them meeting for tennis."

"Hmm, that's a suspicious thing if ever there was one."

"Why, do you think Noel has it in him to have killed Joseph?"

"I didn't until he turned up here, asking for me to go back home. Noel was nice at first, but once he realised I wasn't going to do what he wanted, he wrecked the place, throwing things, shouting stuff about women he loved leaving him and this was the second time."

"What did he mean by that?"

"I can only assume he meant his mam dying, because he'd never had a girlfriend before me."

"Did he become violent?"

"I called him a lunatic. He punched me in the stomach — and let me tell you, it shocked the shit out of me. He dragged me over there to the sofa, then pinned me down, saying he could strangle me if he wanted to."

Karen was strangled. Carol remained calm. "And did he?"

"No, I told him if he didn't get off, I'd ring the hospital, the police, and tell them what he was doing. He'd lose his job, or so I hoped. He got off me, stormed to the door and told me I'd come crawling back soon enough. I think that's why he set up his own clinic so I wouldn't be able to grass on him to anyone, but that's stupid of him because I checked online. He'd still get in trouble because all doctors are licensed under the same governing body. Prior to that and the night I left him, he'd never shown any sign of being aggressive towards me, so you can imagine how surprised I was when he turned like that."

"What happened on the night you left?"

"I'll admit I was bolshy, high on adrenaline, chuffed I was actually leaving him, so I probably came across as a nasty piece of work. I got to my car, and he came out, saying he'd do whatever I wanted, something like that. Begging. When I told him to get lost, he got right in my face and shouted that I was a slag and a 'fucking whore bitch'." Emma shook her head, maybe to dislodge the memory so it couldn't make itself at home, sticking around to taunt her. "I ignored him and drove up here, although it shook me quite a bit."

"So because of his aggression and the assault, you believe he's capable of murder?"

"I want to say no, because I thought his behaviour was down to the split, him panicking that I wasn't going home, but the look in his eyes . . . Put it this way, he's obviously got two sides to him, and he only shows the other one in certain circumstances. Like I said, he hadn't been weird with me before all that. He was frustrating more than owt. Obsessed with his patients, and I did bring it up. Probably like you two get from your other halves if you've got them. I told him he was married to the job, that I came far down his list of priorities."

Dave kept a poker face, but Carol sensed *he* had memories returning too — of his ex, moaning about him always being out on something to do with work instead of going home to her.

"That's why I turned to Joseph," Emma said. "I got more attention off him in the hour or two we'd have together than I ever got from Noel. First it was medical school, then his foundation, then core surgical training. That's a lot of time, and I stuck it out because I'd known from the start what he wanted to be, but once he continued being immersed in work for years after that, I wondered why he'd even married me."

And now I'm wondering why he wanted a proper relationship with me if he wasn't attentive to his wife, if he isn't relationship material. He's still obsessed with his patients, so what's the point of wanting me?

Carol brushed that aside. "Do you know a Karen Stokes?"

Emma nodded. "Only because she's one of those women who went missing, and Geordie was with her for a bit, plus I saw it on the internet yesterday. Do you think *Noel* did it?"

"You sound surprised, yet you just told us you thought he was capable of murder."

"Oh, I do. I've often wondered if Noel killed Joseph then went straight to Tesco on purpose. I did tell the detective at the time to double-check that, but I got the impression the copper thought it was sour grapes on my part, that I wanted to get back at Noel for whatever reason. Noel was cleared. There was no evidence, and the timing was so tight, they said he couldn't be in the Backstreet and Tesco at the same time. So I let it go. But I can understand him murdering Joseph — he was hurt and angry, and I'd say it would have been a spur-of-the-moment thing — but why would he kill Karen? And wouldn't that mean he'd abducted her and the others?"

"We don't know. As I said when we first came in, we have to build a picture before we make any decisions. Noel might have been violent towards you, but obviously, it doesn't mean he's a killer." Carol sipped some Fanta and moved on. "Have you heard about Tom?"

"What about him?"

"I'm sorry to have to tell you, but he was also murdered. Last night."

"What? *Blitz*? How?" Tears bulged and spilled over, but Emma managed to keep her composure.

"He was attacked and run over."

"Oh my bloody God!" Emma pressed a hand to her neck. "Why would anyone *do* that to him?"

That was interesting. Emma's mind hadn't gone straight to Noel being the culprit, yet he'd had a go at Tom and Geordie in the Castle — he had motive, albeit years after the event.

"We're unsure at the moment, but with Karen and now Tom, it's concerning us that it's the same person and they'll do it again."

Emma shook her head, rubbing the tears from her cheeks. "God, let me just get myself together." She blew out a steadying breath. "Okay, okay, I'm fine. At a push, Noel could have got arsey with Tom and it took a nasty turn, but not with Karen. I don't think he even knew her."

Carol thought of the similarity between Emma, Karen, Lesley and Teresa. Noel didn't need to know the other women. The fact they resembled Emma would be enough. They were a targeted type, women who'd have caught his eye. Carol didn't want to accept Noel was behind this, but now she'd heard about his dark side, she'd be stupid not to. What if this Jekyll had always had Hyde in him, but he'd hidden it too well?

And if it isn't him, who the bloody hell is it?

"Does Dolly Parton and the song 'Jolene' mean owt to you?"

Emma seemed confused. "Err, should it?" She blinked. "Hang on, Noel told me I looked like her once."

Carol couldn't see the resemblance, but it at least tied in with the weird disguise. "Do you see him at all these days?"

"Not if I can help it. I warned him to keep away from me after he came here, and if I *do* see him, it's in town, stuff like that, so I go in another direction." She paused. "I just thought. It can't be him. Noel wouldn't do owt to endanger his precious job. It's his reason for getting up in the morning. Why would he risk being struck off if he was caught for murder and kidnap?"

"I agree that wouldn't make sense. Okay, if you can keep this chat to yourself. We can't go around accusing him unless we have evidence." Carol passed over a business card.

"Can't you search the cottage or something?"

"Not without probable cause. As it stands, he says he was home on both the nights we're interested in, and until we can prove otherwise, we have to leave him be. He's already answered our questions. If it *is* him, I'd prefer that he doesn't know we're looking at him so we can get all our ducks in a row, do you see?"

Emma nodded. "I won't be saying owt, not even to the group. If he's done all that bad shit, I want him to go down for it. Have you told the others about Tom?"

"Not yet."

They said their goodbyes, leaving Emma crying at the door, the news about Tom sinking in, and Carol finished her Fanta as they walked towards the car park.

Noel? Really?

She sat in the driver's seat and waited for Dave to buckle up. "What do you think?"

"A man with his hands around his wife's throat, angry and upset she's left him, isn't in the same league as all the other crap. Yes, he could have done it, but he didn't seem fazed at all when we spoke to him, unless you count him going pale when he realised we knew Knitty is his cleaner."

"I wonder why that bothered him."

"No idea."

"Me neither, and it's getting right on my tits."

CHAPTER TWENTY-EIGHT

The Incident Room

The team gathered around Michael's desk and stared at his computer screen. Michael had paused the internal CCTV footage from Sainsbury's at the best shot of the customer who'd bought the Freddo. He stood behind a customer in line, waiting for his turn to be served. The conveyor belt held the first shopper's items, then the Freddo and what seemed to be a spray bottle of Flash. It appeared the Queen herself had nipped out of Buckingham Palace and popped into the supermarket, except it wasn't the Queen at all but a man with the same build as the Dolly Parton person who'd purchased the pay-as-you-go phone in Tesco.

"So he likes to dress up," Carol said. "Do Dolly and the Queen have owt in common? Is there a link?"

"Not as far as I know," Katherine said. "I'm envious of his legs, though. Look at them!"

Dave squinted. "Has he got tights on?"

"Seems like it, unless he's got a tan." Carol peered at the outfit. A skirt suit, blouse, court shoes and a string of pearls drooping around his neck. "How many outfits does he have? Is it just a disguise or does he like dressing up? At least we have an avenue to go down now — finding out where those masks are sold. Are they one-of-a-kind efforts or mass-produced? For someone who needs to remain hidden, he's done a good job of getting noticed."

She didn't see Noel as the dressing-up sort, but then again, she hadn't seen him as someone who'd become violent either, and if Emma was to be believed, Noel had a dark side. This . . . this was just plain weird.

"I did a quick search," Michael said. "Those types of masks are readily available online, but these ones look custom-made. There are some made in China and shipped to various online retailers and brick-and-mortar shops, but there's one company that crafts them specially to order. It's in Middlesbrough. I've already emailed the shop owner to see if they've sold either of those masks — there was no reply when I rang. I asked them to check back five years in case they were bought before the women were abducted."

"Could go back even longer if dressing up is something he's always done," Katherine said.

"Five years will do for now." Carol folded her arms. "We can always ask them to go farther back if it comes up blank. Katherine, did you check to see if any other people went missing besides our three?"

"I did, and all of those cases were closed as the women and men returned home or settled elsewhere — they're in the system as working, et cetera."

"Thanks. Michael, what about the online stores?"

He clicked off the footage and showed her his on-screen list. "I've contacted all of them."

"Cheers. Press play again, let's see what he does once he gets to the cashier." What she really wanted was to see if she or Dave recognised his movements as belonging to Noel. The height was a bit taller than him, but that could be the heels, and the boobs were doing well in hiding his real shape.

Michael flicked back to the footage and did as she'd asked.

Queenie fiddled with the pearls, his hands covered with white gloves. Carol spotted a handbag draped at his elbow, just how the Queen carried one, and he dipped his other fingers inside and brought out a woman's purse.

The first customer gave him a weird look, took her shopping and walked away, and the cashier glanced up at him with a smile which froze in place, her eyes widening at the sight of him. He said something, and she flung her head back and laughed, a hand to her chest, then swiped his items, her mouth moving as she chattered away. He'd likely fobbed her off with some excuse as to why he was wearing a creepy-as-eff mask while shopping. He paid using cash and didn't bother with a carrier bag. He put the Freddo and Flash in his handbag, the spray trigger bit sticking out, and went out of view. The walk wasn't Noel's, unless he'd changed it on purpose. It was more of a regal swoosh-shuffle, as if he'd got right into character.

Michael clicked the stop icon.

Carol had a thought. "Can someone look up where there are men-sized women's shoes available, please. Noel has large feet, so maybe an eleven, but of course, check all sizes in case it isn't him."

She'd written all about Noel on the whiteboard, filling Michael and Katherine in earlier. Neither of them knew him so couldn't offer any advice as to whether they thought he was capable of kidnap and murder.

She sighed. "I'll make some tea then think about where we go next."

"Knitty?" Dave suggested.

"She'll be at work, but I get where you're coming from. Some insight into Noel and the others. Does anyone know Craig's status?"

"Still in holding," Michael said, "complaining about his breakfast last I heard. Upset he didn't get a fry-up."

"Cheeky shit." Carol shook her head in disgust. "We'll just have to wait and see what the CPS say about sending him in on remand or letting him go on bail. I've also got to check in with Richard in case Oliver passed on any info about the driver in last night's murder. But . . . tea."

She went off to make it, trying to slow her racing mind. Once Noel had come into the picture, and with the surgeon angle, she'd been unable to stop thinking about him, but without solid evidence, there was nothing they could do but find it, then go after him — hard.

She handed the teas out and stood drinking hers by the whiteboard, reading everything from start to finish to see if something clicked.

Nothing did.

Carol's phone rang, and she glanced at the screen and swiped, placing her cup on the spare desk. "Hi, Whitney, how's it going?"

"Lindsey didn't come home last night."

"What? Why didn't you get hold of me *then*?"

"I left it until this morning because Tristan said she sometimes stays elsewhere — with men, I mean — but she's always home by the time they need to get ready for school. I did let Alton know, and he logged it. Tristan took Sammy to school earlier, but the Stokes girls have refused to go, and in the circumstances, I thought it best they stayed here. I'm annoyed, because Lindsey told me she wouldn't be out past eleven."

"Shit."

"When she didn't phone me back last night, I popped upstairs to ask Tristan if that was normal, which is when he said about her staying out sometimes. I'm trying to keep the girls occupied, but I'm getting on their nerves, I can tell — someone else should be here really, not me. Oh, and shall I ring Lindsey's ex-husband and let him know what's going on?"

"Yes, do that. We should speak to him anyroad, see what he was doing last night. And I'm not sure what's happening with Craig Stokes at the minute, so we'd need someone else to care for his girls if Lindsey isn't there to do it. You can't be expected to." Carol tapped her foot, hating having to make such a horrible choice..

She left her office and went downstairs to the holding cell. Mulholland was around, so she asked him to go with her to speak to Craig.

She opened the flap in the door. "Craig, I need a wor—"

The stench of excrement floated out, and she gagged.

"What have you done *that* for?" she asked.

Shit peppered the walls and floor, and Craig sat on the bed, naked, his permitted clothing in a pile. "No one would bring me a fry-up, and I'm sick of shouting for someone to feed me properly. Thought this might get your attention." He smirked.

"Do you realise how gross this is, someone else having to wipe up your mess?"

He shrugged.

"Where has yesterday's attitude gone? You were all for taking your punishment."

"Bog off."

So he'd had time to think, to become bolshy. Lovely.

"Where are your girls going? Two options: your Welsh family or social services."

"Fuck you. I can't make that choice."

"Well, someone's got to, because Lindsey can't watch them anymore."

He sent her a sharp glance. "Why not?"

"Do you want me to decide?" She stepped back to get fresher air.

"My family. I don't want them going to strangers."

"I'll still have to call social services for them to deal with the handover."

"Fine. So I'm not getting out on bail, then?"

"Not at the moment." She slammed the hatch shut and looked at Mulholland.

"Fuck's sake," he said.

"Sorry . . ."

She left him to organise the clean-up and went back into the incident room, talking through everything she'd learned since being there last. "Katherine, can you go to Lindsey's house and be there for when social services arrive and help Whitney with the handover? Quickly find out who Craig's next of kin is in Wales and contact them first, then phone social services and arrange to meet them there. Michael, I need you looking into Lindsey as well as the masks and those shoes — also see when her phone last pinged a mast, and get her call records. Christ, we don't have enough people here — ask Richard if you can borrow a uniform to help you. I'll phone Whitney back, then find out whether anyone saw Lindsey in the Little Devil last night."

"Maybe she's overslept at some fella's gaff," Dave said, "and she'll walk in any minute."

"I hope so."

Carol thought about the poor Stokes girls having yet more trauma in their lives, shunted from pillar to post. Hopefully, they'd be placed in the same foster home until the family could collect them. "I've got a horrible feeling, haven't you?"

Dave nodded. "Abduction number four?"

"Hmm. *Fuck.*"

Michael went to work on his computer, and Dave said he'd take over dealing with the shoes. Carol wandered to her office again so she could concentrate while making a to-do list.

First, she got hold of Whitney. "Katherine is on the way. It's social services for now, I'm afraid. I advise you not to tell the girls, they might bolt. Wait until whoever gets there, then explain it to them. Did you get hold of Lindsey's ex?"

"Yes. He'll pick the kids up from school and take the boys to his. He'll phone Tristan to let him know, plus the schools. There's not much else I can do here once the girls are taken care of."

"Where are they?"

"Still in bed."

"Did they have a late night?"

"Yep. One of them was crying."

"That's bloody sad." Carol hurt for them. "Okay, ask the ex if he feels he needs you for Tristan and Sammy, and if not, once the girls are sorted, go home and get some kip."

"Will do."

Next on the list was Richard. "Hi, are you in the station?"

"Yep, but I'm leaving in ten minutes to check in with the uniforms who've gone back out to do house-to-house enquiries near the woodland. Some people didn't answer last night."

"Have you got a list of everyone in the Devil?"

"Yep, hang on." He clacked at his keyboard. "Who are you after?"

"Lindsey Reynolds. We spoke to her about Karen, and she was looking after the Stokes girls, but she didn't come home last night. Her eldest son said that happens sometimes, but I'd have thought she'd have a bit more sense when she's got Whitney and extra guests at her house. I'm worried about her being number four."

"Christ, I can imagine. Well, Lindsey isn't on the list, although Reg did say she'd been in there because she'd left the pub after Tom, saying she might get lucky before she went home."

Carol's stomach rolled over. "Shit, so she could have witnessed the accident, the murder."

"You think the killer took her?"

"What I'm leaning towards is *she* was the bloody target and Tom got in the way."

"Shit. Owt I can do for you?"

"Please. As you're going that way, I could do with you finding out if anyone saw her. I realise a lot of people will have been in bed and already said they heard nowt to do with Tom's murder, but surely someone would have seen Lindsey walking through the estate to go home."

"Not if she didn't even *get* to the estate."

"You have a point. Got owt on where the vehicle went last night?"

"Not a thing after it was seen leaving the scene."

"Bum." She went on to pick his brains about Noel and bit her lip, waiting for his answer.

"I know who he is. It was Piston who went out to that altercation at the Castle. What are you thinking, Noel Bartlett could be your man?"

"I'm not sure. I know him personally, and Dave sort of does too, although we're not friends. Noel drinks in the Lord. He doesn't strike us as having the balls." She told him about the dress-up outfits. "That doesn't fit with him either, neither does the temper his ex-wife said she'd discovered after they'd split, but I believe her version of events."

"People have secrets, you know that."

"Too true. Okay, I need to phone Rib, so if you discover owt, can you phone me direct?"

"Yep. I'll nip to the Devil and have another word with Reg about Lindsey."

"Thanks."

She checked her emails and saw something from Rib:

Carol,

I've finished Karen's examination. Four hundred and seventy-five cigarette burns in various stages of healing. I'd say she'd been burned from when she was taken up until the day of her death. My report is attached. I'll be getting to Tom's this morning.

Carol glanced at the clock. Somehow, it was nearing midday, the time since they'd got back from seeing Emma whizzing by. She'd chance her arm and see if Rib was available.

It rang a few times.

"Morning, Bird."

"Morning, almost afternoon. How are things?"

"Tom's a mess. It's going to take me a fair while, but I'm sure it's as I said — knocked over first, struck with the weapon, then the vehicle drove over him. His insides . . . ruined. If he hadn't been murdered, I don't think he'd have survived being run over the second time. I heard back from Todd: there are marks on the road that suggest someone stopped sharply just before the body. The width of the tyres indicate a large, wide vehicle. I didn't spot them because of the blood on the road."

An SUV? Did Noel really sell his last week, or was he lying?

"God, I had a feeling it would be this," she said then realised she'd spoken out loud.

"Would be what?"

She told him about Noel. "What do you think?"

"Noel? That wet lettuce you were seeing? Oh, come on!"

"I know, but I've got a nasty feeling in my gut." She explained about his friends and what had happened in the Castle and to Emma in the caravan. "Four of them have come up in this investigation. Knitty, Geordie and Tom, plus him. And get this, Emma looks just like the missing women did before they were taken. And another woman hasn't come home. She's slimmer, but she has the same hair — and she was seeing Tom. Geordie's brother at one time, too."

"Bloody hell. It sounds headache-inducing."

"It is."

"Good luck with that. I must get on. I've left my assistant measuring the wounds on the skull."

Carol squirmed. "Right, thanks for that image. I'll wait for Tom's report off you, then."

"Yep. Give me another hour."

She said goodbye and leaned back, closing her eyes for a moment. There was so much going on at once, and she needed a second to recalibrate.

Just five minutes . . .

Jesus, take the wheel.

CHAPTER TWENTY-NINE

Bunning's Breakers Yard

Carol had made the decision to speak to Lindsey's ex first, then Knitty. With the important golden hour of Lindsey going missing long gone, they were behind in trying to find her. The manager had informed them Mark Reynolds was operating the car crusher, so they'd been waiting for five minutes for him to come and see them.

Mark approached, a brawny sod with slicked-back brown hair and thick eyebrows that met in the middle. He reminded Carol of a wider version of Vinnie Jones, Mark's features and walk much the same.

He stopped in front of them in the concrete yard and gestured to an office. "Want to go in there?"

Carol nodded. "Might be best."

They followed him across the yard and into the building. One side was a break area, tables and chairs dotted around, and the other had two desks piled with paperwork. He led them to a table closest to a vending machine and left them to sit while he fed money into a slot and jabbed at buttons. A beige plastic cup flew down, and brown liquid squirted into it.

"You want one?" he asked over his shoulder.

"No, thank you." Carol glanced at Dave: *Is he going to be difficult, d'you think?*

Dave shrugged.

Mark sat with them and stretched his legs under the table. "So, Lindsey. I'm telling you, she'll be with some bloke. She's had a load of them since we split up. Granted, she's never not come back before, not staying out this long anyroad, but she's a crafty cow. If she knew a copper was at her house, that's a free overnight babysitter. I take it Hayley went home?"

Carol passed on what they knew. "Where were you last night?"

He chuckled darkly. "I knew that was coming. We were at the in-laws — well, my girlfriend's parents' place."

"We?"

"That's me, the missus and the baby." He gave the parents' address and phone number. "I haven't got the number of all the other people who were there. You'll have to ask Paula, my bird's mam. They were all her friends. Paula's birthday bash, see?"

"What time did you leave?"

"This morning, about seven. The party went on for ages, I had one too many to drive, so we stayed over. Should have booked the day off work really. Got a banging hangover."

He seemed a bit casual, not bothered about Lindsey at all.

"So you're not worried about your ex-wife, then?" Carol asked.

"Nah, Lindsey's a bad penny. She'll show up. I'll keep the boys until she gets home. I don't have them much, what with the baby and everything, but I'm sure they'll be okay."

"Can you tell me a bit about Geordie — Lee Ike — and Tom Cubbins?"

He chuffed out a laugh. "Lindsey doesn't think I know about them, but I do. She was seeing Geordie's brother when we were married. I happened to be seeing someone too, so it didn't faze me, although I let her think if I caught her playing away, she'd be in the shit."

"In the shit?"

"Yeah, you know, me having a go at her. It was pointless, because she never listened to me, always did whatever she wanted despite me pulling her up on it. That's the reason I left. She got bolshy after Sammy was born, being awkward for the sake of it, so last year, I'd had enough. As for Tom, she's seeing him now. Did you check she isn't there?"

"Tom's dead."

Mark sat straighter. "You what?"

"Killed last night. Did you know him and Geordie well?"

"Fuck me, that's a shocker." He stroked his chin. "Been neighbours with Geordie for a long while until I moved out of Kipling, and I got to know Tom through him. They're all right, even if Geordie did keep it a secret about his brother poking Lindsey's downstairs muffin. I don't hold it against him. I should, but I don't. Other men are welcome to her. What are you interested in those two for?"

"It's part of another investigation." *Or it's all linked together.* Talking of Geordie had reminded her — she ought to speak to him, too. He'd surely heard about Tom because his brother had found him in the road. They ought to speak to Evan as well. A busy afternoon, then. "Do you know owt about the group they hung around with, the ones with all the nicknames?"

"Fucking hell, are that lot still meeting up?"

"What do you know of the others?"

"Well, there's Nosy Knitty — Christ, she's into everyone's business since her husband walked out on her. Got nowt better to do, I s'pose. Another reason why I'm glad I moved away. Living opposite her was a nightmare. Always at her window when she was home. You know about Tom and Geordie, then there's Emma — shit business about Joseph being bumped off — and there's that other fella Emma was married to, used to go into the Devil a lot a few years ago. Noel the Knob."

Carol's heart thumped then lost a beat. "He went to the Devil? What do you mean by a few years ago?"

"Dunno. Maybe around the time those women went missing, but don't quote me on it. There was a joke going round that it was him, because he stopped going in after that apart from once in a blue moon."

Carol felt sick. "What sort of person is he?"

"One of those blokes who tries to fit in but doesn't. Butts into conversations when he's not wanted, you must know the type."

That had happened in the Lord a while ago, and Noel had got punched for it. The idea that he'd stopped going in the Devil sent a shiver down her spine. She didn't glance at Dave in case her face gave her away, she didn't need Mark picking up on anything, but Dave would know as well as she did, the finger of suspicion pointed firmly in Noel's direction.

"Okay, we'll be in touch with Paula. Just a formality." She stood. "Someone will let you know if Lindsey turns up. Thanks for your time."

Mark picked up his cup. "Can you hang about in here for a bit so I can have a longer break?"

She shook her head at the cheek of him and smiled. "No, afraid not."

Outside, she stared across at someone else using the car crusher. If she didn't believe Mark had nothing to do with it, she'd wonder if Lindsey's body was in among all that crumpled metal.

* * *

Kipling Close

Carol had phoned Knitty and arranged to meet at her house later. She'd also phoned Geordie and asked if they could chat. He'd given them directions to the site he worked at and said the foreman would come and get him when they arrived.

First, Evan.

She knocked on the front door, and he answered, a deep-set frown and signs of tiredness wreathing his face.

"You here about last night?" he asked.

"Yes. Can we come in?"

He walked off, so Carol and Dave followed him inside. Evan sprawled out on the sofa, leaving two chairs for them. They sat, and Carol studied him. He appeared haunted, nothing like the man they'd spoken to before. Something had changed in his eyes. Finding a body would do that to you.

"I'm sorry you found Tom," she said.

"So am I. Fuck me, it was the worst thing I've ever seen. I shook him, but he wouldn't wake up." He swallowed. A lump most likely.

"You gave a statement, yes?"

"Yeah, to one of the coppers last night. Didn't get to bed until three."

"Sorry to ask this, but would you mind going through the basics again? Sometimes, memories come back the next day. We really need to know about the vehicle."

"It was too far away for me to make out what it was. I just saw the taillights. It turned right at the end of the road."

"Towards Tesco, that way?"

"Yeah, or it could have been the estate. They might have gone down one of the side roads."

True. "When you left the pub, was Lindsey there?"

"Nah, she went out a minute after Tom."

"Are you aware she's missing?"

Evan closed his eyes and placed a hand over them. "You're shitting me."

"Sorry, I'm not."

He lowered his hand, letting it fall into his lap. It appeared he was wrung out. "Where could she have gone? I didn't leave that long after her, maybe five minutes, and Tom went first, so she'd have seen him in the road. There's no way she'd have walked past and left him there because she was with him, you know, kind of a couple but not." He paused. "Oh fuck. Do you think . . . ?"

"We're going on the assumption she saw something and was taken away."

"Jesus Christ."

"What time did Geordie arrive home?"

"He had to walk the long way round, through the Backstreet and past the town, because of the cordon and that, so it was about one. That's what he said this morning, anyroad. I still wasn't home so can't confirm that. There was a lock-in, and he stayed there gassing about what had happened, plus he had to speak to the police. He was in the Devil all night with me, so it wasn't him."

"We don't think it was. This group he hung around with since he was a kid . . ."

"I'm older so didn't join it, but yeah, they meet up once a month in the Castle for a get-together. There was a falling-out after one of them died, Geordie got punched, and that bloke doesn't meet with them now — the one who thumped him, I mean. He stopped talking to them, got the hump."

"Do you know much about him?"

"Who, Noel? Only that he's rich, some surgeon or other. I didn't have anything to do with that lot, they were Geordie's mates."

They chatted for a while longer, going over Evan's movements, but he had nothing new to give them. They left and, upon spotting Knitty's moped in her front garden, Carol and Dave walked over there.

Knitty opened the door before Carol had a chance to knock. "I've just heard about what's going on, had a copper calling not two minutes ago asking about Lindsey." She showed them inside, and in the kitchen poured tea for everyone. "What's happening around here?"

"She didn't come home last night." Carol accepted the tea, thanked her and added sweetener.

"So I gathered. What can I do to help? I saw a woman in a suit going into her house as I pulled up."

Carol wasn't about to tell her it was probably the social services lady. "We need your help. Have you heard about Tom?"

"Yes, another copper got me out of bed about it last night. It's criminal. He was one of my best friends."

"Tell me about the group."

Knitty launched into a story about how they'd met at school, and she explained everyone's nicknames, something Carol was glad about, because she'd been trying to work out how she'd ask what Noel's meant.

"Grim Reaper — as a kid, he used to boil ants alive in the sun with his magnifying glass."

Carol jolted. *Sick bastard.* "Oh. That's not nice. I hope he didn't do owt worse."

"No, just the ants. He's . . . well, until the night at the Castle, he was a quiet person, laid-back, devoted to his job. Once Emma left him, he changed."

"In what way?"

"Well, he got arsey with us lot for a start, and Emma said he'd been to the caravan to have a go at her. He didn't even attend Joseph's funeral. I can kind of understand it, considering what Joseph and Emma had been getting up to, but in that case, why meet him and play tennis? I just don't get it."

Me neither.

Knitty picked at a fingernail. "Thank God he isn't there when I clean his house. Which reminds me, I have to go out there again later to sort his washing machine and whatever."

They chatted and drank tea, Carol consoling Knitty when she finally broke down about Tom. As always, it was difficult to see someone cry, but unfortunately, it was part of the job.

Carol only hoped there weren't more tears before bedtime.

* * *

They left Knitty's just as the Stokes girls were getting in the social worker's car. Carol held back, feeling like a coward, not wanting to see their faces and how much turmoil they were in, so she phoned Michael and asked him to look into Mark's alibi.

The car drove off, and Whitney beckoned them over.

In the kitchen, Whitney packed some clothing ready for Mark to collect after he'd done the school run — the cheeky shit had asked her to do it like she was some skivvy — and Katherine sat at the table.

"How did the girls take it?" Carol asked.

"Pretty well, considering," Whitney said. "It's like they're used to life's blows, you know?"

"Poor cows," Dave said.

"I really felt for them." Katherine rubbed her eyes. "It's like they're so used to things going wrong, they just get on with it. I really hope the family in Wales are good people and take care of them. I'm going to be worrying for days now. I know they're down for stealing around here, but they're just kids at the end of the day."

Carol's phone went off. "Oh, what's he want?" She accepted the call. "Everything okay, Rich?"

"I've been thinking over what you said about Lindsey being number four. Is it all right for a couple of us to go to hers and have a look around? The usual missing persons thing."

"Yep. We're here now, although we have to nip and see Geordie, but I'm sure Katherine won't mind hanging around to let you in. Whitney really needs to get some shut-eye."

Katherine nodded. "I can stay for a bit, but I should get back to the station and help Michael. Can someone stay here for Mark to collect the boys' things?"

Carol passed that on to Rich.

"I'll get hold of him and say he has to collect it while we're there," he said. "We're not here for his convenience."

With that settled, Carol and Dave left, waving Whitney off as she drove away. It felt like one thing after another today, flitting from person to person, but it kept Carol's mind off Noel and whether he'd taken to killing more than ants, switching his magnifying glass for blunt objects. Cigarettes. Surgery on a dead woman.

The thought curled her toes in a bad way.

* * *

Geordie spoke to them in a mint-green Portakabin. Dusty footprints covered the floor, and the orange chairs and Formica-topped tables were straight out of a secondary school dining hall. He flumped down onto a seat and rested his elbows on the table. Carol and Dave sat opposite.

"Look, all this is doing my head in, and I'm scared," he said.

"Scared?" Carol frowned.

"First it was Shark — sorry, Joseph — and then Tom. What if someone's after the group?"

That was a possibility Carol hadn't contemplated yet. What if the missing women were associated with the group in some way? Karen had been having it away with Geordie, and Lindsey had dabbled with Evan. What about Lesley and Teresa? How did they fit in?

"By the group, I take it you mean your old friends from school." She listed the names.

"Yeah. All right, there's a gap between Joseph and Tom being killed, but still, it's put the shits up me. I was just drinking with Tom last night, then he fucking well gets murdered!"

"Were any of you seeing Lesley or Teresa?"

"Not as far as I know."

That put the brakes on her theory, then. "Who do you think is after you, assuming someone is?"

"That bloody Grim. He's had a beef ever since Emma left him."

"Noel Bartlett, you mean."

"Yeah. Dickhead. He got nasty with Emma, so he's got it in him."

Dave wrote in his notebook. "Is the beef you have influencing that opinion, or do you really believe Mr Bartlett is picking you all off — that *is* what you're saying, yes?"

"Yes, that's *exactly* what I'm saying. It can't be anyone else, can it? He's cut all ties with us, all because we didn't grass on Emma." His cheeks flushed — anger building?

"Has anyone spoken to you about Lindsey?" Carol asked.

"No, what about her?"

Carol took a deep breath. "She's missing."

"What the actual *fuck*? When?"

"Last night, around the time Tom was murdered."

"Jesus effing Christ!" Geordie shot up and paced. "I can't get over this. Four women in the past three years, and no one knows where they are? What do you lot do all day, twiddle your thumbs?"

"We do exactly what we're doing now," Carol said. "Speaking to people, working out her movements, asking who'd have a grudge against her or why she'd be a target, so we can find whoever did this."

He plonked himself on the chair again. "Sorry, it's just my nerves are wrecked. This is all a bit mental."

"Does Noel know Lindsey?" she asked.

"Not that I'm aware of. What, you think he's snatching women?" Geordie laughed. "It'll be about the only way he can get one after Emma."

Carol's cheeks heated. *He got me.* "Why's that?"

"He's not relationship material. Emma fucked off with Joseph because Noel was hardly around. He probably gets his kicks from the naked bodies on his operating table, that's why he'd gone off Emma in bed."

The idea of that was revolting.

"Do you really believe that?" she asked.

"Nah, I'm just spouting off, aren't I?"

"What time did you get home last night?"

"About one." He massaged his temples. "My brain's full, so I could be out by a few minutes."

I know the bloody feeling. "Other than Noel, is there anyone else you think may have killed Tom and taken Lindsey?"

"Nope."

Well, that answered that, didn't it?

* * *

Despite Noel saying he was busy today, it had to be done. They'd spoken to all of the other group members again apart from him and Emma, and Carol didn't think Emma needed another visit, so after scoffing a sandwich on the way and taking a toilet break, here they were at the clinic, hoping Noel wasn't in surgery.

As it happened, he was in his office doing paperwork, so Isla showed them in. He looked up from what he was doing, his face brightening at the sight of Carol in the doorway.

"Carol!" He gave a conspirator's smile and rubbed his hands. "Are you alone?"

Oh God, he's vile.

She realised he'd been this leery before, when they were hooking up. To be honest, it had flattered her that he'd wanted her so much, but now, he just came off as a pervert, the flasher type in a beige rain mac.

She stepped inside to allow Dave to come in after her.

"Oh." Noel pouted. "What can I do for you?"

"You said you were home last night," Carol said, determined to lead this time.

"Yes. I told you, I was in bed." He bared his teeth in what he seemed to think was a sexy grin.

It was anything but.

"Lindsey Reynolds. Do you know her?"

His eyebrows rose. "Should I? Is she a patient of mine?"

"I heard you're fond of your patients, so surely you'd know if she'd been one or not."

"Ah, someone's been talking. Emma, by any chance? To answer your question, I don't think I know this Lindsey, no. Why do you ask?"

"She's missing."

"Oh, that's not good. And I suppose, because you brought up where I was last night, that you're checking if it was me?" He shook his head. "You don't know me at all, Carol."

Something about those words made her feel uncomfortable.

"Tom Cubbins was murdered last night." Carol had said it out of the blue to shock him, but going by his expression, her tactic hadn't worked.

Noel rested his forearms on the desk, steepled his fingers and propped his chin on the tips. "Again, not good. I suppose *that* was me as well, was it?"

He was humouring her, and it rankled.

"We'll be on the lookout for your SUV, just in case." She watched him.

Something had to scare him, but it clearly wasn't what she'd just said. He didn't even flinch.

"A waste of your time. I told you, I sold it last week to a traveller. Besides, I have no idea what my car has to do with Tom's death."

She was surprised he didn't seem bothered about his former friend. Yes, there'd been the row at the Castle, they'd lied to him by omission, but the group were closely bonded for many years, so surely he felt even a smidgen of grief about Tom?

"He was run over," she said.

Noel sighed. "That's unfortunate for him, but I'm not in the habit of doing that sort of thing."

"Why did you stop going to the Little Devil around three years ago?"

Once again, her question hadn't riled him.

"Because it's full of ingrates and smelly fishermen. Now, I finished my surgeries earlier than expected, this afternoon's lady bottled out, so if it's all right with you, I'd like to go home. Should I get CCTV set up there so I can prove that's where I'm going?"

Carol smiled tightly. "No one's stopping you."

"My bed's available if you can spare half an hour." He let out strange giggle.

It froze Carol on the spot, and she glared at him. Half an hour? He was more like a five-minute kind of man, and once again, she wondered why she'd continued seeing him for so long. Why wouldn't he get the message that their night-time activities were over? Why keep being suggestive?

Anger rose, and she gritted her teeth. "Not. Interested."

She walked out, leaving Dave glowering at him, and it felt as if all the ghosts of the dead ants Noel had supposedly killed came alive on her skin. She left the clinic, getting in the car to wait for Dave, whacking up the air-con to get rid of the clammy sweat that had broken out.

That giggle. She'd never heard him laugh like that before.

And she never wanted to again.

CHAPTER THIRTY

Piper Place

Grim disliked Dave so much he contemplated adding him to the list. The only thing stopping him was Dave had also been cheated on, and the cheated needed to be cut some slack. If Dave didn't get to spend all of his working day — and his home life — with Carol, Grim supposed he might like him. One thing Grim admired about the man was his fierce loyalty to her, always there as her guard dog, snapping his teeth at anyone who dared to piss her off. It didn't sit well that Carol reciprocated. She might have thought she'd schooled her features when he'd deliberately baited Dave about his wife having an affair, but he'd seen her intense hatred for him rising to the surface.

Interesting — and heart-breaking. *Was* there something more than being work partners going on with them? *That* had to be what the problem was, why Carol wouldn't enter a proper relationship with Grim. She had the hots for Dave!

Grim would process that when he had more time. He sat in his car round the back of Piper Place, a quiet cul-de-sac on the top edge of Coldwater, his car parked in some trees out of view.

Lesley's body had been in his boot all day, and he found it amusing that police officers had been so close to it and hadn't had a bloody clue that it was baking in the heat. He was surprised it didn't smell.

He needed to dump the corpse. This spot wasn't ideal. It was too enclosed, too secluded. So he'd made up his mind to take a risk in the daylight and deposit her against a tree closest to the rear of the cul-de-sac. Easier for the police to discover.

He reached into the back seat for a fresh set of overalls and dressed in the front seat — a bit of a squash, but he didn't want to do it outside. Hood on, mask up, gloves covering his sweaty hands, he slid booties over his shoes and left the vehicle.

At the open boot, a strong recollection of Shark entered Grim's mind, how battered he'd been, how undignified his death, how savage. Grim sighed, pushing the images away, hefting Lesley from her tarpaulin-protected cubby and carrying her to the biggest tree. She was stiff, the rigid foetal position awkward in his arms, so putting her on her back had to go out of the window. He placed her on the ground on her side, annoyed he hadn't factored rigor into things. Now he couldn't position her in the way he liked, the way that sent a message. He'd folded her into the boot during the night. If he'd used the SUV, he could have laid her out in the same position as Karen, but thank God he hadn't, what with Dave mentioning that vehicle earlier.

Had someone else seen him leaving Tom on the road, was that why they were interested in the SUV? He was sure nobody had been around apart from that person tending to Tom.

He left Lesley and walked to his car, reaching into the box on the passenger seat. He smiled, took the item to the body and balanced it on her cheek. Next, he collected her handbag and the plastic storage box from the rear footwell, pouring the contents of the latter next to her head. Skin, lots of baggy skin.

Make of that what you will, Carol.

He'd shed the women's excess by cutting it off, their old skin representing the old them, and now, like Karen, Lesley was a new woman.

Clean.

But she was never dirty in the first place.

Grim chose to ignore that. He'd already forgiven himself for making a mistake. He'd heard the conversation about the affair, the word Lesley instead of Lindsey. A terrible error on his part, but he wouldn't do that again. No more women and a lot more punishing the group. After that, it was Operation Get Carol Back. Emma was a lost cause now, he'd finally accepted that, but he was sure he could win Carol over. Force her to love him.

And never leave.

CHAPTER THIRTY-ONE

The Park

It had been a horrible day so far. Bones's stomach didn't feel too good, all knotted, and he'd lost his appetite after the phone call. Things were spiralling out of control, and there was nothing he could do to stop it. Life had thrown him yet another curveball on top of everything else he kept hidden on his phone, laptop and inside his head.

He kicked a stone on the tarmac and sat on a swing. Wished he was little again, although that was a lie. Being little meant extra punches and kicks and cruel words aimed at him, day after day, bruise after bruise. Other people had been there at the time, and they hadn't done anything. Couldn't, else the Bully would turn on them, too. All of them put up with it through fear.

Bones prayed things would work out.

What else was there to do but that?

CHAPTER THIRTY-TWO

The Incident Room

Carol and the team had gone through the case from the beginning, trying to piece things together. Everything pointed to Noel as the prime suspect — he was the common denominator regarding the group, but for the life of them, they couldn't link him to Karen, Lesley, Teresa or Lindsey apart from them all resembling Emma. Still, that was enough in Carol's book, that curly blonde hair, but she couldn't go storming over to his place and accuse him of anything because they had no solid evidence, nor had he given them a reason to grill him on the two occasions they'd spoken to him today.

"It's looking likely it's him, we just have to prove it," Dave said, "although I'm still trying to come to terms with the fact he's involved. Mr Drippy Arse, a kidnapper and killer. Why, though? If he's picking off the group members, I get that, but the women?"

Michael leaned back, his chair squeaking, and gestured to PC Lloyd at the spare desk. "Lloyd's been through their social media for the past hour or so after Katherine did it, and there's no mention of Noel. He's not even on any platforms."

"That we know of," Katherine said. "He could have been at one time but deleted the accounts. He could be spying on everyone with a false name. I'll go through it all again. There might be one name they all have in common on their friend list."

Michael nodded. "I hadn't got around to that yet. I took over looking into the shoes for Dave then dealt with the masks."

"What did you get from that?" Carol asked.

Michael consulted his notes. "The shoes are available from a variety of places, and I've asked them to let me know if there were sales of high heels for the Dolly outfit plus the court shoes for the Queen — I sent them cropped images of the stills from the footage to make it easier for them and specifically asked if any purchases had been sent to Scudderton. That's for the online shops. The high street ones are few and far between, and they're searching their sales records, but as you can imagine, that might take some time. Some stores are farther afield, so he'd have had to travel to collect them rather than have them sent to his address. If so, I bet he paid in cash like he did with the burner and the Freddo."

"The masks, got owt back from anyone?" Carol pulled the tab of an orange Fanta.

"Yes, it came through just now. The fella from the custom-made place in Middlesbrough did make Dolly and Queen masks for the same client, but he also made one of that actress, the one in *The Split*. Nicola Walker."

"You look like her, Carol," Katherine said.

Carol's body chilled, and she stared at Dave, her mouth gaping. "Do I?"

"A bit." Dave frowned. "It's *got* to be him, that fucking Noel."

"I know, but what can we bring him in on? There's nowt."

"Then we'll have to find something. We *could* go to his place and give him a better talking-to, see if he slips up."

"But he could switch it around on us and complain we're harassing him," Michael said. "I've had his phone pinged, and with the local mast, he could have been anywhere within a certain mile radius regarding Karen and Tom, which means Scudderton and the surrounding areas. We could ask for a warrant for his phone records, try to get a better pinpoint. Shit, it's so frustrating. Our hands are tied until we have something solid."

"Where did the mask fella deliver to?" Carol asked.

"The buyer paid cash and collected Dolly and Queen from the shop. No CCTV footage, but he remembers the bloke because he arrived wearing a clown mask. The other one was bought a while after Emma left Noel."

A clown mask? So even then he was hiding his identity. Carol rubbed her forehead. "Katherine, you get on with digging into mutual friends of the women on social media. Lloyd, are you okay to still poke through all the comments and posts, go through them again?"

"I'll do that now."

Carol went to the whiteboard to add to the vast amount of information already on there. She stared at the images of who she now believed was Noel standing in line at the tills in the two supermarkets. She studied the build, the height. It could be him, but it could be one of a thousand other men in the area, too. She was as frustrated as Michael about not having a proper reason to bring Noel in, but like she'd said to Emma, she didn't want him knowing they were onto him. On the other hand, if they didn't move fast and he'd snatched Lindsey . . .

She contemplated for a while, Michael drawing her into the present.

"No ANPR sightings of either of his cars, so maybe he took public transport."

"He knows exactly what he's doing," Carol said.

Her phone rang. Joy on the front desk.

Carol tried to sound upbeat. "Hi, love."

"Sorry to be the bearer of bad news . . ."

"Oh God, what?"

"We've had another phone call about a body. Same voice as the one to do with Karen Stokes."

"Have officers been dispatched?"

"Yes, to the little forest behind Piper Place. I'm waiting on a call back from them."

The edge of Coldwater closest to Tesco . . . Noel said he was leaving work . . . Did he go home or . . . "What did he say this time?"

"I'll send you the recording."

"Send it to Michael as we're in the incident room."

"Okay. Good luck working out what it means."

Carol said goodbye and walked over to Michael's desk, calling out to everyone, "There might be another body. Michael, Joy's sending you a voice clip of the triple-nine call."

Michael opened his email browser and clicked on the one from Joy. He opened the file and pressed play. They listened to the usual wordage at the beginning of the call, then:

"*It's me again.*" The Texas accent. "*There's a body behind Piper Place.*"

"*Can you repeat that, please, sir?*"

"*There's a body behind Piper Place.*"

"*Did you discover it?*"

"*No, I put it there.*"

"*You put it there?*"

"*Islands in the stream, that is what we are — that's what we were* supposed *to be, fuck it!*"

"*Can you explain that, sir?*"

"*Dolly has been a bad girl. She's killing herself because I can't do it. Goodbye.*"

The call cut off.

"What the fuck was that about?" Dave said. "Is he delusional and thinks Dolly is doing the killing, not him?"

"Or does he want to kill whoever Dolly represents?" Carol said. "He wants to kill her — let's say it's Emma — but he knows he'll be the first person we look at for it."

Katherine *hmmed*. "Think about the words to that song he mentioned. It says something about 'no one in between'. Emma had an affair . . ."

The fan whooshed a welcome sweep of cold air over Carol's rapidly heating face. "Fucking hell, he's lost it. He's . . . how did I never see this in him?"

"I didn't either," Dave said, "so don't take the blame for not spotting owt. What do we do, go and see him now, ask where he's been since he left work?"

Carol nodded. "It'll be interesting to see if he's at home, whether he's calm and collected or jittery and hyped up if he's just dumped a body." Her phone rang again. "Hi, Joy."

"Sadly, the caller wasn't messing us about. Female, deceased, covered in cigarette burns, and there's signs of surgery and strangulation."

"Shit. We're going to see a suspect now, then we'll go Piper Place and speak to Rib and Todd. Ta-ra." She put her phone away. "It's got to be one of the women. My thought is, is he killing them in the order they were taken? Are we going to find Lesley?"

She closed her eyes. Another meeting with Noel was just around the corner, and this time, she'd take a much better gander at his cottage. The days of her rushing upstairs to his bedroom and taking no notice of her surroundings were over. It was time to get nosy.

"While we're gone, I need you to look into every operation Noel has performed. The ones at the hospital will be easy for staff to track, but perhaps not at his clinic — his employees aren't likely to hand over the information without his say-so. Find out if he has to inform some kind of governing body what operations he's doing privately. My reasoning is, did any of our women need plastic surgery for owt? Could that be the link? Rib will let us know of owt to do with Karen, but we need to know about the others."

All the strands floated outwards in Carol's head, the tendrils of a jellyfish, wavering, none of them tying together, but she'd make a shiny bow out of them if it was the last thing she did.

* * *

Truth-Hunt Cottage

Despite the red sports car being parked in the driveway, there was no answer to Carol's knock and, frustrated, she left Dave out the front and prowled around the outside of the property, looking for something, anything that would give them a solid clue.

Nothing.

He didn't have a garage, so there was nowhere to hide the SUV — she had a strong suspicion he hadn't sold it but ditched it somewhere because there'd be evidence on it from knocking Tom over. All the while she thought this, there was a nagging doubt in the back of her head. So many things pointed to it being Noel, but there was still a chance he was innocent.

But Emma mentioning Noel killing Joseph, those words wouldn't go away, and Carol had to face it that her ex-lover was possibly capable of so much more than collecting storage boxes.

He may also collect women.

The words of Dolly's song played in Carol's head. A devoted couple, never to be parted. The sea surrounding an island so nobody could get to them. Was that how he'd seen his marriage to Emma, even though she'd said he was more devoted to his patients than her?

Carol stared at the rear garden. It was immaculate, and nothing seemed untoward on the moors beyond. A well stood in the middle of the grass, so she walked over to it and peered down. It smelled faintly of shit, piss and damp, but that could be wet earth, and she was relieved it wasn't the odour of anything more sinister.

She turned and inspected the back of the cottage. The usual. Windows, brick facade, a grate or two in the patio slabs, a hose coiled around a holder on the wall. She stepped forward and nosed through the kitchen window. No appliances out, and to anyone who didn't know him, it'd look like the place was empty, except she knew different. He'd said he liked everything put away, neat and tidy.

She walked around the left-hand side and stared through the nets in the living room window. On the inside wall to her left, three large pictures hung. Minimal furniture, something she'd expect from him, and no knick-knacks or anything that gave a home that cosy air. The only odd thing out of place was a small stepladder propped against the wall beside a closed door.

She continued down the side of the cottage and joined Dave on the driveway. "I wonder where he is if his car is here?"

"Probably getting himself an alibi somewhere, or maybe he's inside and just not answering."

Carol seethed and phoned the station to get an APB out on Noel's SUV — yes, he'd said he'd sold it, but maybe he bloody hadn't. If he wasn't inside, his red car being here didn't make sense. It'd be a long walk to wherever he'd gone for his alibi, unless he was out on the moors for an afternoon stroll.

She'd get him in the end, but in the meantime, the clock was ticking.

Too fast for Carol's liking.

* * *

Piper Place

The protective clothing added another uncomfortable layer. Carol stood in the just-erected tent with Dave, Rib and Todd.

"Lesley Johnson," Todd said.

"Ah, shit. So he's going in the order they were taken." Carol stared at the body, the pile of skin and the handbag. What did the skin *mean*? "A cupcake on her cheek, what's that all about?"

"That's from Buns 'n' Bread," Rib said. "I had one last week and recognise the sugar flower on the icing. Red velvet cake."

Carol nodded to answer Dave's silent query for him to contact the owner of the bakery. He moved to the corner of the tent closest to the flap and took his phone out.

"Someone will have noticed a man in a disguise buying cakes, if that's what he did," Carol muttered. "But maybe we'll get lucky, he didn't dress up, and someone recalls who bought a red velvet."

"You're joking, aren't you?" Rib said. "She makes fifty a day, and all of them are gone before lunchtime. Will she remember fifty people times however many days?"

"Whatever she can remember is better than nowt."

Todd frowned. "You said dressing up . . ."

She explained about the outfits and wigs. "He clearly doesn't want to be recognised, so it's someone from around here. We've got Noel Bartlett down for it, and something about his cottage is bugging me, but I can't put my finger on it." It had pestered her ever since she and Dave had left it.

"The surgeon?" Todd asked. "Going by the state of Karen and Lesley, he isn't very good at his job."

The same green thread had been used on Lesley, and on the visible wounds, the cuts were ragged again. Because of the body's position, she couldn't see all of them, and she wondered, once Rib straightened her out on his table, whether she'd have a cut on her abdomen.

"The cigarette burns must mean something," she mused, sickened by the sight of them. "Or maybe it's just a perverse way to torture."

"Does Noel smoke?" Rib asked.

"I've never seen him doing it, put it that way." She didn't add that she hadn't tasted or smelled it when she'd kissed him. God, she wanted to throw up at remembering she'd let him touch her. Be intimate.

Dave came to stand beside her. "The owner's compiling a list."

"So time's being stalled again." Frustrated, Carol gritted her teeth at how some investigations just couldn't get going because of waiting on information. She pointed at Lesley's neck. "Noel's wife, Emma, said he'd threatened to strangle her. This might sound nuts, but I've got a theory. If we add everything together, all the tidbits, this is what I think's happened. Noel thought he had the perfect marriage, but then Emma left him. He tried to get her back, but she wasn't having any of it. He possibly killed her lover, then got fixated on Emma, but instead of pinning his focus on her, he took women who look like her. He's got to have kept them somewhere all this time — Rib, you'd know if Karen had been frozen after death and stored, wouldn't you?"

"Yep. She wasn't. She had a relatively fresh sandwich in her stomach."

Carol continued with her theme. "Alongside the Emma obsession, there's the group. Unless other group members end up dead, I believe Tom's death wasn't intended, that Lindsey was the target and Tom got in the way. That it just so happened to be a man Noel has known for years and had a beef with is neither here nor there. We've got our suspicions but no forensics, sightings or owt we can use as a reason to charge him. He's been clever. If we nab him without it, we all know the CPS will wonder what the hell we're playing at and tell us to release him."

"Something's got to give, Bird." Rib squatted beside Lesley. "She died hours ago. I'm talking very late evening or just the other side of midnight. The timing's tight for killing Tom, abducting Lindsey, then killing Lesley. Brave of him to dump her in daylight."

"Maybe he had to," Todd said. "In case Carol and Dave visited his cottage."

"We already have," Carol said, "except he wasn't in, which leads me to believe he's gone somewhere to be seen so we can't pin this on him. Let's just say it really is him. He created an alibi with Joseph by going to Tesco. He had a flimsy one regarding the dumping of Karen's body by saying he'd been at home, so I wonder what this one will be." She sighed, Lesley filling her vision. "He was starving them, don't you think?"

Lesley was painfully thin, and it seemed her bones could split her skin, they were that prominent.

"Looks like it to me," Dave said. "Owt in her handbag apart from ID?"

Rib nodded. "Lipstick, a packet of tissues, a purse with her ID, debit and credit cards, a tampon and sanitary towel, but the same as Karen, no phone."

"Yet she had one because Katherine read through the old files on all of the women. Each pinged the nearest mast around the time they were abducted. Michael's looking into Lindsey's to see what's going on there, but with the radius covered, all it will show is she was in the area. For Karen, Lesley and Teresa, nothing weird was going on via phone usage — as in, no off messages or threats — and all calls, I assume, were from people they knew. I say assume, because Katherine didn't flag owt to the contrary."

Dave adjusted his mask. "We've got a hell of a lot of information. I can't believe there isn't some part of Noel somewhere."

"With Karen being washed," Rib said, "and, I suspect, her hair combed through to remove owt, there was nowt on her except for a few minute fibres, plus any grit and whatever that was picked up from the alley she was in. The fibres could shed some light on things. Lesley may also have some on her body, and if they match . . . I was going to say then we'd know the same person did this, but given the state of each woman, that's obvious anyroad."

"I'll cling on to any evidence at this point," Carol said. "All it takes is one small thing to link him to this, then he's ours."

* * *

Skully Street

Lesley Johnson's parents had buckled under the pressure of the news, crumpling into each other on the sofa, the father's sobs harsh, the mother's wails heartrending. Carol and Dave had waited for the storm of grief to subside somewhat, then asked the intrusive questions. Carol discovered Lesley had been a nice woman, would be greatly missed, and this couple now had a gaping, daughter-shaped hole in their lives that could never be filled.

She had come to the end of the usual questions and now had to broach the subject that could give the team what they needed if the answers were what she wanted to hear. "Does the name Noel Bartlett ring any bells for you?"

Val Johnson frowned and wiped her red nose with a crinkled tissue. "Yes, he's the surgeon who put a graft on my arm." She rolled the sleeve of her blouse up to reveal it. "Why?"

"Are you still in contact with him?"

"No, but he does send me a Christmas card each year, which is kind of him."

So I was right. He does *remember all of his patients. Him wondering if Lesley was one when we spoke to him was a bluff.* "Did Lesley know him?"

"No. I don't understand. What has Dr Bartlett got to do with . . . with everything?"

Carol smiled. "We're not sure yet, but several names have come up in this investigation, so I'll ask you if Lesley knew them. Lee Ike, known as Geordie?"

"She's never mentioned him."

"Evan Ike?"

"No . . ."

"Tom Cubbins and Joseph Viticci?"

Val shook her head then turned to her husband. "Do any of those names mean owt to you, Norman?"

"No, but I wish they did, then the police would have someone to look into."

Oh, we've got someone, we just can't touch him yet. "Okay, you've been very helpful. We'll leave you be for now, but if we hear owt, we'll be in touch. Someone will be in contact regarding when you can view Lesley — we'd like a formal identification if it's not too much for you. If you feel you can't go through that, we can do it via DNA." *Like we'll do with Karen now Craig's banged up.*

"No, we'll do it," Norman said. "I can't have my baby wondering where we are and why we haven't visited."

His reply concerned Carol. Was he fooling himself into thinking he was visiting a live daughter, one who'd smile and cry upon seeing them, holding her arms out for a hug?

"She's dead," Val said dully. "She won't know whether we're there or not." She closed her eyes and bit her lip.

"I know, love, but I wanted to pretend for a minute."

Carol's eyes leaked.

* * *

The Incident Room

"Got owt from the hospital on those surgeries yet?" Carol asked, entering the room, Dave behind her.

"It's going to take them time," Michael said.

Carol kicked a desk leg. "Exactly what we don't have. What about ANPR?"

"No hits on either of his cars lately."

"Where the fuck *is* he?" Carol gripped the sides of her hair. Much as she didn't want to, and time being against them, she accepted she needed to remove herself for a moment. "Okay, we'll break to clear our heads, then we get back to it. We'll review all the information and get our heads together on what we need to do going forward."

"Oh, I've got an email from one of the shoe people." Michael clicked it open and read. "A shop in Middlesbrough — interesting that the masks were from there, too — sold them in one transaction in May 2018, cash payment. No store CCTV, and none of them can recall who it was, which is understandable. I'll check with Middlesbrough council on whether they still have street footage from that long ago, but I don't hold out much hope, do you?"

"No," Carol said, deflated. She clapped. "It's breaktime. Go. Leave the building, take a walk. Distance yourselves. Be back here in an hour."

She left, bypassing the DCI's office, his door open.

"Everything okay, Carol?" he called out as she went by.

"Yep, closing in, sir."

"Good, good."

She went downstairs and out of the building, wanting to run, to find somewhere to be alone. She rushed down the street and turned right then right again into the communal gardens behind the station. She chose a bench beneath a flowering tree and watched people enjoying time with their little kids by the duck pond, others having a picnic on the bandstand, yet more sunbathing on the grass. Guilt prodded her for allowing her team to lose an hour of work, but everyone was stressed and needed time out. A rest away from everything associated with the case would see them eager to dive in when they got back, brains fresher.

Carol couldn't take her own advice, though. Her mind just wouldn't clear.

She sighed. Plenty of time for that when this was all over.

CHAPTER THIRTY-THREE

Scud Stream

This was perhaps a silly place to set fire to a car, but Grim felt he had no choice. It was dangerous for him to be out and about so soon after dumping Lesley, but he had a horrible feeling Carol was closing in on him, so he'd driven home and left the red car out the front, then ran round the back to get in the SUV parked on the patio. He couldn't risk leaving it there, and his Google search of bodies of water in the area where he could push it beneath the surface meant he'd be captured on those bloody ANPR cameras. So it had to be here, water definitely in abundance but not deep enough for the SUV to submerge. He could jog around the edge of Coldwater afterwards and trek home behind the hedges alongside the road, which would shield him from anyone going past.

What would he say to Carol and Lapdog Dave if they asked him where he'd been again, though? He smiled — he'd walk farther along, well past his cottage, then go on the moors there, wandering around as though he'd just had a little stroll. If they were waiting for him at home, he'd appear, hands in pockets, and they couldn't prove he'd been anywhere else. He hadn't seen anyone while driving the red car to or from Piper Place. Other than that, he'd say he was taking a nap and hadn't heard them knocking.

His forensic gear and everything to do with murder sat on the driver's seat, and he'd poured petrol on them from the spare can in the back, ensuring he didn't get any on himself. He'd also sloshed some in the footwell on top of the tyre iron he'd killed Tom with, plus on the back and passenger seats. Someone would see the smoke, a driver going by perhaps, but everything that needed to be burned might be wet by the time someone got over here to investigate. The only thing that would give away the fact the SUV had been in an accident was the dent in the bonnet, maybe Tom's blood on the tyres, but the water might help with that, and anyway, Grim could blame it on the traveller and hope for the best.

Things had gone slightly out of control, but he'd have to get on with it and maintain it was nothing to do with him. He'd cleaned the steering wheel after he'd parked here, just in case, so now it was time to set the front seat on fire, wait for it to destroy the evidence, then push the vehicle into the stream.

He reached in and took the handbrake off, holding his breath as the petrol stank. Stepped back to light a match. It reminded him of the times he'd sparked up a fag and burned those Emmas, and he giggled. It would be okay, wouldn't it? Everything would turn out all right in the end.

He touched the flame to a rag and threw it and the match onto his clothes, slamming the door. Fire whooshed up and pressed its blazing body to the glass. Putting new gloves on, he walked to the back of the SUV and pushed, the bloody thing not budging at first. He pushed harder, ran with it, and it rolled down the slope of the bank and into the water, the momentum sending it into the centre of the stream, where it stopped.

He turned and headed for home, praying he'd done enough, and grinned at the thought of Knitty arriving later.

A silver lining.

CHAPTER THIRTY-FOUR

Undisclosed Location

Bones waited for the slap, the shouts, the meanness, but they didn't come. Maybe the Bully was pretending they were nice these days since they had an audience, or maybe they'd turned over a new leaf. Whatever, Bones would take whatever reprieve he could get.

CHAPTER THIRTY-FIVE

Truth-Hunt Cottage

At five o'clock, Knitty had entered the cottage, the scent of Grim's aftershave lingering, so he'd not long been here. She tucked kitchen roll into the washing machine seal and poured bleach on it. By the time she'd cleaned his cooker, fridge-freezer and dishwasher, the bleach might have worked its magic. Grim had left a note to say he'd gone to the Lord for dinner, so she had plenty of time as he wasn't coming back until nine.

It took two hours for her to finish up, but the mould in the seal hadn't quite gone. The smell had been overpowering earlier, so she'd propped the back door in the kitchen open and sprayed and wiped the life out of the other appliances. She'd give the bleach another half an hour, then she was going home. She made herself a cuppa and took it into the living room, frowning at a stepladder beside the door.

A quick glance around, and she knew something was off. Two of the pictures that were usually on the far wall had been taken down, propped beneath the window, and two built-in bathroom fans whirred, steel squares on hinges beside them, string pulls to turn them on.

That was well weird, so she popped her cup on the sideboard, a coaster beneath it, and grabbed the stepladder, opening it out beneath the fan on the far left. She had that strange feeling again of being watched, but she shook it off and climbed the ladder, ready to look through the fan to the other side.

A set of eyes greeted her, and she screamed, clutching the top of the ladder for support. She squinted in case she was seeing things, but no, there were the eyes, a nose and a mouth, and what looked like big freckles all over the skin, the lazy speed of the fan blades chopping the features.

"Hello?" she said, then felt daft.

"Get help . . ."

"What are you *doing* here?" Knitty thought of the cottage layout. What was behind there, a room? Was there another door along the hallway like the one to the living room that was disguised as the wooden panelling?

"He kidnapped us. Please, phone the police . . ."

"Us?" Oh shit, was this one of those poor women?

"He's coming, I can hear his car."

Knitty cocked her head. She couldn't hear anything except for the noise from the fan. "Hang on, I'll . . . Oh God, I'll phone the police."

Knitty hated to leave that face, but she got down from the ladder and ran to the kitchen for her phone. *Grim* had taken the women? She pounced on her bag on the table and rooted around inside, her hands shaking, her heartbeat too erratic, just like when she'd . . .

She couldn't think of that now.

Phone in hand, she struggled to access her contacts with her sausage fingers and cursed herself. "Come on, come on . . ." She jabbed at Carol Wren's name — thank God she'd had the foresight to save the number off that business card — and held the mobile to her ear.

It rang and rang, clicking to voicemail.

She ended the call and jerkily sent her a message: *At Grim's. Kidnapped woman is here. Help!* She jabbed send then rushed into the hallway, thinking about phoning 999 as well, just in case, but she wanted to save the woman so stuffed her phone into her cleaner's apron and felt along the panelling for a secret door. She pushed each of the wall panels, desperate to get to that poor lady.

Near the front door, a section of wood clicked open when she released the pressure, and she flung it aside, expecting to see the fan woman standing there. What she saw threw her mind into confusion. Strips of horizontal grass and three paths lined with flowers. Three front doors, red, blue and pink, each with a number, a ribbon bow, a knocker in the shape of a cow's head and a letterbox. She quickly gauged where the woman had been in relation to the living room and rushed to number three, pushing the door, hoping it would spring back like the panelling.

It didn't.

She tried to open the letterbox, but it was stuck down. Knitty spun and spotted a mural of a street, and her stomach seemed to leave her body. She recognised it. The street Grim had grown up in, where she used to go and play, stay for tea, the pavement to the right where he used to murder the ants.

"Oh fuck, oh fuck, oh fuck . . ."

She swirled towards the hallway, intent on finding something to open the pink door, but stopped short at the person who'd come in, a scream building in her throat. It was a tall woman — at least she thought it was a woman until she looked closer. A mask, and it looked a bit like Carol Wren. A wig the same style and shade as the detective's hair.

Chest tight with pain and fear, Knitty snatched her phone from her pocket and held it up. "I've rung the police."

"You always have been nosy," Fake Carol said with Grim's voice. "And you've just fucked everything up."

He advanced, and Knitty screamed.

CHAPTER THIRTY-SIX

The Police Station

Carol itched to see who'd phoned and messaged her a few minutes ago, but at the moment, she was about to view some footage. Todd, who stood beside her, said she'd love digi forever because of what they'd discovered.

Unable to settle, to go home, she'd stayed at the station after Michael and Katherine had gone, Dave saying he'd hang around with her. The team's discussion about the case from start to finish had left them all frustrated as there wasn't one thing they could pin on Noel.

Now, there might be something at last.

The digi tech, Roy, brought up a load of stills, the top one a dark, blurry image. "I don't think you'll want to watch all the videos from start to finish because there are a lot and you'll want to go and make your arrest. What we've got here is footage of Karen, Lesley and Teresa being abducted. There's Tom's accident, too. Also stuff showing the Stokes girls doing their muggings and burglaries. Then there's Karen and Lee Ike in compromising positions, but the most disturbing ones for me are a rape and a murder."

"What?" Carol glanced at Dave then back to the computer screen.

Roy explained, and Carol felt sick. She'd been fooled, had believed the murderer to be a good person, and as for the rape . . . Michael would be crushed.

"Who does the laptop belong to?" she asked.

Roy told her.

"What? So he filmed all this shit and never *told* anyone? Jesus Christ! So who abducted the women, as if I can't guess?"

Roy clicked on a few squares to minimise some stills and stopped on a side shot of an SUV. Noel sat in the driver's seat, side-on, and Karen was beside him as a passenger, her head back, eyes closed.

"Just prior to this," Todd said, "he'd elbowed her in the face. Oh, and I've got a small team out at Scud Stream. There's an abandoned SUV registered to Noel Bartlett."

"Fucking lying bastard. We've got to go. Thanks!"

Carol ran from the room, down a corridor, and through reception, Dave's pounding footsteps behind her. She burst out of the station and got in the car, adrenaline flowing, and took her phone out of her pocket. She slung it across to Dave when he got in and asked him to access her messages to see who'd got hold of her earlier. Carol sped off, siren going, lights flashing.

"Shit," Dave said.

"What?"

"Knitty's at his place, and she says one of the women is there."

"Oh God . . ."

Carol floored it, zooming towards the outskirts, switching the noise and lights off once she got to the road that led to Noel's cottage. She sped along, worry gnawing at her, and veered onto his drive, pelting up it and parking by the open front door.

Open. Front. Door.

"Fuck, look at that," she said. "Did he come back? Her moped's there, but his car isn't."

Carol got out of her car and entered the house slowly, Dave at her back. The hallway was as she'd remembered it, all the panelling, but a section closest to the front door was ajar. She slipped gloves on and pulled open the panel, shocked at what she found inside. And that was what had been bothering her about the cottage earlier: no windows. The living room at the back ended too short for this to be a part of it.

She went inside, walking over fake grass to the row of front doors and hammered on one with her fist. "Can you hear me? Is anyone in there?" She turned to Dave, who stood on the threshold, the whole room a surreal creep-fest.

"Can you hear that?" he asked.

Carol strained her ears. "No . . ."

"Faint shouting."

He disappeared, and Carol went after him. Another door in the panelling stood open, and she went inside the living room. Yes, she heard it now, along with a hum. Dave stood by a sideboard, a full cup of tea on it, and narrowed his eyes, listening. He glanced up at the same time Carol did.

Extractor fans?

"Help us!" a woman screamed.

"Oh my fucking God! Get that ladder, Dave, quick!"

Dave snatched it up and opened it, placing it beneath the fan closest to him. He climbed up and peered through. "Lindsey?"

Carol got on the phone to call for backup and an ambulance, leaving Dave to calm Lindsey and possibly Teresa. While she spoke, she checked the kitchen. The back door stood open, the scent of bleach and cleaning products strong. Next she went upstairs, her skin crawling with those ants again as she searched through Noel's bedroom, then the bathroom, the spare room and back downstairs. Her call over, she slid her phone away and returned to the hallway panelling, pressing it on the opposite side to the other two doors.

A section popped open, and she held her breath, bracing herself for Noel to jump out at her. "Police!" She flew inside, scanning everything, and gaped.

An operating theatre, and on the shelf ahead, large jars containing what looked like globules of fat and skin in liquid.

"Fucking hell . . ." She gagged and backed out, going into the living room.

Dave stood on the ladder at the other fan. "We're here. You're safe. We'll get you out."

"Teresa?" Carol hoped.

"Yep." He grimaced. "Both have fag burns on their faces, and Lindsey's got a broken nose."

The sound of sirens whined, and Carol ran out the front to wave them in. Todd had come with a team, and two squad cars followed him in. An ambulance sped up in the distance, and Carol breathed a sigh of relief. The women would be rescued and cared for, but where the fuck were Knitty and Noel?

Carol's phone rang with an unknown number, and while the SOCO team and everyone else got suited up to enter the cottage, she stood by her car and answered.

"Hello?"

"It's Emma."

"Is everything okay?"

"No, he's here, he's here, outside my caravan, and he's got a knife to Knitty's neck. Geordie . . . Geordie came because Noel told him to meet him at my van, but fuck, oh my God, Noel's trying to get in! He's got a mask on!"

Jesus Christ. "Do *not* open that door. Tell Geordie to dial 999, but we're on our way. Keep safe until we get there, you got that?"

"Yes, okay, okay . . ."

"Hang on a sec." Carol caught hold of Todd's arm in the hallway. "I've got to keep my phone line open, so can you ring for armed response and backup?" She gave him the caravan address. "An ambulance, just in case. Noel's got a knife."

Todd nodded.

"Stay on the line," Carol said to Emma. "I'm going to pass you to Dave in a sec while I drive."

"Okay. Oh God, hurry up!"

Carol legged it to the living room door. "Dave, we have to go. *Now!*"

CHAPTER THIRTY-SEVEN

Sunshine Caravan Park

Breathing heavily behind his Carol Wren mask, Grim was aware of people around him, phones out, either videoing him or calling the police. He hadn't thought this through, had imagined knocking on Emma's caravan door and entering with Knitty, giving the speech he'd learned word for word, then setting fire to the van with the traitors in it while he watched them burn from outside, then he'd take Emma home and force her to apologise. It was too early, holiday-makers still around — why hadn't he waited in the car somewhere with Knitty until it got dark?

But she told the police, so you'd have been caught either way.

He hated his rational side butting in, now wasn't the time for sarky self-criticism, and if he could rewind the years and do things differently, he would. He'd had a shower once he'd got home from ditching the SUV, taking down the pictures so the bitches in boxes could have the fans on, and if he hadn't forgotten to put the pictures back for when Knitty got there, he wouldn't have returned. He'd planned to go to the Lord, be seen and hope no one noticed what time he'd walked in, then meet them all at the caravan, but his error had him turning around and driving back to the cottage. He'd seen Knitty's moped and crept upstairs to put his outfit on, then went back down to confront her.

He still couldn't believe he'd found her in Guilt-Ridden, standing in his creation and sullying it with her presence. Lindsey or Teresa must have called out through the fans, and Knitty had worked out where the room was.

He held the blunt edge of the knife at her throat, but it still terrified her, that pressure, the thought that it *could* be the sharp part and he'd slit her skin any minute. She shivered in his hold — he stood behind her, one arm across her belly — and her breathing had turned tattered the moment he'd dragged her out of Truth-Hunt, punching her face and shoving her in the car. He'd engaged the child locks, and instead of screaming and fighting, she'd sat still, staring ahead, tears falling.

"Open the door, Emma," he shouted. "I just want to talk."

"Fuck off," came the muffled reply. Thunder, the twat from Newcastle.

No one knew who Grim was, these people were all from out of town, here for a nice summer break, his mask concealing what he looked like, but his car, that would give him away when he escaped.

Shit.

The sense of everything unravelling curled around him, squeezing tight.

"Emma, I mean it, I'm just here for a chat, that's all, nowt else."

"She doesn't want to talk to you." Thunder's shape came to the full-glass door, his edges distorted behind the starburst patterns. "Let Knitty go, and we'll say no more about it."

Let Knitty go? On your fucking bike.

"No, let me in, *then* we'll say no more about it."

Grim dug the knife harder, and Knitty whimpered.

"Please," she said. "I won't say owt. I'll even say we were messing about, having a laugh. You've got a mask on, so it could work . . . a joke, like."

"Shut up, just shut up for a minute so I can *think*."

The moan of distant sirens cut into his thoughts, and he switched the blade round. "You feel that? Feel the difference? One slight move, and it'll cut. Like *this*." He jerked his hand slightly.

"Nymph!" Knitty screeched. "Nymph, open the fucking door!"

Thunder inched it open and widened his eyes, probably at the blood. "Jesus Christ, Grim, what the hell's *wrong* with you?"

"Let us in." Grim pushed Knitty forward, closer to the steps. "If you don't, I'll kill her."

Thunder flung the door wide, and Grim manoeuvred Knitty up the steps and into the van. Grim kept Thunder in his peripheral but looked at Emma — he could hardly call her Nymph anymore, she was no longer a waif — cowering on the sofa unit among loads of clothes, her phone facedown beside her. Such a scutty, disgusting bitch. The van stank of old rubbish.

"Lock us in," Grim said to Thunder.

His old friend twiddled the key this way and that, then stepped backwards into the kitchen area.

"Don't even think about running out of that door at the other end," Grim said. "Lock that as well, then get back here and sit by Emma, or Knitty gets a second smile."

The sound of sirens grew louder.

Thunder did as he was told, and Grim's ego inflated — Thunder had never obeyed him before, always had some reason not to, and the gob on him . . .

With the remaining members of the group in his sights, Grim got ready for his speech.

"Keep your traps shut until I've finished. Any talking, and Knitty gets it."

The silly cow whimpered again, getting right on his nerves.

"All this, it's your fault, Emma." He gave her a wicked stare and couldn't believe he'd once loved her, that he was doing all this because of *her*. "If you hadn't left, none of this would be happening. Shark would still be here — I said *don't* speak until I've finished, Thunder." Grim fought the urge to slice Knitty and be done with it, to prove he wasn't joking. "Yes, I killed him, if that's what you were going to say. I bashed his stupid head in and stuffed him in the boot, satisfied? Now, those women going missing, it was *me*, because they looked like you, Emma, *you*, and I wanted you back, I wanted you to say sorry and mean it, to admit what you'd done was wrong, but none of them did, *you* didn't, and I just . . . I just wanted everything to go back to how it was."

He thought of the constant denials from Lesley, and Karen seeming proud of cheating on Craig, and Teresa, she was *glad* she'd been seeing that married man. He hadn't had time to work on Lindsey yet, and now he never would, because this stupid, nosy, bastard bitch in his hold had spoiled it all.

"You two keeping the secret wasn't on," he said. "Knitty, Thunder and that fucking Blitz, you *all* knew what Emma and Shark were doing, and that's why we're here. I sorted Shark and Blitz . . ." He laughed at Emma's and Thunder's expressions. "Yes, Blitz was me, too. Fucking convenient he was there when I went after Lindsey." He inhaled deeply. "Now it's your turn. I want you gone, traitors that you are."

"Now, fucking hang on." Thunder finally lived up to the reason for his name and shot up, coming closer, an exploding storm. "You can't just go around killing people."

Grim smiled, although Thunder wouldn't see it behind the mask's mouth slit. "Oh, I think you'll find I can."

He sliced Knitty's throat from left to right, and she sagged, her knees giving out. Grim let her drop to the racket of Emma screaming and Thunder getting down on his knees saying, "Fuck, oh fuck. No, no . . ." and Emma drawing breath and yelling, "You've killed her!"

"I mean what I say." Grim raised the knife and stabbed Thunder in the back.

A bloke screaming was different from a woman, louder, more robust, and Grim loved the sound. Thunder sucked in air, then tried to get up.

"If I take that knife out, you're fucked, *pal*, so if I were you, I'd sit nice and still — and *shut up*, Emma, you noisy bitch!" Through the manky net curtains, Grim caught a glimpse of Carol with a phone to her ear outside, Lapdog beside her as usual, and several officers, some in all-black clothing holding guns, headgear on.

So she's brought the big boys in.

Grim was without a weapon, and he didn't like it. He snatched the knife from Thunder's back and brandished it at Emma, Thunder moaning and muttering "Shit! Oh shit!" over and over.

"Close the curtains," Grim said to his ex-wife. "Do it, or I swear to God . . ."

Emma scrabbled up and did as she'd been told, stalling at one point — she must have seen the guns, the holiday-makers gone, the van surrounded. She let out a weird groan, sounding like the cow she was, and snapped the curtains shut.

"It's just you and me left," he said.

She sat again, looking straight at him. "What have you become?"

"It's your fault, so don't try and blame this on me."

"No, it's *your* fault. *You* chose to do all this, no one else. If we boil it right down, you ruined our marriage, you drove me to Shark because you acted like I didn't exist. Didn't you even notice I was depressed? The state of the fucking cottage should have told you that. I didn't clean, I couldn't be bothered, didn't see the point when you were rarely there. I was alone apart from the group." She stared at Thunder. "He needs help. Please, just let him go outside. I saw ambulances . . ."

"He doesn't deserve to live, liar that he is." He took his box of matches out of his pocket. "One move, and you're—"

"Noel Bartlett, give yourself up," came from outside, loud, like someone had spoken through a megaphone. *Someone*, not Carol.

She doesn't care about you either.

Grim placed the knife on the table. "Move, and there'll be trouble, got it?"

Emma nodded, and her eyes shot to one side. To her phone. "What are you doing with those matches?"

"You'll see."

"Are you going to set fire to the place?"

He struck the match against the side of the box.

"Thunder didn't lock the doors," she went on. "He locked it then unlocked it again."

Grim cottoned on. "Are you letting *her* know what's going on? Is that who she's fucking listening to on the phone? You silly, silly girl." He dropped the match on the carpet then lunged for her, punching her in the face to derail her, giving him enough time to run to the closest door, turn the key and check it was secure.

Emma sobbed and held her hands to her face. "You've broken my nose, you bastard."

"Wouldn't be the first time I've done that to a cheater. Get up, come over here."

Thunder moaned. "Em, don't do it . . ."

"Noel Bartlett, this is your final warning . . ."

Annoyed by whoever that was, Grim kicked Thunder in the head, once, twice, three times, the man going silent, his eyes closing. "See what happens when people don't do what I want? I said . . . Get. Up."

Emma stood, glancing at the fire spreading, creeping to the wall and climbing up the curtains by the table. It moved to the next set around the seating area, orange tongues lapping, reaching for Emma. She darted away, her gaze going to behind him.

"I don't fucking think so, woman."

Grim snatched at her hair and dragged her down the caravan to the other door. The silhouette of someone in black was on the other side of the glass, and Grim twisted the key and checked the door was locked.

"Back off," he shouted to the officer, a squirming, clawing Emma getting right on his wick. "Back off or she dies!"

She's going to die anyway. There's no taking her back home now.

He towed Emma by her hair to the other end of the caravan and shoved her onto the seating. Some of it raged with flames, the clothing going up, smoke billowing. Emma coughed, and Grim found it hard to breathe beneath the mask.

He hauled her to the floor, then climbed on top and put his hands around her throat. At last, he was strangling the real Emma, flames licking all around them, her trying to buck him off, her eyes bulging. Thick smoke slithered into the eye holes of the mask. The sound of breaking glass had Grim laughing — the heat must have busted the windows out — and he squeezed harder, wanting her gone, dead, so no one could be hurt by her again.

The smack to his shoulder had him turning to look over his shoulder. Two men in black aimed guns at him, and Carol peered from the farthest doorway, her expression a picture as she stared at a version of herself on his mask through the smoke.

"Let her go," someone shouted. "Hands behind your head!"

Grim ignored them and continued to stare at Carol, yet another person who'd cheated on him, going off with that fucking Dave, moving in together, all cosy, leaving him behind.

Hands grabbed his upper arms, and he lost his grip on Emma's neck. Grim inhaled to shout obscenities, but smoke clogged his throat, and he coughed, struggling for breath. Two officers yanked him and Emma down past the kitchen and out of the door, the fresh air fanning the flames. Grim couldn't see Carol, his eyes watering, but he felt her stare and gauged what was going on. People going inside the burning caravan, shouting that they only had limited time and, "It's too late, we can't get in . . ."

Cold cuffs clipped around his wrists, and Grim screamed out his pleasure.

They were being left to burn.

* * *

Carol, shaken from seeing herself in that mask Noel had on, leaned against the back of a caravan two along and tried to calm her racing heart. She'd left everyone to it, a fire engine arriving far too late to save the van — the flames had taken too much of a hold, Geordie and Knitty still inside, officers unable to get past the wall of fire to save them.

"You okay?" Dave asked.

"I will be. It was just a shock. That mask."

"I said you looked like her a bit. The actress."

"I didn't see it myself until . . . He even had a wig like my hair." She shuddered. Thought of Geordie. "Do you think it was significant, Geordie being stabbed in the back?"

"Seems that way to me. I expect, if Noel talks, we'll know what his reasoning was."

"I heard enough from his little speech in the van when he was busy blaming everyone but himself." She sighed. "I'm not interviewing him, I've decided that much. You can do it with Katherine, unless the DCI wants in. It's for the best anyroad, what with my affiliation. Even though I wasn't with him anymore . . . it's better for me to take a step back."

"Good call. What do you want to do now, stay here or go and see what's happening at the cottage?"

"The cottage, but first I want to make sure Emma's okay."

She pushed off the van and walked out to the clearing in front of Emma's ruined home, the fire engine rumbling, the flames put out. The holidaymakers in the nearest vans had been herded away from the scene. One ambulance had gone off, not needed now, but Emma sat inside the other, someone checking her over.

"Did I do okay?" Emma asked.

"Yep, brilliant." Carol smiled — she'd coached Emma before Noel had gone into the caravan, getting her to keep Noel talking then to describe what he was doing and his position. She addressed the paramedic. "Are you taking Emma to hospital?"

"Smoke inhalation, so yes. A broken nose and sore neck, but otherwise, she's fine physically."

"Do you need me to phone someone for you?" she asked Emma. "Somewhere to stay?"

"I'd have gone to Knitty's, but . . ."

Carol nodded. "I know, I know."

"I'll go to Mam's, see about renting another van."

While Carol owned one, she didn't offer hers. If she did, that would mean Dave wouldn't have a winter bolthole if he needed time with any ladies that might enter his life in the future. Plus, Carol liked the idea of coming up here for a week when it snowed, being alone.

"Okay. As your phone's wrecked, do you want to borrow mine to contact your mother?" Carol held it out.

Emma took it. "I only know her home number off by heart. I hope she's in."

Carol moved away to let her have some privacy, and Dave walked with her.

"I wonder how bad Knitty and Geordie are," she said. "What state they're in. The fire . . . it went up too quickly . . ."

The oxygen from the open door had given it a boost, and the fire had engulfed the end of the kitchen area, heading for the bedrooms.

"Don't beat yourself up." Dave draped an arm around her shoulders. "Come on, let's get your phone and drive to the cottage."

Carol bit back tears. They had someone else to visit too. It wasn't only the Stokes family who had tried to bury the past.

CHAPTER THIRTY-EIGHT

Truth-Hunt Cottage

The pink evening sky with peach streaks looked too pretty above the picturesque cottage that had seen untold horrors, and as Carol stood in the hallway in full protective gear, she gathered her courage to explore.

Todd and his team worked diligently. He'd sent Ben Asher and a second, smaller team of SOCOs to Scud Stream, and they'd finally lifted the SUV from the water and had moved on to Knitty's back garden with yet another excavation team. The discovered footage had revealed Knitty striking a man on the back of the head with the heavy base of an iron bird bath — her ire apparently giving her the strength to lift it despite its weight. The person recording it had been standing in the alley at the bottom of the garden, the fence slatted so they'd had a good view through one of the gaps. More footage from an hour later showed Knitty digging a hole, and eight hours after that, morning almost calling, she'd put the body in the grave.

Her husband hadn't left her at all.

Had the camera person stayed there all night, watching? Or had they gone home, getting up early to capture the burial?

So much had happened since this case had started, so many people's guilty secrets coming to light, some involving her own family filling her head too, and with little sleep, Carol was flagging. Still, she'd keep going, try to get everything done before darkness finally scoffed the beautiful pastels from the sky, then they might be able to nip to the Lord for a quick drink before last orders, going home to eat a takeaway.

Dave had gone upstairs once they'd found out Lindsey and Teresa had been taken to hospital. Carol had phoned Michael prior to entering, asking him to do her a favour and give the Fetts the good news that their daughter had been found alive. She'd also phoned Mark Reynolds, who'd agreed to meet Carol and Dave later.

It was nine o'clock, and she could afford to spend half an hour here. She wandered into the weird room, keeping out of the way so the techs could get on. All of the front doors were open, revealing what lay inside the boxes.

Carol went cold. Boxes. She remembered what Noel had said last summer.

"If everything is in its place, you know where to find it."

"You can't put me in place," she'd said. *"I don't belong in a box and I don't want to be found."*

"But it could be a pretty one with a pink bow . . ."

What if he'd been planning to grab her next? With an empty box in the middle, who knew if he'd earmarked that for her, but ah, she wouldn't have been in the middle box but at the end, the one with the pink front door. The pink bow on it . . . she wanted to be sick. Another wave of coldness went through her — she'd been here, having sex with him, while these boxes had been occupied. She hadn't had a clue what he'd really meant.

She stared at the mural on the wall. A street. Houses. Cars parked at the kerbs. She peered into the painted distance at a boy, crouching, a magnifying glass in hand, a beam of light going through it.

The boy was smiling.

She turned away from it, unable to process the change in Noel — or, more to the point, the way he'd been able to put his two selves into compartments. But why wouldn't he? She reckoned he'd have imaginary storage boxes he'd placed them in. From listening to the phone call, the conversation going on in the caravan, he'd allowed one persona to bleed into the other, overtaking his somewhat quirky side. She had questions, ones she'd get Dave to ask him in the morning. Tonight, he was on his own in a holding cell, on suicide watch as he'd threatened to kill himself when he'd been taken away.

She studied the boxes one by one. Lindsey had been in the first — had that also been Karen's prison? Blue plastic covered the mattress, and Karen was creeped out thinking about being the wrong side of that Perspex screen with the little hatch. At least there was a toilet and shower, a beside cabinet with a lamp on top. Oh, and a book with a couple on the front in a romantic pose, the title *Second Chance at Love*. Close to the front door stood a wooden chair. Was that where he'd sat? She shivered and moved on to the middle box. A tech was in there, and he pointed to a paper plate. On it, a cupcake case.

Lesley's room, then.

She sidled along to number three, which was identical to the others, except for what looked like a crossword puzzle book and a pencil on the bed. So he'd cared enough to provide entertainment with the reading material and crosswords, then. A small mercy.

She walked out into the hallway and avoided the operating theatre — one look at those jars of skin and fat had been enough, thank you very much. Another panel beside it stood open, and she stared in at some steps.

A cellar.

Down she went into what she could only describe as a weird setup. Towers of black storage boxes, containing God knew what. Three large receptacles with water in them, and in the ceiling, three grates. This must be where the shower water went. But how the hell did he empty them?

She asked a SOCO.

"Bilge pump's over there," he said. "And if you look up there, you'll see the sky if you squint. Those grates are in the back garden."

She'd seen those when she'd looked around earlier and thought they'd been storm drains or something. "So, what, the pump goes up there?"

"Yep, he must take the grates off and use the garden hose. I suspect he emptied the water in the well. There's an officer down it, checking. It stinks of shit, so maybe the caravan toilets were emptied in there an' all."

She had to get out of there, so she climbed the stairs and entered the kitchen, stopping beside an officer taking inventory of the fridge. A tea plate of red velvet cupcakes, some sandwiches in clingfilm, cut into big triangles, and several Freddo bars. Bottles of water filled the salad box, and a blender jug contained something thick and green.

Carol went upstairs and joined Dave and a SOCO, who stood in front of a built-in wardrobe. She went to the bedside table and peered down at a bingo game set, the box showing it contained a mesh globe with a handle to turn the balls, a pad of bingo cards and four daubers. What had he done, played fucking bingo with them all?

She walked over to Dave and jolted at the sight before her. "Oh."

On a shelf above the hanging rail, two masks mounted on what she assumed were polystyrene heads, wigs on top. Dolly and the Queen. The clothes they'd seen on the footage hung beneath, the shoes on the floor. Farther along, what appeared to be a Santa outfit — Teresa's fancy dress from the Christmas party at the Devil — and other women's clothing, likely items worn by the women when they'd been abducted. After that, Noel's regular clothes and . . .

"I wonder if he wore those forensic overalls when he dumped the bodies," she said. "Those fibres Rib was on about. Reckon they'll be a match to his SUV?"

Dave nodded. "Yep, but either way we've got shitloads on him. There's enough DNA in those box rooms downstairs to show the women were kept here."

"What if he cleaned Karen's room so well there's nowt of her in there?"

The SOCO laughed. "There'll be something, believe me. It'll be in the fans. Hair, I bet you."

Carol nodded. It was enough to put him away for years. "I can't get over—"

"Don't," Dave said. "You didn't know. Put it out of your head and treat this like any other case. He was nowt to do with you when he came up on our radar, and when he wasn't anyone to be concerned about, you didn't realise there was owt to look for."

He was right, but unless Noel pleaded guilty, she'd be going to court as a witness as well as the DI, and she'd have to explain everything. How would that look?

"Are you telling this court, DI Wren, that you had no idea women were incarcerated in that cottage while you engaged in sexual behaviour upstairs?"

Tears pricked her eyes. It was time to move on before she lost it. Sometimes, things became overwhelming.

She peered at a transparent storage box beside the shoes. "Phones."

The SOCO nodded. "You can put money on them belonging to the victims. There's a clown mask stuffed behind the others."

Carol smiled despite everything. Yes, they definitely had him. Noel was fucked.

* * *

Marlborough Street

Mark lived in a semi-detached with all the mod cons, the interior flash and fancy, lots of bling — crystal doorknobs, sparkling chandeliers, the type found in Home Bargains for a lot less than the real thing. It wasn't Carol's bag, but she had to admit, it did look nice, although how it remained so clean with kids about was a mystery.

Mark sat beside his girlfriend, Henrietta, on a white leather sofa. Sammy was in bed, but Tristan was up, sitting on a recliner. Dave filled the doorway, while Carol took the chair beside Tristan's. She let them know everything was okay with Lindsey and that she'd likely be allowed to leave hospital tomorrow.

"But that's not why I'm here really."

Mark frowned. "Eh?"

Carol looked at Tristan. "Would you like to talk about what we found on your laptop?"

Tristan got up fast and tried to bolt, but Dave stopped him.

"It's all right, lad," Dave said. "We just need to know why you never said owt."

Tristan glanced at his father and hung his head.

A telling sign?

"What the fuck's this about a laptop?" Mark's demeanour had changed in an instant, and he shot to his feet, stomping over to Tristan and slapping him around the side of the head. "What's going on, you little prick?"

"Hey," Dave said, holding a hand up. "*Don't* touch him again. That's assault of a minor."

"Assault? He's my fucking kid, and I'll punish him however I bloody want to."

Henrietta remained quiet, her cheeks red.

"Do you want to press charges, Tristan?" Carol asked.

"I don't . . . I don't know . . . what . . ." He shook from head to foot and whispered, "He's the Bully."

The Bully?

Mark bowed his arms. "You'd better bloody not get me done, lad, else you know what'll happen."

"Right, let's end this here." Carol glared at Mark. "We need to speak to Tristan, and I don't feel he's safe with you, nor do I feel Sammy or your baby are for that matter." She glanced at Henrietta. "Your baby is in bed?"

She nodded.

"Do you need help?"

She nodded again.

"You fucking what?" Mark rounded on her and held a fist up. "What have I told you, eh? What have I said about opening your fat gob?"

Carol herded Tristan out into the hallway and phoned for backup while Dave tried to placate Mark. This had gone from zero to a hundred within seconds, the turn of events startling her, because Mark hadn't given her the impression he was that type of man.

Tristan sat on the stairs, his forehead on his knees, sobbing.

Carol dealt with her call — they were stretched for officers, so it'd be a miracle if anyone could get here quickly. She knelt in front of the boy, Dave cuffing Mark in her peripheral.

"Is that why you couldn't tell anyone about the videos?"

Tristan lifted his head. "He'd have killed me for being out late, not to mention Mam having a go. I . . . I go out when it's dark, and no one knows."

"You've been doing that for a long time."

Tristan nodded.

Carol rested a hand on his shoulder. "That's a lot for you to keep inside for years. Does your father scare you *that* much?"

"Yeah. He . . . Honest, he'd have laid into me and might not have stopped if he knew I was sneaking out. It was easier after he left, but if Mam knew, she might have told him, and he'd have got to me anyroad."

"Too fucking right I would have," Mark shouted from the living room.

Carol got up and closed the door, then returned to Tristan. "What's going to happen now is an officer will take you down to the station, where there will be an appropriate adult present while officers ask questions. Tomorrow, you should be able to go home to your mam."

"What about Sammy? He's a shit because of Dad. He's played up since he was about two and got worse when Dad left."

"I'm sure Henrietta will take care of him for tonight because your father will be down at the station — they'll be safe, understand? You don't have to press charges, but we will." She waited for a response, and with nothing forthcoming said, "Did you see your mother being taken?"

"No, and I didn't think owt of her not coming back because she's done it before. I didn't add it all up that the surgeon had taken her until Dad phoned to tell me he was picking me up from school."

That took Carol aback. "So you know him, then?"

"Yeah, he patched me up when I had . . . an accident. Called me Bones, said I was part of his gang now."

Carol cringed at that. "An accident or . . . ?"

Tristan jerked his head to the living room door.

"Right. The Bully hurt you. Do you want to tell the officers about that at the station?"

"Yeah. I'll tell you lot everything. Maybe then Mam will, too. She's kept it all quiet. I used to let him hit me so he didn't pick on my brother, but Sammy watched it, and that's why he's a shit."

Carol felt for the lad. He'd obviously hidden more than the footage. For a child to have that burden, no wonder he was introverted and Sammy was a nightmare. The boys had coped with it in different ways.

"We'll fix everything," she said. "I promise."

* * *

Kipling Close

Once more in protectives, Carol and Dave stood in Knitty's kitchen by the back door, staring out into the garden. A tent had been erected, so she couldn't see inside, but she could imagine what was going on. As the footage had shown the exact location of the grave, the team would be able to get on with things, although it'd be a painstaking task.

She'd come here first rather than go to Evan's over the road to give him the distressing news about his brother, putting off the inevitable, her selfishly needing a breather after the shocking goings-on at Mark's place. He'd railed at the officers who'd come to collect him in a meat wagon, and Whitney had been called in to sit with Henrietta and the other kids while Tristan had been driven to the station.

She joined two SOCO officers in poking around Knitty's, not knowing what she was looking for, maybe something that would explain why she'd killed her husband — if that was who the body was. Had guilt burned through her at what she'd done? Or had she been relieved? He might well have been a replica of Mark and Craig.

It was frustrating that with Knitty dead, they might never know.

Upon finding nothing — digi would sift through her laptop and iPad — Carol couldn't hold off any longer. She'd spoken to Alton on the front desk prior to coming here, and he'd said Knitty's sister, the only remaining relative, was the next of kin. She lived in Devon, so local officers would visit her. News of tents being in two back gardens would likely hit the tabloids tomorrow, speculation rife. Alton had also said Evan was Geordie's NOK, their father dying when they were little, their mother two years ago, other relatives an uncle and two aunts.

She returned to the kitchen, noting the time on the wall clock. Evan might be in bed, but if he'd been to the Devil and didn't stay for a lock-in, he'd be home by now.

"Let's get this over and done with," she said.

"We've missed our bevvy at the Lord."

"Yep, but we might get to the Chinese in Mollengate before it shuts."

"Good, I'm starving. We haven't had owt since that sandwich around lunchtime."

"That feels like days ago."

They took their protectives off at the door, placed everything in a bag and signed out of the log, PC Pitson manning the front of the house.

"All right, Alan?" Carol asked.

"So-so."

She smiled and walked across the road, her muscles and bones aching, her head throbbing from an oncoming migraine where she hadn't had a drink for so long. Light shone through the flimsy curtains at Evan's, and she knocked on the door, taking a deep breath, holding it, then letting it go.

He opened the door and looked at Carol, then Dave coming up the path behind her. She didn't need to say anything, he knew.

"I fucking *told* him not to go to Emma's. Oh God. *Fuck*."

"Inside," Carol said. "Come on."

Time to tell a broken man his brother had been stabbed in the back and burned to death, all because a woman had an affair.

Tragic.

CHAPTER THIRTY-NINE

Interview Room Two

Carol had slept solidly, which was a surprise, as she'd thought the memory of Evan's howling would keep her up all night. It had been a harrowing experience, and they'd ended up staying with him until around 1 a.m., neither of them hungry for a takeaway any longer in the face of such grief.

She sat in the viewing area on the other side of interview room two and stared at Noel sitting beside his brief. The DCI and Dave sat opposite. Dave would lead, as the DCI wasn't up to speed with all the goings-on. The spiel had already been said for the tape, and Dave had asked, "What do the disguises mean?"

Everyone waited for Noel's answer, but it didn't look like he was going to provide it.

"Listen to me, I've already said I did it all, so why are we talking about it? Why do I have to explain myself? I kidnapped, I killed, whatever, just send me to prison."

"We'd like your side of it for our records. Yes, we have an idea why you did what you did, but don't you want to get it off your chest?" Dave asked.

"No."

"Are you pleading guilty?"

"Yes."

Carol's shoulders slumped in relief. No lengthy trial. She wouldn't have to reveal to a jury that she'd had sex with a killer.

"What's the significance of Dolly Parton and the Queen?" Dave said.

"I've just said I don't want to talk about it."

"Are they Emma and your mother?"

"Don't speak about my mother." Noel gave Dave a filthy look.

"So I'm right. Fine. Why dress up as them?"

Noel glanced at his solicitor who nodded.

Is he telling him to talk?

Noel sighed. "I wanted them close to me. They left me."

Carol shivered. He'd also had a mask of her. He must have also wanted *her* close. If she hadn't been so involved, she'd have felt sorry for him — three women had left, and to be near them, he'd had masks made, a way to be with those people again. But she *had* been involved, and anything to do with him left her cold and unsettled.

"What about the storage boxes?" Dave went on. "We found so many of them at your cottage, in cupboards, loads in the cellar, and your home was bare apart from furniture. What's that all about?"

"Emma was a slob, and I needed it tidy. I had to get her out of my cottage, all of her. But I wanted her back, and when she didn't come, when the money didn't make her see sense, I . . . I took the women. They didn't do it for me, so I reckoned I should pick someone else, someone who wasn't like Emma. I chose Carol, trying to start again with her, but she wouldn't do it, she didn't want me either."

She sucked in a breath at her name being mentioned. She'd explained all to the DCI, so at least that hadn't come as a shock to him, but it still felt strange to hear herself being spoken about.

"She told you she only wanted sex," Dave said. "So why did you think she'd want more than that?"

"Because I *wanted* her to." Noel thumped the table. "She was learning. She'd cleaned her house out and got her flat all nice, she said so, and I knew she'd be right for me then."

The solicitor whispered something in his ear.

"Carol never knew owt about the box rooms or my operating theatre. She just came in the front door and went upstairs. The only other room she went in was the kitchen the first time. We had wine."

Perhaps the solicitor had advised him to tell the truth about Carol being in the cottage as it might go in his favour.

"Moving on," the DCI said.

"You provided entertainment for the women," Dave said. "We found a book, crossword puzzles and a boxed game of bingo."

"The book was for Karen. I wanted her to read it and see the wife went back to the husband in the end, she gave the marriage a second chance and was happy. All I wanted was for Karen to go back to Craig and stick to her marriage vows."

"Why didn't she get that chance?"

"Because she wouldn't do what I said. She didn't feel bad for cheating on him. Three years I kept her, and in all that time, she never once said she was sorry. She told me she'd move to London, leave him and her kids behind, that she didn't even *like* her girls. What's that all about? The book didn't work."

"Did Lesley read it?"

"No, because I made a mistake with her. She didn't even have an affair, it was *Lindsey*." He clenched his teeth.

"So Teresa was given the crossword book. Any reason?"

"Yeah, she liked doing them. They had things they hated and things they liked. If they were good, they got the nice stuff. I gave Teresa the crossword book because . . . I was going to kill her next, you know, take Guilt-Ridden down and stop snatching women."

"Guilt-Ridden?"

"That's what I called the estate they were living on."

"The estate?"

"That bloody *room*! The *women*. God!"

"So that room containing the box homes, that's Guilt-Ridden, yes?"

"Finally, he gets it."

"Did you all play bingo?"

"No, that was for Lindsey. That's one of her favourite things. We didn't get around to playing because of that fucking Knitty."

It made sense yet was confusing at the same time. He clearly wasn't going to explain why the good things were significant, and honestly, they didn't need to know. Teresa was coming in today to give her statement — it might span several days, depending on how much she had to tell — so they'd likely get answers then.

"Why did you botch the surgery?"

Noel rolled his eyes. "Now I thought you were a bit dim, but for fuck's sake, isn't it obvious? I'm a surgeon, so if I'd done it properly, you'd have got me earlier. I didn't want to advertise it was me."

"The green thread?"

"For envy."

"Do you want to elaborate?"

"Nope."

"Let's talk about the money withdrawals after you abducted the women. You forced them to go to a cashpoint. How did you get them to do that?"

"None of your business."

"And why did you make them do it?"

"Someone had to pay for their keep!"

"From where I'm sitting, you didn't feed them much, so I'd say they'd been short-changed, wouldn't you?"

Noel grunted.

"We've done some research and have discovered you did plastic surgery on Harry Smith's stump after his accident at the clothing factory. The man who orchestrated last summer's murders. Did he give you the idea to do what you did?"

"No!"

"Why did you burn the women?"

"Why not?"
"Let's move on to the hair. Why did you shave it off?"
"So they were like Pixie Emma."
"Can you explain that for us?"
"No."
"What about the cow knockers on the front doors?"
"Jesus, isn't it obvious? *Emma*'s a cow." Noel sulked.
"The bow on the front doors . . ."
"Ask Carol. I want my mother."
"But she's deceased."
"No, I want her close."
Ah, the outfit.
"I'm afraid those items are evidence now." Dave glanced at the DCI. "I think we need a medical evaluation before we go further, Noel. I don't want to ask you any more questions until I know it's okay to proceed."
"What, do you think I'm mad?"
The pause seemed to go on forever.
"Interview suspended at . . ."

* * *

Kipling Close

Carol had been unable to get a part of a conversation she'd had with Lindsey out of her mind. The woman had been uneasy, so Carol wanted to clear it up. She sat at the kitchen table having refused a cuppa — she didn't plan on staying for long.
"Did you know about Karen's first affair? The one before Geordie?"
Lindsey nodded. "We were mates, I kept it quiet."
"You've heard what was found in the Stokeses' back garden, yes?"
Lindsey's mouth dropped open. "Oh God . . ."
"Hmm."

* * *

Carol's Office

Michael sat on the other side of Carol's desk and stared at her. "It was Grandad who raped Lesley, wasn't it?"

Carol nodded. "I'm sorry. There's footage, plus photos of him and Lesley at the scene."

Michael sighed. "I don't know what to say."

"You don't have to say anything. I get where you're coming from. I thought I knew Noel, so . . . Yeah."

She got up to look out of the window, her back to him in case he needed time to process. Instead, he came to stand beside her and draped an arm around her shoulder.

"Now it's my turn to give *you* the chat," he said. "You're not Noel, and whatever he did isn't a reflection on you."

She smiled. "I know."

"Good."

They stared out at the sea in the distance, nothing more to be said.

CHAPTER FORTY

Scudderton Cove

Summer evenings at the beach were precious. Carol and Dave had come down to Cove to sit on the wall with their fish supper from June's Chippy. Carol looked at a sea kissed by a lilac-and-orange sky, the sun sitting on the horizon, ready to go to bed. Everything had been wrapped up, all the paperwork done, and they'd left work earlier needing to ground themselves.

The CPS had decided Craig Stokes would be held in remand while the evidence was being processed. The little one's death and burial was a crime too big to allow him out on bail. He'd admitted to it all, so no trial, and evidence on the blanket had proved he'd handled it, plus some of his blood had landed on the baby — he'd nicked his finger with the knife he'd used to cut the umbilical cord.

That whole episode, the sheer horror of it, still upset Carol weeks later. Probably always would. The team had called the baby Malek, an Arabic name meaning "messenger", as his discovery had given all of them a message: to look beyond the surface, to see behind the carefully constructed veils and find what lurked beneath. It had been the theme of the whole investigation really. An Arabic name had been chosen as tests had shown Malek hadn't been Craig's, he was half Egyptian, so Karen had been playing around with someone else as well as Geordie.

Maybe that was why she'd been shoved down the stairs? Perhaps Craig had found out he hadn't fathered the child and he'd intentionally killed it. He wouldn't speak about that when questioned, remaining tight-lipped, his face full of anger, and when asked why Karen had kept the secret of the death, he'd said guilt had played a part, she'd hated herself for having an affair. Carol didn't believe that. If she'd felt so guilty, why start something with Geordie?

The search for Malek's father was ongoing.

The Stokes girls had settled well in Wales — their nan, Craig's mother, over the moon to finally meet and get to know her granddaughters. There had been no sudden rise in muggings and burglaries in that area, so it was safe to say they were behaving themselves.

In consideration of his helping the police with their enquiries, no charges had been pressed against Tristan. Lindsey had taken her boys and moved away, farther north somewhere, their names changed; she wanted to start again without Mark around. Being held hostage in the box room, even for just a short amount of time, had changed her, and she'd gained a new perspective on life. She'd given a statement about her marriage to Mark, the abuse, the gaslighting, and he was out on bail awaiting trial. Henrietta had done the same, and she'd also moved away, down to Cornwall near her mother, taking her baby for a fresh start.

Mark lived in a bedsit, alone.

The fibres Rib had found were a match to the carpeting in Noel's SUV.

The team had attended many funerals recently. Geordie, Tom, Knitty, Karen and Lesley, all laid to rest in the same cemetery. Carol had felt so close to Karen and Lesley during the investigation, their lives picked apart for all of the team to see. The saddest part was Lesley had been a case of mistaken identity and had paid for it dearly.

Carol sighed at the weight lifting off her shoulders. Amazing what a bit of sun and sea could do, not to mention the lush chips with lots of salt and vinegar. "I wonder how Teresa's doing."

"What, in therapy?" Dave asked.

"Hmm. I hope it helps her. She held it together brilliantly, despite being kept there all those years."

"It's like she said, she had faith she'd be found and held on to that throughout."

"Amazing woman."

"You're telling me."

As always when a case ended, Carol marvelled at how life went on. The people affected coped as best they could with the remnants they had left, some with people missing from any new family photos, others wishing they'd said "I love you" more before death had come calling. And Carol would move on too. She'd had a few words with herself and accepted she couldn't have known Noel had two sides to him — how could she when he'd only shown her the one? And she'd also accepted that lugging around the heavy burden of guilt regarding her mother was a load she shouldn't be carrying.

Last night, she'd allowed herself to think about it all instead of pretending she couldn't remember that night. The row, Mam shouting, saying she'd had enough, that she was leaving with Carol. That recollection had rendered Carol numb — she'd blocked it out, thinking Mam had left her behind with a monster, when she'd been intending to take her child with her.

Something else had slithered into her mind too. Carol taking her punishment in the barrel on the patio, the water so cold, Dad telling her she had to go in it up to her neck. All that time, Mam had been so close, and Carol hadn't known.

"I think he killed her," she said.

"What? Who?" Dave paused with a chip halfway to his mouth.

"Sorry, just thinking out loud. About Mam and Dad."

"Oh . . . Are you serious?"

"Yes. I . . . thought of some things last night. It was the burials in the gardens that set me off. Unlocked the vault, if you see what I mean."

"Shit . . ."

"I know."

"What are you going to do? That house belongs to someone else now."

"I feel for them." Last night's memory soaked her again. "He dug a hole that night and laid a patio the day after she supposedly left."

"Christ. You're going to have to call it in, you know that, don't you?"

"Tomorrow."

"Are you going to be okay until then?"

She popped a piece of fish in her mouth. Chewed. Swallowed. "Yep. I've got chips, my best buddy and a beautiful view, so why wouldn't I be?"

"Don't kid a kidder, pal. This is your mam we're talking about. A possible murder. You can't keep bottling things up. Look what it did to Tristan."

"I can't help it, I don't like thinking about back then. It'll be hard to deal with, but at least I'll know where she went. At least I'll know she never left me."

And for the first time since she'd realised Noel was involved in the case, she understood. No one liked being abandoned.

They finished their food to the symphony of the waves, the gulls calling to one another, and the sight of a delivery boat on its way to Hull. Peace floated over Carol, despite what lay ahead, and it was as if her mother whispered to her on the breeze.

"You found me, my sweet lass. You found me."

THE END

THE JOFFE BOOKS STORY

We began in 2014 when Jasper agreed to publish his mum's much-rejected romance novel and it became a bestseller.

Since then we've grown into the largest independent publisher in the UK. We're extremely proud to publish some of the very best writers in the world, including Joy Ellis, Faith Martin, Caro Ramsay, Helen Forrester, Simon Brett and Robert Goddard. Everyone at Joffe Books loves reading and we never forget that it all begins with the magic of an author telling a story.

We are proud to publish talented first-time authors, as well as established writers whose books we love introducing to a new generation of readers.

We have been shortlisted for Independent Publisher of the Year at the British Book Awards three times, in 2020, 2021 and 2022, and for the Diversity and Inclusivity Award at the Independent Publishing Awards in 2022.

We built this company with your help, and we love to hear from you, so please email us about absolutely anything bookish at feedback@joffebooks.com

If you want to receive free books every Friday and hear about all our new releases, join our mailing list: www.joffebooks.com/contact

And when you tell your friends about us, just remember: it's pronounced Joffe as in coffee or toffee!

ALSO BY EMMY ELLIS

DETECTIVE CAROL WREN MYSTERIES

Book 1: SPITE YOUR FACE
Book 2: HOLD YOUR BREATH
Book 3: GUILT BURNS HOLES

Printed in Great Britain
by Amazon

27648998R00158